KEITH FINNEY

A NORFOLK MYSTERY

DOUBLE CROSS

VINCI

BOOKS

By Keith Finney

The Norfolk Mysteries

Dead Man's Trench

Murder By Hanging

The Boathouse Killer

Miller's End

Dead… Again

A Yuletide Mystery

Double Cross

The Lavender Killer

Murder RSVP

For Joan

Vinci Books

vinci-books.com

Published by Vinci Books Ltd in 2025

1

A CIP catalogue record for this book is available from the British Library.

Paperback ISBN: 9781036700973

Chapter One

AN UNEASY SILENCE

LYN SAT ALONE in Stanton Parva's ancient church, waiting for Ant to arrive. She fixed her gaze on the remnants of an ornate wood rood screen that once separated the clergy in the chancel from worshippers in the nave.

Edward VI has a lot to answer for when he ordered the screen in every church to be torn down, thought Lyn.

As the minutes passed, Lyn mused over how often she'd sat in the time-worn pine pews over the years.

The sound of the east door opening reverberated around the bare, white-washed walls, snapping Lyn from her reflections.

At last, she thought, expecting to see Ant's cheery features.

'Sorry to disturb you, this'll only take a jiffy.'

Lyn's disappointment faded as she admired April's speed, carrying a vase of flowers to a side-chapel. April replaced faded hellebores with fresh blooms, being careful not to drop any petals from the old spray. She then waved to Lyn and disappeared through the east entrance.

As Lyn once again sat alone, she pondered how it would feel to be walking down the aisle in her wedding dress.

Ten minutes later, a man's voice pierced the silence. 'I can explain.'

She didn't need to turn around to recognise who the voice belonged to.

This should be good, she thought as Ant stooped to place a kiss on her cheek, then sat down next to her. She turned to her right and gave Ant a whimsical look.

Allowing a few seconds to pass, he scratched his head and sighed. 'George, the bull on Home Farm needed seeing to. You know what livestock farming is like. I couldn't leave his injury to fester, so I called in a favour with the vet.'

Lyn watched with amusement as her fiance tried to suppress his breathing to hide how out of breath he was.

'If I were you, I'd get myself down to the gym in Aylsham. You're out of condition, or is it just your age?'

Ant frowned. 'You cheeky thing. I'm in my prime.'

'If you say so, darling. Your breathing doesn't seem to agree.'

Ant nudged his companion, a sure sign he was trying to apologise for being late. 'Will lunch get me out of trouble for being a bad lad?' Ant stole a second peck on his girlfriend's cheek.

'I want the full works, not just a sausage bap from Lil's Chuck Wagon,' said Lyn.

Ant laughed, then checked himself for making a racket in the church.

'What about a mixed grill in the Wherry Arms? You know it's Jed's specialty.'

'I'm not sure that's saying much, but at least it's nearer to the school. I've got a busy afternoon coming up. One thing though. Don't order the mushy peas—It's not normal.

Ant sighed and shook his head, 'Then wouldn't a bap at Lil's be—'

'Don't even think about it. My rules,' replied Lyn with a knowing smile.'

'Alright, the Wherry Arms, it shall be.'

Lyn's look of satisfaction wore off as time passed and Ant fidgeted with his car keys, which tested her patience. 'Will you keep still?' She looked at her mobile. 'It's twenty-past already. I know the Reverend Morton is in the vestry because I heard him earlier.'

Ant looked towards the oak-panelled door that separated the chancel from the vestry. 'Let's see what's going on.' Without waiting for his intended, he was off, leaving Lyn to follow in his wake.

'The vicar might have someone with him. Perhaps that's why he's not appeared. I don't think we should—'

'Then he ought to have had the manners to pop out and apologise to us,' interrupted Ant, already tapping lightly on the gnarled door as Lyn caught up with him.

'Hello, anybody there?'

'Good Lord,' said Lyn in a breathy tone. She turned towards the back of the church to see a small, thin figure dressed in black trousers and a shirt, save for a white collar, showing the woman's vocation.

Ant looked over Lyn's shoulder. 'Seeing that collar, I thought it was the reverend for a second or two.'

'Don't be daft, can't you tell the difference between... oh, never mind.'

'Oops, sorry to put the wind up you,' said the woman in

a bright tone as she walked down the aisle. 'I'm always getting told off for doing that... surprising people, I mean.'

By now she stood less than ten feet from the intrigued pair, Ant's right hand still on the door handle of the vestry door.

'I'm Alison. Well, the reverend Alison King, to be formal about it. Everyone calls me Ali.'

The newcomer's confidence, enhanced by her beguiling smile, transfixed Lyn. 'Nice to meet you, er, Ali. I'm Lyn Blackthorn and this one, for my sins, is my fiance, Anthony Stanton.'

'Steady on,' protested Ant.

'Get used to it when you're married, Ant,' laughed Alison. 'Maybe you'll do your bit to prove the stereotype wrong?'

'Isn't that another stereotypical viewpoint?' quizzed Ant.

'This is all getting a little confusing for me,' said Lyn as the threesome laughed, before lowering their tone to show respect for their surroundings.

As the levity abated, Ali fixed Ant with an enquiring eye. 'Stanton. Any connection with the village name?'

'Ha, ha, you've been found out,' said Lyn as she gazed at her blushing husband to be. 'He's the son of the Earl of Stanton.'

Ali took a step back. 'I see. Am I supposed to genuflect or something? And how do I address you, "My Lord"?'

Ant's blush intensified. 'Anthony will do, and if my fiance doesn't stop stirring it, I'll put her back on the shelf.'

Lyn moved closer to Ant and gave him an affectionate peck on the cheek. 'You're not getting out of it just like that. Once we've seen the vicar to fix the date, it's a done deal.'

'Ah, so that's what you're doing here. In that case, I'll leave you to it. I only called in on the off chance of introducing myself to the Reverend Morton. I'm new in the area, and it's the done thing to do the rounds of the local churches to break tea and cake, so to speak. Please give my regards to the vicar and tell him I'll call back soon.'

With that, Ali said her goodbyes and retraced her steps to the church entrance, covering the distance as if she didn't have a care in the world.

'What a lovely woman,' said Lyn as she watched Ali exit the sacred building.'

'She frightened me to death.'

'That's because you don't like confident women who have a mind of their own.'

'And you wouldn't fall into either of those categories, then?' replied Ant as he returned Lyn's earlier peck on the cheek. 'Anyway, let's get on with why we're here before you lay anymore verbal booby-traps for me.'

'As if,' replied Lyn with a devilish grin.

He tapped on the door and waited. No response. This time he knocked with more urgency, before half-opening the door and announcing himself. 'Vicar, it's Anthony Stanton. I've got Lyn with me. We have an appointment to discuss potential dates for our wedding service and so on.'

Both looked around the half-open door.

We'll look stupid if the reverend opens on us, thought Lyn.

'Are you there, reverend? We don't mean to interrupt, but—.'

Ant felt a rush of turbulent air as he opened the entrance door. The vicar's papers flew into a frenzied cyclone, making the room take on the appearance of a winter storm with oversized snowflakes.

'Shut the door,' exclaimed Lyn as she pointed to the heavy timber door.

Ant commented, 'That was savage,' as he leaned against the closed door and watched the papers fall.

Only then did something dawn on the pair.

'I'm stating the obvious, but there's no vicar,' said Lyn.

'And I'm about to do the same. Something isn't right here.' Ant looked around as he picked his way through the paper debris and crossed the stone floor to the vicar's disorganised desk. He moved his hand to lift the heavy receiver of an old-fashioned telephone on the vicar's paper-strewn desk, before thinking better of the idea. 'Oops, don't want to contaminate potential evidence and confuse Peter Riley with my fingerprints.'

'Now that would be funny, you know. Him having to deal with you as a suspect.'

'No, it wouldn't,' replied Ant with a deep frown forming on his forehead.

Feeling an inside pocket, he retrieved his mobile and selected the police station from his contacts list.

'Aren't you overreacting?' commented Lyn as she chided her companion as he held a finger over the call button.

'Don't ring the police station, at least not yet. We'll look like right idiots if we call Peter Riley, only to watch the vicar follow him through the door a few seconds later.'

'I'm surprised. I thought you might be the one keen to report the vicar missing, so I'm not sure why you're having a go at me. What am I supposed to do?'

Lyn raised her eyebrows, 'Do? Nothing for now. First you make me cover my fingers to close the door like some latter-day Agatha Christie character, and then you call in the cavalry.'

He smiled. 'The local police force are many things, although likening them to the Coldstream Guards is not one of them.'

Lyn tiptoed between the untidy paper trail and neared her betrothed. 'Listen, smarty-pants. For all we know, the reverend may be in the vicarage making himself a cup of tea to go with the chocolate digestive biscuits Cybil Dawson keeps him supplied with.'

Ant roared with laughter. 'Cybil Dawson. Is she still going? I thought teaching you self-defence last year might have seen her off. She must be seventy, at least—'

'Seventy-six if you must know, and no one has "seen her off". In fact, she runs two classes a week now and would take the vicar tomorrow if he'd have her.'

Ant screwed up his face. 'Yuck, the thought of it?'

'You are stupid. I meant as his housekeeper, not his wife!'

A scratchy voice came from Ant's mobile.

'Ah, yes, oops,' replied its embarrassed owner. 'Wrong number, bye.' Slipping the phone back into his inside pocket, Ant frowned. 'Fred Battersby will have recognised me. You know there's not much he misses.'

Lyn laughed. 'You're right. Then again, the station's lovely desk sergeant will assume you're being as absent minded as ever.'

'Oi,' complained Ant. 'Less of the "as ever" bit.'

A quick exchange of smiles soon faded as the potential seriousness of the situation sank in.

'What about a robbery? There's been a few churches targeted over recent months for their silver plate,' commented Lyn as she looked around the desolate space. 'His books are on the floor. And look there,' she added, pointing at two open drawers in a small desk. 'His diary is missing. He always keeps it in the left one.'

Her companion gazed at the open draws, then at the stout wall cupboard that held the church plate. Rattling the

KEITH FINNEY

small oak doorknobs, he tried to gain access to its precious contents. 'Still locked... and I don't see a thief bothering to lock it again after nicking the silver, do you?'

If it wasn't a robbery, what's happening? thought Lyn as she frowned in confused agreement with Ant.

They moved around the vestry, looking for clues, taking care not to disturb anything to preserve the scene in case they called Inspector Riley.

Their search for clues came to a sudden end as a sharp crack of a Norfolk latch being lifted filled the air.

'There, I told you he'd just nipped out and left the door open. I bet he went back to the vicarage to check his diary.'

Within seconds, a sudden gust of wind caused the lying paper to take to the air again like a maelstrom and dashing Lyn's hope of welcoming the vicar.

'It's only me. Goodness, what's been going on here?' The tall, upright frame of Thorndike, the village doctor, almost fell in the room on a strong following wind. He shut the door and leaned against its ancient timbers. 'Thank goodness for that. The forecast says we're in for more squalls. It's awful out there.'

Thorndike gave both a confused look as a snowstorm of paper fell. 'I came to see the vicar.'

'So did we,' replied Lyn.

The doctor gazed at the interior door as Lyn briefed the doctor on what they'd found.

'And that's how we ended up here. Did you have an appointment too?'

Doctor Thorndike shook his head. 'Not in so many words. The vicar rang me at home last night to say he wasn't feeling himself, and might I pop in when passing.'

Ant jangled his car keys as he tried to get to grips with the timeline of events. 'A little odd him ringing you at home instead of waiting for the surgery to open, don't you think? How did he sound to you?'

Thorndike thought for a few seconds. 'As you know, few people have my home number. I'm ex-directory for a reason. It means only the emergency services, and a few selected ... like Lyn and you have my number. So does the vicar. I assumed he rang me, worried about a parishioner—you know how involved he gets sometimes, usually to his detriment. You ask how he sounded? I'd say, unsettled.'

'Unsettled?' repeated Lyn.

'Yes, unsettled rather than out of sorts. Oh, dear, I'm not making sense, am I? What I mean is that I didn't get the feeling he showed any outward signs of illness, and he wouldn't elaborate further. After he asked me to call, he seemed to regret making the request. He said he didn't mean to have disturbed me and not to worry.'

'But still you came?' said Ant.

'If a patient goes to the trouble of calling me at home, knowing how I value my privacy when "off duty," then apologises and says not to bother. Well, that's when alarm bells ring. Reverend Morton is many things. However, a time waster he is not. I thought I'd—'

The doctor's mobile interrupted his flow. Pressing the icon on his handset to accept the call, he placed the phone next to his ear and listened to the voice. 'Right, I'll be with you in a couple of minutes.'

'Trouble?' asked Lyn.

A few seconds later, Thorndike closed the call. 'Jenny Palsgrove thinks she's going into labour. I'm sure it's a Braxton-Hicks, but I'd better check her over and put her mind at ease.'

A concerned look spread across Lyn's face. 'But she told

me the other day as she picked up her eldest from school that she's about thirty-weeks along?'

Thorndike nodded. 'That's right, but her previous child was four weeks premature, so mum's more cautious this time. Understandable, of course, but I'll put my best bedside manner on and calm things down.' He looked at his watch. 'Better get a move on. Keep me updated about the vicar, will you? Something isn't right.'

Thorndike braced himself against the windy conditions, opened the door, then closed it behind him before too much paper flew about again.

'Poor Jenny, I hope she's alright,' said Lyn in a concerned tone.

Ant came closer to his fiance and coupled her arm in his. 'Don't worry, Thorndike is the best. He'll sort her out, yes?'

Lyn gave him an uncertain smile.

The vestry returned to its earlier settled state as they looked around the dishevelled room.

'I don't think there's much doubt that we should call Peter Riley in, is there?' suggested Ant.

Lyn uncoupled her arm and wandered over to the open drawers of the vicar's desk. 'I keep thinking of his diary. He's never without the thing.' She turned to him and said, 'I'll make the call.'

'No, don't touch it.'

Ant's urgent call took Lyn by surprise, causing her to retract her extended arm as if the telephone were on fire. She froze.

'Apologies, Lyn, It's just—'

'Fingerprints. Yes, I know… what was I thinking about?'

He gave her a reassuring peck on the cheek. 'You were thinking about Jenny, that's what. Listen, she's in excellent hands. Everything will work out. Come on, I'll ring from my mobile.'

Seconds passed before the call connected. 'Ah, it's you again, or do you need Hammond's Bakery, or perhaps Sid and Carol's chippy?'

Ant turned to Lyn and mouthed, 'Fred knows it's me.'

'It's not the dark ages, you know, they'll have call recognition. Of course, he knows it's you, silly,' whispered Lyn.

He resigned himself to his fate and tried to explain.

'Never mind that now, young man, I'll get the inspector to you, tout-suite,' replied the desk sergeant in a calm, jovial tone before ending the call.

'Serves you right for not explaining what you wanted.'

'But you told me not to call.'

'I don't think I did?'

'Yes, you did, and you know it.'

'Never mind that now. He'll be here in five-minutes.'

Ant shook his head in disbelief at how easily his fiance had a knack for reinventing the past to her advantage.

The time passed quickly as they gathered their thoughts for the detective's imminent arrival.

'I told you, here he comes.' She looked towards the outside door as the latch lifted. 'Well, here we go.'

In walked the rain-soaked figure of Detective Inspector Peter Riley. 'Is that right?' said Riley as he removed his dripping gabardine and looked for somewhere to hang it.

'Be careful you don't disturb any evidence, Peter,' said Lyn as she gave Ant a triumphant look.

'Er, yes,' replied the inspector before finally deciding. He rolled up the damp coat and stuffed it under his arm.

'Won't that soak your suit jacket?' asked Lyn.

Riley glimpsed his damp coat, shrugged his shoulders, and frowned.

'Now, back to my question. Who told—'

Ant got in first. 'My fiance thought the vicar had just nipped out for a self-defence class with Cybil Dawson.'

Riley frowned as he gazed first at Lyn, then at the turmoil strewn around the vestry.

'You well know I said he'd gone to the vicarage to check something in his diary,' asserted Lyn as she grimaced at her intended.

Inspector Riley closed his eyes in bemusement and held up his left arm. 'Enough, you two. That call disturbed an interview I was conducting with a known villain. And for what? To listen to two thirty-five-year-olds bickering like kids?'

His targets stood with their heads bowed like ragamuffins awaiting their fate outside the headmaster's office.

'We're both thirty-two, if you must know.'

Ant let out a schoolboy giggle.

'Oh, I give up. What's the point?' said Riley in a weary tone as he removed the wet jacket from under his arm and inspected the damp patch in his suit jacket.

The objects of his displeasure looked at one another and exchanged guilty looks.

'We apologise for not taking the matter seriously.'

'I should think so. My desk sergeant told me who phoned him.'

'Actually, it was him.'

'There you go again. I'm not bothered who picked up that telephone. My job is to find out if someone has committed a criminal offence here. It's as simple as that.' He fixed his look on Ant. 'And I hope you wore gloves when you pawed that phone?'

Serves him right for going on at me about compromising evidence, thought Lyn. She smiled, the edges of her mouth moving upward just enough for Ant to take the point.

'Nope. I rang the police station on my mobile. I know better than to touch anything,' replied Ant.

'You could tell me why you called,' Riley continued.

The two miscreants looked at each. This time Lyn struck first by explaining the events leading up to the call.

'That's it? You heard a noise and assumed it was the vicar, then found he'd vanished? I assume you've checked for clues, or were you too preoccupied to notice the missing key on the rack?'

His friends gave the rack a blank stare before Lyn had a burst of inspiration.

'If I'm not mistaken, the missing key fits the old records chest by the west door. Heaven knows when it was last opened.'

Riley walked towards the connecting door from the vestry to the chancel. 'Perhaps it's time we looked?'

The inspector did his best to avoid standing on the paper lying about the floor as he passed through the doorway, with Ant and Lyn following close behind.

I love this church.

Lyn first looked at the altar, behind which stood an oak table holding several pieces of ancient pewter plate.

She wondered about the medieval images that were covered over when all churches received the order to whitewash them in Tudor times. Lyn knew they'd found a fragment near the belfry loft opening years ago and wished the parish could have found the money for a full investigation.

'Come on you,' whispered Ant as he urged Lyn to get a move on.

'Coming,' she responded as she brought herself back to the problems of the present.

They stood in a row a few feet from the heavy timber chest that had wrought iron banding around its body and cross-ways on the arched lid. A magnificent escutcheon plate hid the keyhole, which gave access to its secrets. Inspector Riley stepped forward and inspected the escutcheon plate.

'There's a trace of fresh blood on this. Whoever turned the key needs help. We might ask ourselves if it belongs to our elusive vicar?'

Chapter Two

HE SAID, SHE SAID

THE WHERRY ARMS was unusually busy for a Wednesday lunchtime as Ant and Lyn settled into a corner table and eagerly awaited Jed's famous mixed grill. As he set two hot plates in front of them, the feast met with two different reactions. Ant's face was full of anticipation at the treat to come as he took a gulp of his pint of Bodger Ale.

'Isn't this fab?' oozed Ant.

Lyn's reaction could not have been more different.

I should have gone for Lil's sausage bap, she thought.

'If you mean the odd-looking gammon, undernourished chop, and anaemic chips, then I suppose, yes, it's a treat.'

The conversation about mushy vs garden peas paused when Fitch arrived at the pub.

'Do you two never stop arguing? What is it this time, whether the rain will set in, or will the sun crack the flags? Or, who's going to pay for that… er, what is it?'

Ant gave his friend a pained look. 'Mushy peas—and don't start.'

Fitch indulged in a few seconds over-acting as he bent forward to inspect his friend's lunch. 'With a mixed grill?'

Lyn pointed to her fiance's plate with her knife. 'There, I told you we should have ordered garden peas. Even Jed gave you a funny look, which says something coming from the culinary philistine that he is.'

Ant muttered as he gathered a large portion of the offending legume onto his fork. He gave his friends a look of defiance as he scoffed it all in one go.

Fitch shook his head. 'Time to move on from peas. What have you two been up to then? If he's paying for this lot, there must be a reason. Come on, spill the beans... or should that be peas?'

Ant continued to ignore Fitch as Lyn took a sip of her lemonade before placing the glass back on the small circular pub table.

'So, there you have it,' said Lyn as she finished reprising the events of that morning.

A twinkle shone from the mechanic's eyes. 'So let me get this right. The vicar has run for it rather than meet with you two to talk about wedding dates? He sounds like a sensible chap to me, does our reverend?'

At that moment, Jed sauntered over. 'Everything all right here? 'Who did you say is running?' Having your usual, Fitch?'

The mechanic smiled at his host. 'Yes, please, and it's the vicar who has scarpered.' Jed put a hand to his right temple in a faux salute, turned, then stopped. 'The vicar, you say. More likely he's still running from that Cynthia Hake.'

Three pairs of ears pricked up. 'Cynthia?' exclaimed Lyn. 'What's she been up to?'

Jed shrugged his shoulders. 'All I know is that a couple

of my regulars said they saw Reverend Morton and Cynthia arguing in the churchyard last night. It seems the vicar stormed off and left the poor woman standing there. At least that's what I heard.'

Ant and Lyn exchanged eager looks.

'It looks like there are things we don't know about the vicar. Maybe he's a discreet philanderer, pursuing the unmarried women in the area?'

Ant burst out laughing. 'Remember we're talking about Stephen Morton here. He may be a little eccentric, but hardly one to chase the ladies.'

'And don't forget the drinking,' chipped in Jed.

'Drink? He doesn't… does he?' exclaimed Lyn.

'Don't you believe it. He's a good customer of mine on the quiet.'

The three men continued to exchange racy banter until Lyn brought a measure of sobriety to bear. 'Let's not forget that the inspector found fresh blood on the old parish records' chest. I know it's tempting to make light of the situation, but something is wrong here. Who told you they'd been arguing, anyway?'

Jed's smile faded at Lyn's timely reminder of the potential seriousness of the situation.

'Bootsy Williams.'

The same expression of surprise spread across the bar owner's customers.

'Bootsy?' exclaimed Ant.

'He's a nut,' added Fitch.

'Never mind what he is,' interrupted Lyn. 'It's years since any of us have seen him and perhaps he's changed from when he was a kid. I thought he'd gone for good.'

Jed shrugged his shoulders. 'Seems his dad died a while ago and he's back to claim his inheritance.'

All four realised they could hear a pin drop in the bar.

'What are you lot staring at? Have you nothing better to do than earwig people's private conversations? Get on with your drinking or I'll put the towels over the pumps.'

The threat of being deprived of alcohol was enough to persuade Jed's regulars to mind their own business, or at least not to make eavesdropping so obvious.

Fitch continued to revive memories of his youth. 'I never saw him in a pair of ordinary shoes... always boots.'

'That family was as poor as the proverbial church mouse. His dad was a dock hand in Great Yarmouth, so was always in and out of work. It must have been hard for them. I assumed he wore work boots because that's what his father got hold of. I remember they never fitted him... always too big,' said Lyn.

Ant let out a chuckle. 'I guess that's why he was full of bruises from tripping over his own feet.'

'That wasn't the boots,' added Fitch. 'It was his father.'

'What?' said Lyn in a shocked tone.

'Fitch is right,' explained Jed. 'I saw Bootsy once after he'd felt the back of his father's hand. He told me he couldn't wait until he left school because he'd take off at the first chance. It turns out he was as good as his word.'

'You must have come across the same issue in your professional life?' commented Ant.

Lyn sat pensively, listening to the shocking revelation. It took several seconds for her companion's question to sink in. 'Not so much the bruising... I, er... I suppose parents who are that way inclined know we'll pick up on it straight away and call in Child Services. Then again, you don't have to smack a child to damage them. So yes, I suppose today it's the same, only different.'

The mood around the table deteriorated as they each took in Lyn's devastating conclusions.

A voice shouted, 'How about a pint, Jed? I'm spitting feathers. So is Albert here.'

The question was enough to lift the mood as Jed let out a sigh before turning to leave the gathering and headed back to the bar. 'Alright, alright, don't get your knickers in a twist... and as for Albert, is he asleep again or is he dead this time?'

The regulars laughed as Albert's table companion gave the old man a nudge.

'Mine's a pint,' mumbled the newly conscious regular.

Jed shook his head. 'I'll swear those will be Albert's last words. Perhaps we should pay to have it inscribed on his headstone.' The pub owner's quip raised a second chorus of laughs as he poured the old man's beer by giving an ornate ebony and brass pump handle a hefty pull.

Thank heavens that's over. Thought Lyn.

Taking his cue from the tone of levity in the bar, Ant shouted over to Jed, 'So, where will we find our mutual friend?'

'Their old place down Sheep Dip Lane. You'll know it when you get to it. There's an old tractor in what's supposed to be their front garden. Must have been there for twenty years or more. Just a warning. Don't forget he has a temper. If I remember correctly, he hated you because you were, now, what did he call you? That posh bu—'

'No need, I remember.'

Lyn reflected on Jed's words by remembering all the times she'd rescued Ant from Bootsy's angry fists at school. I never understood why he never fought back.

'Nothing for it,' said Ant. 'We'll have to find the man,

flying fists or not. He might just have information that leads us to the vicar.'

They spent the next few minutes agreeing on the best approach to take with Bootsy, together with Fitch agreeing to tell inspector Riley what they were up to.

'The inspector will have to wait until I've finished old man Eccles' car. I've got it on the ramps, and he wants it back today, although what he sees in that pile of rust is beyond me.'

Lyn smiled, 'A bit like that rubbish you drive around in… when it's working, anyway.'

Ant gave his best hurt little boy look. 'You know perfectly well that my Morgan is a classic sports car. Isn't that so, Fitch?'

'Don't bring me into this. My little lovebirds, you can fight it out between yourselves.'

'Coward,' giggled Lyn.

'Too right I am,' answered Fitch as he made for the pub door.

———

SHEEP DIP LANE was one of those country roads that time seemed to have bypassed. The road was so rarely used that grass tufts grew through the disintegrating tarmac, giving it a wild garden appearance. Overgrown hawthorn hedges and mature Juniper trees blocked out light on both sides of the track.

Bootsy's cottage hid behind vegetation, tucked away from the road. Remnants of a front garden long abandoned remained with an occasional rose attempting to make itself known to the world. Ant brought the Morgan to a controlled stop, making no effort to pull off what passed for a roadway, judging it unlikely any vehicle might need to pass.

'Are you sure this is the place?' said Ant as he surveyed the rundown property.

Lyn hopped out of the open-topped sports car and pushed open the remains of a handsome garden gate. 'Well, there's the old tractor, and there doesn't seem to be anything else down the road.'

Ant shrugged his shoulders and joined his companion at the entrance to the dilapidated property. 'Notice anything weird?'

'No, I don't hear a sound?'

'Spot on. It's as if the wildlife has given up the ghost and done a runner. It's not natural.'

Lyn scanned a line of trees and thick undergrowth. 'I can't disagree. This place gives me the creeps. Come on, let's get this over and done with, then get back to civilisation.'

'So that's what you call Stanton Parva on a busy day?'

'You are silly sometimes, my little Lord Fauntleroy.' She watched as her intended scrunched his nose, knowing that he found the term irritating.

'Hah ha, I don't think,' responded Ant. 'Come on, let's see if the man is at home... or whatever this place passes for.'

He knocked on the tired-looking door, causing loose flakes of old paint and bone-dry putty from a small glass pane to fall away. 'Nothing. The place looks deserted. I reckon Jed got it wrong or mixed it up with another place. What do you think?'

Lyn was attempting to see into a ground-floor room through a grime-covered window and ripped net curtain that had long past any chance of repair. 'I agree and don't see how anyone might live in this place. Why not give it one more go, then we'll get off?'

Just as Ant rapped on the weather-beaten door for a second time, an angry male voice filled the still air. 'Get off my land.'

They turned toward the voice.

'Steady, fella. Put that shotgun down, you'll hurt somebody with that. I assume you're Bootsy?'

The agitated man levelled the gun at Ant. 'Not somebody, mate. It'll be you if you don't shift. And take her with you while you're about it.' The shotgun remained aimed at his unwanted visitor's chest. Yet he hesitated.

'Wait a minute, I know you. You're that posh bu—'

'You still have that chip on your shoulder, I see?'

Bootsy pulled the shotgun tighter into his right shoulder. 'Careful, Lord Snooty. I'm the one in charge now. I wondered how you knew my nickname. That makes you Lyn Blackthorn, I suppose? Still protecting the lord of the manor's son, I see?'

Is he angry enough to pull that trigger? thought Lyn. She tried a smile to see if the gesture might take the heat out of the confrontation. His eyes are cold as ice. I don't like this at all.

'That was a long time ago. What say we start again? We need your help.'

Lyn's words shocked Bootsy. Before long, he loosened his grip on the shotgun and lowered the deadly weapon. 'You want my help?' Now there's a turn up for the books. It wasn't like that at school, was it? You two were like all the others. At me all the time because I didn't dress like the rest of you. I hated every one of you... and still do.' He stiffened his grip on the gun.

'Steady,' said Ant in a calm, confident voice while holding an open palm out to the agitated man.

I wonder if there's another way, thought Lyn.

'Does that include Jed?'

Bootsy narrowed his eyes. 'Don't bring him into this. He was different from the rest of you.'

Where do we go now? Perhaps it's time to stretch the truth a little.

'Jed wanted to come with us today … He told us you were back and where to find you.'

She noticed Ant giving her a side-glance.

Come on, Bootsy, take the bait, thought Lyn.

The man's eyes shifted between his uninvited guests before settling on Lyn as he played with the safety latch on the shotgun. 'Don't try to trick me. Jed was the only one who ever listened to me. He understood because he didn't fit in either. If you're lying to me, I'll—'

'No trick,' replied Lyn as she took a mobile from her jacket pocket and held it out to him. 'I'll put the number in. You can talk to him yourself. OK, I fibbed about him wanting to come with us, but the rest is the truth. Here, you can ask him.' Lyn urged the man to take her phone.

Bootsy looked at the mobile, then back at its owner. He relaxed before putting his guard back up. 'Stop lying to me.'

Lyn kept her gaze fixed on the aggressor while retracting her arm and dialling in Jed's number. She watched as Bootsy narrowed his eyes.

Got to stay calm Ant… and please be at home, Jed.

After what seemed like an age, a voice crackled down the line. Lyn looked at the signal's strength.

We're in the middle of nowhere surround by tall trees. I hope I don't lose the line to Jed.

'Give me the phone,' barked the gunman as his level of agitation reached a new height.

'Calm down… here… here's Jed for you.'

Bootsy switched the shotgun into his left hand and let it fall to his side. He grabbed the mobile from Lyn's right hand and thrust it to his ear. 'That you, Jed? Did you tell 'em where I lived?'

I hope Jed's got his serious head on and doesn't muck about with Bootsy, thought Lyn.

She could tell by Bootsy's loosening grip on his shotgun that Jed was saying the right things.

Thank goodness for that. Perhaps we will see the day out after all, she thought, looking at Ant's relieved features as he, too, got the drift of the mobile conversation.

'See you soon, mate,' was all that Bootsy said before closing the call and handing Lyn her mobile. 'He says you're alright. We'll see. Jed told me what you wanted. Why should I care about the vicar? His lot did nothing for me.'

'This is a man's life we're talking about. Don't you care about anything but yourself? For goodness' sake, grow up,' said Lyn, unable to hide her agitation.

Bootsy raised his shotgun again. 'Jed said you'd changed… he's wrong. Now get off my land or I'll shoot the both of you.'

Ant tried to calm the escalating situation. 'Now you know what I have to put up with day after day,' He offered Bootsy a knowing smile.

Lyn flashed Ant an angry stare as she watched the two men exchange knowing smirks.

If I get my hold of that gun, it'll be me who's doing the shooting around here, she fumed to herself.

Ant tried to build on his newfound rapport with the angry man. 'Look, anything you can tell us might just help find the vicar.'

'Stop asking me stuff about a man I can't stand. Given

half a chance, I'd knock him for six,' replied Bootsy, now in full-on confrontation mode.

Lyn spoke, only for Ant to touch her arm. She took the hint.

'I guess Jed told you why we're here. We just need a name. Who was the woman arguing with the vicar? That's all we need to know, and we'll leave you in peace... please.'

Jed seemed amused at the power he now had over Ant, then his eyes narrowed. 'Wait a minute, I've got nothing to do with anything. Just because I said I'd like to smack the vicar. It doesn't mean—'

'No, no, of course not,' replied Ant.

'She was giving it to him, I tell you. He looked scared to death.'

'A name? Please, it will help so much.'

Bootsy thought for a few seconds and gave Lyn a cursory look before concentrating on Ant. 'I dunno, but I've seen her working up at the cafe on Stanton Broad. Doesn't look as though butter would melt, but seeing her go for him in the dog collar. It was something wicked.'

The two men exchanged a second knowing look and smiled.

'I know what you mean, mate. But listen, thanks for the info and as I promised, that's it. We'll leave you to get on with your day.'

Ant turned to Lyn and ushered her toward the gate. For now, she kept her counsel and complied.

As they left, Ant turned back to Bootsy, whose shotgun tracked their every move. 'Thanks again for the information. Are you thinking of sticking around?'

Bootsy glared at his inquisitor. 'That's my business, posh boy.'

Ant took the hint.

Once through the gate, Lyn pulled her arm away from his gentle grip. As they reached the Morgan, Lyn turned to her intended. 'I didn't appreciate being talked down to like that. Don't you think you took "the little lady" stuff a too far?

He paused while looking back at Bootsy's cottage. Feeling for Lyn's hand, he turned back to her. 'I'm sorry if it came across like that. I was more interested in saving our lives.'

Chapter Three

YOU FIRST

THURSDAY MORNING BROKE with an overcast sky and a threat of heavy rain as Ant gazed into his half-drunk mug of coffee in Fitch's disorganised office. 'And to cap it all, Lyn's told me to stay at Stanton Hall.'

'Well, how on earth did you expect her to react?'

Ant shrugged his shoulders and took another sip of his coffee. 'Not like that. For heaven's sake. All I did was try, successfully, as things turned out, to get us a name and not get us shot and off she goes like a rocket. There's gratitude for you. And to top it all off, she says I've to move all my vintage car memorabilia out of her house as well.'

Fitch rose from his dilapidated typing chair and took the two steps needed to reach the paint-splattered sink. He rinsed his coffee mug with cold water and scoured the inside with an oil-stained index finger. 'Well, that's no bad thing. I've been telling you for years that most of it is old tat.'

Ant gave his friend a tormented look.

'It's no use you looking at me like that. You say you told Lyn to grow up? If you ask me, I—'

'I didn't,' moaned Ant as he drank that last of his coffee.

'That's what I mean. It's time for you to grow up. We're not at school now and she won't pander to you every time you play the little-boy-lost card.'

Ant stood, stepped to the sink, and gently nudged his friend to one side. He placed his empty mug onto the drainer, making no attempt to wash it out or make eye contact with his closest male friend.

'I'll wash it, shall I?'

Ant didn't respond, as he turned and shuffled over to a window that gave a grime-covered view of the garage forecourt.

'See what I mean,' continued Fitch. 'Not dealing with it doesn't make it go away. I tell you what, if you'd have spoken to me like you did to Lyn, I'd have punched your lights out.'

Ant again did not react.

Fitch decided he'd had enough of his friend's moping. Crossing the floor until he stood behind his friend, he grabbed an arm and spun Ant around so that they faced each other with just inches between them.

'Whichever way you look at it, it's not the way to treat women, especially the one you expect to marry. I say "expect", because the way you're going, that's about as likely to happen as... well, how many pigs do you see flying out there?'

Ant still couldn't look at Fitch and didn't resist being manhandled. 'All I said was—'

'you've told me all that stuff and it doesn't change a thing. You've got some grovelling to do and not much time to get it done. If you let Lyn stew in her temper with you, she'll convince herself you're not worth the trouble. Just because we all grew up together, don't think the affection she has for your mum and dad will change the way she thinks.'

The tiny office fell silent.

Several seconds passed as his unseeing gaze focused on his friend. A tear trickled down his cheek as he pulled back and looked over to the rear door of the garage office.

'If you run away again, Anthony, you're giving Lyn up. Do you understand? The thing is, are you going to take what looks to you to be the easy way out, or will you fix this... and I mean fix it now?'

Ant took a last look at the back door before finally acknowledging Fitch's presence. He fixed his look on the man before lowering his gaze.

'It's already too late. Lyn made that clear last night.'

'Rubbish,' shouted Fitch, making Ant jump. He looked at his wristwatch. 'It's coming up to twelve, so they'll break for lunchtime soon. I suggest you get yourself over to her office and make your peace. Say whatever you need to say... so long as you mean it. I dunno, take her out somewhere nice for lunch—and I don't mean Jed's mixed grill or a Cornish pasty from the bakers.'

A few seconds that felt like an age passed as Ant processed his friend's advice.

'I suppose so, but I still say it got us to find out where that woman works.'

'And at what cost, you stupid man? Is it something in your aristocratic genes that makes you believe you can't ever be mistaken and "ordinary" folk are supposed to bow and scrape to you?'

'Don't be stupid,' replied an angry Ant.

'That's rich coming from you. Let me ask you something. If your dad was standing here instead of me, what would he tell you to do?'

Mention of his father brought Ant up with a start. 'Don't bring my father into—'

'Why?' interrupted Fitch. 'Because you know I'm right and he'd tell you what you did was wrong and no way to speak to anybody, especially Lyn? That's the truth, isn't it?'

The two men continued to square off as tempers flared.

Fitch looked at his watch again. 'Anyway, I've got a car to recover, so I'll leave you to stew in your own juice. Make sure you snap the lock closed when you leave... by whichever door you choose.'

Ant remained in the untidy office for several minutes before making his mind to move. He knew Fitch's reference to choose by which door he left was a metaphor for sticking around or making a run for it. If he left the village, then what? Back to army intelligence? They didn't want him and yet they wouldn't discharge him either. The stalemate angered Ant, but knew he couldn't resign his commission because of the shame it would cause the family. Ant also recognised he owed it to the personnel he served with not to turn his back on them for the sake of convenience.

'Blast my PTSD,' he muttered.

In the end, he opened the front door to the office, and as instructed, made sure the lock snapped into place, before heading towards Stanton Parva Primary School. Looking up at the heavy sky, he thought it an apt reflection of his mood. During the five minutes it took him to reach the gates, he'd dismissed two greetings of "Afternoon" from locals with only a cursory response. He knew his behaviour drew surprised looks from the bemused villagers. Now he stood gripping the wrought-iron gates to the playground as if his life depended on it.

'Hello, stranger. I hear you're in her bad books?' The voice of Lyn's secretary, Tina Broughton, stirred Ant from his stupor. He turned and looked at the petite woman without comment.

'Blimey, as bad as that, eh? Now I know why madam in there is in such a foul mood. She said you argued, but goodness me, was it that serious?'

Ant looked at the weather-worn stone flags that formed the pavements throughout the village. He shrugged his shoulders.

Tina looked around, then tutted. 'Well, you're here, so I assume you intend to have it out with her and are just plucking up the courage to open the gate? I'll protect you and make sure Lyn can't throw anything at you. Nothing's as bad as we imagine,' continued Tina. 'You, above all people, know that. Come on, let's get this done so we can all resume business as usual. I'm fed up with treading on eggshells with her. She's even been snapping at the kids, which isn't like her at all.'

Tina pushed the gate open and took hold of Ant's arm. 'I've got some fresh ground coffee on and I'm sure I can find some chocolate digestives. Lyn won't waste her favourite treat chucking them in your direction.'

The walk to Lyn's office reminded Ant of the dread he felt when he made the same journey as a boy. Except this time, he knew the stakes were much higher. Would Lyn hear him out or refuse to see him at all? What would he do then? Thoughts of dread coursed through his brain as they covered the last few yards remaining until they entered the administration block.

Passing through the entrance, he picked up the familiar smell of floor polish and dinner being prepared that he remembered so well.

'Come on, I'll tell her you're here. Sit in my chair so she can't see you,' said Tina as she tapped on Lyn's door and prepared to deal with whatever reaction she got from her boss.

'Tell him he can take a run and jump off Yarmouth pier', was all he heard before Tina closed the door behind her and disappeared into the headteacher's office. From now on, all that Ant would hear was the muffled sound of two voices raising and lowering in time to the rapidity of their various rapid exchanges.

Ant wondered if Tina was giving Lyn the same pep-talk that Fitch had given him.

I guess I'll find out the second Tina opens that door.

He didn't have long to wait. The school secretary popped her head around the doorframe. 'The biscuits did the trick.' Tina beckoned him forward with a curled finger. 'And don't mess it up this time... because something tells me you won't get a second chance,' she whispered.

This was one of those times when Ant wished the floor might open and swallow him whole, rather than face the controlled wrath of his betrothed. He took a deep breath in and left the safety of Tina's chair behind as he reached the door.

The secretary didn't allow him to hang around. Instead, she almost pulled him into Lyn's office, retreated and shut the door behind her, leaving the visitor to his uncertain fate.

Lyn sat behind her cluttered desk wearing an inscrutable expression that she knew would knock Ant off his guard, unable to read her mood.

Am I being too hard on him? she thought, as her fiancé stood frozen to the spot, not sure what to do with himself. *What he did humiliated me. Why am I the one that feels awful?*

Lyn pushed her chair back, stood and walked the short distance to the two chequered cloth armchairs arranged at a slight angle. She sat in one and motioned with the flick of her eyes that Ant should sit opposite. He understood at once and complied with the instruction.

Time passed as they looked at each other, before one broke eye contact to fuss with a sleeve before restoring eye contact. The stand-off continued until Lyn's office door opened. Tina entered holding a tray on which sat two steaming mugs of coffee and several round biscuits.

'I thought this might help,' said Tina as she placed the tray on a low table that kept the two armchairs apart.

Lyn offered the slightest of smiles while keeping her eyes on Ant.

'No need to say thank you. All part of the service,' said Tina in a sardonic tone as she glanced at the pair. 'I'm going to say this whether you like it or not,' started the secretary as she stood back from the warring parties. 'You two have been together one way or another for most of your lives, so why are you giving each other daggers? I don't know what happened yesterday. It's none of my business. However, what is my business is putting a stop to this nonsense before it goes too far to be put back together.'

Lyn stared at her coffee while Ant played with a digestive. Neither acknowledged Tina's words.

'Lyn, you are a woman used to getting her own way. This place is your world where what you say goes—but it's not the real world. As for you, Anthony, you're a man who's led, and continues to lead a privileged life. You might control everything that goes on, on your father's estate, but you can't control everything and everyone you come across.'

Tina noticed a flicker of acknowledgement between the two. 'You might well both blush. It's time you learned to recognise how pride and thick-headedness eventually destroy trust, and yes, love. If you ask me, which I know you're not, but non-the-less, hear this. Perhaps this should have happened years ago so that each of you could decide what you wanted from life — and each other. As it is, you're on the edge of the biggest decision of your lives. Don't let pride and expecting your own way to come between you now. Do you hear me?'

Tina withdrew to the still open interconnecting door between her office and Lyn's. 'Oh, and headteacher, you have Mr and Mrs Phelps at one-thirty, so whatever you two decide, you need to get a move on with it. Anyway, I'm off for an early lunch, so tat-ta.' With that, Tina left the room before quietly closing the door on the hurt lovers.

Why should I be the one to always make the first move? thought Lyn as she took a sip from her steaming coffee. It's not as if I've done anything wrong.

She looked at Ant, who'd stopped playing with the sweet treat and sunk back into the comfortable upholstery of his chair.

Out of nowhere, Ant spoke in a muted, almost inaudible tone. His eyes remained downcast. 'I told mum and dad about it last night.' His gaze slowly lifted to engage Lyn's unsmiling features. 'They both said how stupid I'd been.'

Lyn replaced her coffee on the low table. 'And what about you, Ant? Any thoughts?'

The brevity of her reply and direct question caused Ant to briefly break eye contact. 'Looking back, I guess I called it wrong.' He nervously looked at Lyn again to test the reception his admission provoked. 'The thing is, I thought I was doing the right thing.'

'Don't do that "You may disagree with me, but", thing politicians always pull when they're in a tight corner. I—'

'No, Lyn. I'm not saying that at all. I'm trying to say

sorry,' said Ant, leaning forward in his chair, hands grasped together in a tight, intertwined knot.

The bluntness of Ant's admission took her by surprise. Gone was the nervousness he'd previously shown. Now Ant looked at her directly.

Blimey, his parents must have had a right go at him. I can't keep this up much longer, thought Lyn.

'Listen,' began Ant. 'Can we start again? Tina was right. We're mates and its daft for something like this to come between us. If I come across all "Lord of the Manor", like. I don't mean to, but—'

'Don't start with the "but's", you were doing OK until then.' Lyn picked up a chocolate biscuit and offered it to Ant. 'Peace offering?' For the first time, the hint of a smile showed.

Lyn held onto the treat tightly as her visitor tried to take it.

'I know I'm not perfect,' Lyn began. 'You diminished me yesterday, and that was so wrong. I'm sure you thought it a clever move to get what you wanted from Bootsy, but just because it worked doesn't make it right. You know, Ant, once we get into that rut of putting each other down as a tool to get something the other one wants, well, that's the end. I saw too much of that stuff with my parents… always trying to score points—and for what, to feel superior for a few seconds? It's corrosive, Ant, and I want none of it.'

Have I gone too far? He's not responsible for my parents' relationship and what that did to me, thought Lyn.

Ant frowned. 'Like it or not, I suppose we're all products of our childhood and the influence people have on us. I know you had a hard time, and still do with your parents and you're right. I should have found another way with

Bootsy instead of using outdated stereotypes that were never acceptable.'

He's trying, thought Lyn.

Ant felt confident enough now to take a risk. Leaning forward over the coffee table, he waited to see if Lyn would reciprocate his peace offering. The seconds felt like an age as he watched and waited.

His fiance leaned forward with the beginnings of a smile spreading across her face. 'We understand each other better now. Yes?'

'Bet your life.'

'Then let's get on with it,' replied Lyn as she moved closer to Ant. Just as he thought they might kiss, Lyn stood and made her way to the door. 'Are you coming?'

'Coming where?' replied Ant.

'To Staithe Cafe for that lunch you owe me. Anything's better than Jed's mixed grill, don't you think? Let's see if Bootsy's tip has legs.'

Ant stood, still disappointed that he'd missed out on an affectionate peck and turned to face the headteacher. 'Mea-culpa'. He patted his chest with an open palm to reinforce his apology.

'Not so fast, matey. You still have tons of humble pie to eat, so you can stop with that public school rubbish and get your wallet out.'

Tina followed their every moved as they passed through her small office. 'Don't forget the Phelps.'

Lyn returned an ironic smile. 'I suppose even those two will be a light relief after an hour with this one.' She nodded in Ant's direction as she turned the doorknob and passed into the corridor.

'I get what you mean,' commented Tina as she caught Ant's mischievous grin and cheeky thumbs up.

'Hm,' muttered Ant. 'What was that you said earlier about the way I spoke to you?'

'That doesn't count.'

Walking along the spotless black and white tiled floor, their progress ended as Lyn spotted two youngsters running towards them. 'No running in the corridors, James, and Ian, and single file please. You know the rules, don't you?'

The two lads immediately slowed to the required walking pace and moved to their left. 'Yes Miss,' replied the boys in unison as they sped up again, once beyond the headteacher.

'Late for their lunch, as usual. I'm not sure who they take more notice of, me or Milly, our dinner lady.'

Ant wore a look of amazement. 'She isn't still working here, is she? I was terrified of her.'

'The one and only, and she hasn't changed one bit apart from the silver locks and a dicky hip. Her bark is worse than her bite and loves the kids. She's the first one to break out the sweeties and hugs if one of them falls and grazes their knee or such like.'

Memories of childhood encounters with the dinner lady flooded back as the pair exited the building and walked across the playground. The space teamed with eager children enjoying their lunch break. Ant and Lyn wasted no time and arrived at the Morgan with its top down, taking advantage of the sunny weather.

'Best make the most of it,' shouted Ant as he raised his voice over the roar of the sports car's throaty engine. Within seconds of starting off up the village high street, Lyn motioned for Ant to stop the car.

'That's Ian Jefferson. He looks in a right state,' said Lyn as she glimpsed the agitated man racing down the wide sandstone steps of the police station. Before her companion said a word, Lyn was out of the stationary Morgan and trotting over to Jefferson.

'Are you OK, Ian?'

'The vicar. He's missing,' replied Jefferson in a breathy tone. 'I don't know what to do. The police aren't saying anything except repeatedly asking me what I was doing yesterday morning, and can I prove it? They obviously think I've done something to the Reverend Morton. How could they think such a thing?'

Lyn tried to calm the agitated man, who was fidgeting and staring at the ground.

'Everyone knows how much you do for the church and the close friendship you have with the vicar,' began Lyn. 'The police are just doing their job. You know what they're like. Listen, why don't you go home and have a nice cup of tea? I promise that as soon as anyone knows anything more about what's happened, we'll be sure to tell you.'

Jefferson calmed down as Lyn rubbed his arm in a comforting gesture. 'I suppose you're right, Ms Blackthorn. Perhaps I'm being silly, but we work so closely together. Why didn't he say anything to me if he was going away? Something bad must have happened.'

'No, no, Ian. Let's not think like that. As I say, have a drink, then check everything is alright at the church, just as you normally do each day. That's what the vicar would expect you to do, isn't it?'

Personalising the instruction as if she were the vicar did the trick. Moments later, Ian Jefferson nodded while giving Lyn a lingering look. He then turned away and made for his cottage on the edge of the village.

Ant patted Lyn's arm as she clambered back into the Morgan. 'He looked in a right state.'

'It's not surprising. He's never away from the church.

Mowing the graveyard, touching the paint up or mopping the floor, Ian's always doing something to help the vicar. No wonder he's so upset.'

———

STAITHE CAFE SAT SERENELY at the head of what had once been a bustling basin of commercial activity. A place where wherries loaded and unloaded all manner of goods and materials to keep the local community going.

The building in which the cafe now stood began life as a boat chandler to keep the wherries in good repair and supplied with the tools of their trade. As the industrial landscape changed with the coming of the railways and better roads, business at the Staithe declined.

Only in recent decades had the growing interest in sailing for leisure provided enough tourists to make a cafe a growing concern. Now, throughout the summer months, the business did a roaring trade in light snacks and cream teas.

They parked in an idyllic spot overlooking the broad as it widened to provide a wide vista of the Norfolk countryside. The pair took in the intoxicating mix of calm waters and beds of rushes, beyond which lay open fields of wheat dancing rhythmically in a light breeze.

'Can't get much better than this, eh?' said Ant as he raised his right arm, allowing the breeze to smother his flesh in a calming balm of country air.

'I can think of one thing that will top it off,' replied Lyn, with a glint in her eye.

Ant smiled. 'Let me guess, some tea in a China cup and a silver plate-stand of crustless sandwiches and fairy cakes.'

'Got it one,' replied Lyn as she clicked the car door open, hopped out and made for the entrance to the old wooden building. Lyn scanned the empty decked area and chose a corner table for two.

As they waited to be served, the pair continued to discuss the disappearance of the vicar.

'Odd, don't you think, that the inspector hasn't been in touch?' said Lyn.

Ant looked around in vain for a server. 'No, it's only been twenty-four hours. I expect Peter's following up a ton of bits and pieces trying to make sense of whether the Reverend Morton has done a runner, or someone's nabbed the poor fellow.'

Lyn gave him one of her more cynical looks. 'That's one way of putting it, I suppose. Now, where on earth is everyone?' She turned to look at the front half-glazed front door to check the establishment was open for business. 'Yep, it says they're open, so let's hope the woman Bootsy described is on shift today.'

'What was it he said? Something to do with butter?' Just then, a small-framed lady in a black tunic covered with a white apron came around a corner of the cafe.

'Oh, you want serving, do you?' she said, offering her customers a stern look.

Lyn tried not to giggle as the irritated waitress looked away while holding a pen and a small duplicate pad in both hands. 'Er, yes, please. May we have two afternoon teas, please?'

The waitress bristled at her request. 'You need to order them before twelve. They take a long time to prepare, you know.' The woman put her pen and pad into her apron pocket. 'I can do you coffee and a baked scone if you like?'

Ant thought he might push his luck. 'Would that be with jam and cream?' He looked at Lyn and winked.

An icy stare and the briefest of responses informed the pair of their culinary fate.

'No cream, and it'll have to be marmalade. Can I get you anything else?'

It's not worth the hassle, thought Lyn as she exchanged a look of resignation with her intended.

The waitress turned on her heels and made off for the kitchen, leaving Lyn and Ant wondering what might turn up on their plates.

'I don't fancy my chances getting a dessert, do you?' asked Ant.

'I'm not betting on it, that's for sure,' replied Lyn.

Minutes ticked by as they waited for their snack, observing a tourist hire-boat manoeuvring the calm waters.

'Some folks aren't safe being let loose on one of those things. Look, they're not wearing life preservers,' remarked Lyn.

'I've got an idea,' said Ant in an eager tone. 'Why don't you nip into the kitchen and cosy up to the angry one? You never know, she might have information we can use?'

Lyn turned and frowned. 'You haven't heard a word that I've said, have you?'

'What? Yes, of course I have. You were talking about the King.'

'Oh, I give up,' replied Lyn in an exasperated tone.

'What do you think?'

'You don't want to know, Anthony Stanton, but if you mean chatting the waitress up, what's to lose?'

Within a minute, Lyn had reappeared.

'Anything?' asked Ant.

Lyn held her arms up in exasperation. 'All I asked was if she knew the Reverend Morton.'

'And...' asked Ant expectantly.

Lyn shrugged her shoulders, 'And nothing. She looked like she'd put her finger in an electric socket. She froze, then did a runner.'

'A runner?'

'Are you deaf?' replied Lyn. 'Look, there she goes,' said Lyn as she pointed to a compact car making off at speed.

Ant smiled. 'Now I wonder why an innocent person might do that?'

Chapter Four

REFLECTIONS

I BET *he'll be interested to hear about Cynthia,* thought Lyn, as the pair headed back to the church after missing out on lunch at the Staithe Cafe.

Ant turned into the familiar car park of the old church and brought the Morgan to a smooth stop. Without waiting for his companion, Ant set off toward a headstone he knew only too well.

I'd better leave him for a minute or two.

She watched as he stood next to the grave of his elder brother, Greg, and wondered what maelstrom of thoughts coursed through the head of her fiance at that moment.

His life would have been so different had Greg not wrapped his car around that stupid tree.

She got out of the low sports car and quietly shut the passenger door. She noted how reassuring he seemed to find palming the granite headstone, curling his right hand across the still sharp top edge of the memorial.

Lyn snuggled into him and placed a comforting arm around his waist. They stood, oblivious to other people nearby, busying themselves, changing over the flowers dedicated to a loved one.

'Come on,' said Lyn as she nudged Ant for a second time. 'Let's get inside.'

Following her instructions, he lowered his voice respectfully and checked his clothing for correctness. Lyn gazed around the church's interior and its mix of architecture. She marvelled at the Norman arches and rounded window reveals, and medieval flourishes of flamboyance.

'It's crazy to think about the happiness and grief these walls have soaked up over the better part of a thousand years, isn't it?'

Ant looked up at the delicate roof structure that soared above, as if suspended in mid-air. 'Do you believe that?'

'Don't you feel a sense of peace in here?'

Lyn's comment brought on a rare moment of emotion from a man who'd seen many things over a long military career. Added to which, the heartache of his own brother's funeral in the holy space remained raw.

'I'm sorry,' said Lyn. 'That was crass of me.' She cupped his hand in hers and moved into him.

Ant touched her forehead with his own and allowed the faintest of smiles to cross his pain-etched face. 'It's OK, if there was a need for anyone to apologise, you'd be the last in line. Even after all this time, the first thing that pops into my mind when I come through those doors is Greg's funeral. If I close my eyes, I see everything as if was happening right now.'

Lyn gave his hand a tight squeeze. 'Open your eyes and come back into the present. Greg knows you love him. Remember me saying these walls give back what they absorb? What are you feeling at this moment?'

Ant's breathing slowed as Lyn continued to hold his

hand in hers. She watched as he took a deep breath and smiled. 'I remember Greg taking the blame for me when I broke one of dad's precious chess pieces playing cricket in his study, despite being told not to by our mum.'

'Who do you think put that lovely thought into your head?' said Lyn in a low tone.

Her fiance's eyes filled up for a second time. Without saying a word, Lyn smoothed them away with a gentle touch. 'Smiling and tears, eh? You know the answer to my question, don't you?'

Before Ant could respond, the inspector appeared from the vestry. 'Ah, it's you two. Are you that keen to tie the knot that you can't keep away from the place?'

Lyn shielded her partner from the inspector while he composed himself and attempted to lighten things up. 'To get married, we need a vicar, and since he seems to have vanished, it leaves us with a conundrum. Do we live over the brush, or head for the registry office?'

Her confession shocked Ant.

'I'm joking, you silly man. As if your mum and dad would allow it.'

The inspector couldn't help himself as he burst out laughing. 'Can you imagine the future Earl of Stanton with his new lady of the manor in the council offices next to the fish and chip shop saying, "I do"?'

The couple's eyes widened in faux horror as Ant put his head in his hands.

'Don't worry. I'm teasing you, much as it might amuse our friendly detective. If you think I'm going to be done out of my big day in a tiara and posh dress, you can think again.'

The laughter soon subsided. They seemed to self-censor their levity as the vicar's disappearance sank in.

Inspector Riley broke the silence. 'There's something I want to show you. Why don't you join me in the vestry?'

'Blimey, your scenes of crime people have been busy, haven't they?' exclaimed Lyn as she surveyed the constabulary's work. 'I've never seen so much fingerprint powder in one place. Have they found anything?'

Riley sighed. 'That's the problem. Here, you'd better put these on.' The inspector took a fist full of vinyl gloves and handed a set to his compatriots. 'Most times, we're lucky to pick up more than a couple of clean prints. Here, the opposite is the problem. Since so many people use the vestry, we've lifted dozens. It'll take ages to sort them out and identify their owners.'

Lyn looked around at the silver-white powder. 'I see the problem, what with the choir using the vestry, and parishioner meetings the vicar holds here. You'll end up having to fingerprint most of the village.'

Ant laughed. 'I can see that going down well with Phyllis Abbott.'

The inspector let out a sigh. 'Thank you, Anthony. You've conjured up a terrible image in my addled brain.'

Lyn moved further into the room, trying hard not to touch anything. 'Let's not ponder that, shall we? Now, you said you had something to show us?'

'I did,' replied Riley, shaking as if someone had walked over his grave at the prospect of fending off the village gossip's unwanted affections. 'Look at these.' He pointed to a neat pile of envelopes on the vicar's desk. 'They are from the same person.'

'They weren't there yesterday. Where did you find them?' asked Lyn.

Riley tapped the top envelope with a forefinger. 'They were in a secret compartment. I only discovered by chance when I took the drawer out. I realised the inside was shorter than the outside. A bit of fiddling and, hey presto, out popped the false front cover of the secret compartment.'

Riley's friends watch with fascination as he pulled out the drawer and operated the mechanism.

'That's rather cool,' said Lyn in an eager tone. 'What would the vicar of a parish church be doing with a secret drawer in his office desk?' Lyn picked up several envelopes while the other two pondered her question. She scanned their contents, one after the other. 'You're right, Peter. They're all from the same person. A woman, I'd say. To be more precise, my bet is on Cynthia Hake.'

Ant could contain his curiosity no more. 'Here, let me have one.' For several seconds, he appeared totally absorbed in its contents. 'Wow, this is hot stuff. It seems our elusive vicar leads something of a double life.'

Inspector Riley caught Ant and Lyn exchanging a knowing glance.

'I suppose you'll make me wait before you share some nugget or other?'

Lyn retook possession of the neatly folded papers. 'See, each one signed, "C".' Well, the waitress who almost served us at Staithe Cafe was Cynthia Hake.

'What waitress?' spluttered Riley.

Ant explained their meeting with Bootsy and visit to Staithe Cafe. '… And there you have it. You now have as much information as us.'

'You're telling me that while waiting for a cup of tea and a cake, the woman took off?' The inspector chaffed at the idea. 'And as for Bootsy, he's as daft as a box of frogs who's convinced the world and his mother are out to get him. You say he threatened to shoot you?'

You can be infuriating sometimes, Peter.

'Take it or leave it, Peter,' replied Lyn. 'Jed says Bootsy saw an argument between a woman and the vicar, which Bootsy confirmed, and while he couldn't give us a name, he told us where she worked.'

Inspector Riley shook his head in disbelief. 'In the short time I've known you two, you've been kidnapped, almost strangled, or attacked in some other fashion. To this we can now add almost getting yourselves shot. You should leave this stuff to the police.' Riley shook his head as he looked at the two beaming faces.

'The gun wasn't loaded, anyway,' laughed Lyn.

'It was. I saw the cartridges when he broke open the gun,' responded Ant.

'You didn't tell me that?'

'What good would that have done?'

'He might have—'

'But he didn't and we're here to tell the tale. Isn't that right, Peter?' said Ant.

Riley looked at the white-painted ceiling of the vestry. 'I give up. You'll be the death of me.'

As the inspector drifted off into his own world, Lyn picked up an envelope and placed it under her nose. Replacing this with one after the other. 'Yes, "Amore Amore".'

'What?' said Ant while Peter Riley continued to gaze at the ceiling.

'The perfume. It's an exclusive perfume, by the way.'

Ant attempted the same test. 'I can't smell anything other than a bit of damp?'

Lyn gave her intended a scornful glance. 'Then why did you buy me a bottle for Christmas?'

'Christmas?'

'Remember? It's the time of year when the big fellow in

the red suit turns up, romantic men ask their girlfriends to marry them… and buy them expensive perfume.'

By now, the inspector had recovered from his stupor. 'This'll be good,' he said, wearing a broad smile.

'Just testing you,' replied Ant, before breaking eye contact and busying himself with the contents of an envelope.

'Good try, but not convincing,' laughed the inspector.

'I've heard it all now. He's a man who can't tell the difference between damp wallpaper and expensive perfume. To cap it all, he doesn't remember buying it for me. I don't know why I bother!'

Ant tried his best to move from being the centre of attention by asking a question. 'Why would the vicar open every letter? One sniff and he'd know who sent them?'

Inspector Riley handled several of the opened envelopes. 'You may be onto something, Anthony. As you say, why bother opening the letters in the first place?'

Ant looked from Lyn to Riley, then back to the envelope he was holding. 'Perhaps we've got this wrong. Receiving steamy love letters doesn't prove he reciprocated her feelings. But it does at least show he found it flattering. It can't be much fun to run one of these parishes without the help of a partner. She never mentions him by name or gives any hint who the man is.'

Lyn browsed through a couple of pages. 'So, you're saying the vicar felt safe keeping them, because even if they came to light, he could say a male parishioner had given the letters to him for safekeeping.'

Riley shook his head. 'Hang on, hang on. You say he didn't wish to receive the letters. Then you say he got a kick out of receiving them, knowing no one could prove their intended target?'

'I reckon there's more to it than the letters. It makes little sense from a woman's perspective. I'd only write this stuff to a man if more conventional approaches failed, like an amorous look, or picking imaginary fluff from his collar.' She turned to the two men. Ant seemed confused, while Peter Riley looked at his lapels.

'Tell me, Ant. When I smooth your suit jacket down while you're still wearing it, or run my hands through your hair, what goes through your mind?'

'Either my apparel needs an iron, or my hair needs combing. Is that the right answer?' said Ant.

'Don't be stupid,' responded Riley. 'It means you have a mark on your jacket, and it needs dry cleaning, or in the hair's case, she's spotted some of the grey stuff.'

Lyn shook her head in despair. 'No wonder blokes stay single for so long. You're all stupid.'

The men exchanged the sort of look two toddlers share when one steals a sweet from the other, and both victim and thief wonder what to do next.

'All I'm saying is that Cynthia will have tried different ways to get the vicar's attention and make her intentions clear. Only then might she put pen to paper. She's reluctant to name him or give any clue who he is,' said Lyn.

Ant raised a finger as if a great revelation had descended upon him. 'What, a bit like a Valentine thing?'

'At last,' said an exasperated Lyn. 'Two people, attracted to one another, find it impossible to give any hint they recip-rocate their feelings. One lovingly hides the letters in a secret place. The other becomes more desperate to receive a response.'

'You mean unrequited love?' responded Ant. 'What if, in a fit of temper, born out of being spurned by the man she secretly loves, Cynthia caused him harm?'

'You make it sound like a Mills and Boon paperback, but something like that,' replied Lyn.

Riley collected the envelopes and placed them back on the pile, taking note to make sure all were in date order. 'So, we have a man unsure if he wants Cynthia Hake's attention, matched by a woman desperate for his affection. We don't know if he wrote back or attempted to speak to her. What if he told her he wasn't interested? Then the vicar vanishes. That might explain why Cynthia Hake did a runner at the mere mention of his name to her. Perhaps she had something to hide?'

As Ant and Lyn pondered the inspector's hypothesis, a breathless Ian Jefferson appeared at the open vestry door.

'Lord,' remarked Lyn. 'Where did you appear from? You look as though you've seen a ghost.'

Jefferson took several seconds to catch his breath while hanging on the doorframe. 'Didn't mean to startle everyone, but I was walking down the high street when someone told me they'd seen the inspector walking into the church. I'm eager to find out if there's any news about the vicar. His disappearance is so out of character. I can't...' His voice tailed off as he broke down, causing Lyn to offer what comfort she could.

'Everything will be alright, Ian. We're all upset about what's happened, but the vicar depends on you to keep things going. Yes?'

Inspector Riley broke in. 'Hang on, the man's missing, not dead.'

Mention of death caused Jefferson to break down again and hold on to Lyn, as one of her pupils might after falling over in the playground.

'None of this is your fault, Ian. You can't be beside the vicar twenty-four hours a day.'

Lyn's kind words eventually caused Jefferson to calm down. He accepted her offer of a paper tissue and began dabbing his eyes. 'This is so embarrassing.'

Lyn gestured for Jefferson to join them in the vestry. He frowned as he scanned the untidy room full of papers and fingerprint powder, as well as the sheaves of paper laying haphazardly on the stone floor.

'Don't worry about that, Mr Jefferson,' said the inspector. 'In fact, you may help us.'

Riley's frown deepened.

'There's nothing to be alarmed about. Given how closely you work with the vicar, you might hold a nugget of information, or some detail unique to you.'

Lyn reinforced her point. 'The inspector is right, Ian. For example, did the vicar ever mention any unpleasantness from parishioners? Perhaps you might tell the inspector when you last saw the reverend?'

'But I told his desk sergeant all this. Why would he want me to repeat information I have already volunteered to the police? Am I a suspect Lyn?'

The inspector took over the conversation. 'My sergeant must've got his wires crossed. You know what Fred Battersby is like. Don't worry, I'll pick this up with him later.'

Riley's disarming comments settled Jefferson down as he looked for further confirmation from Lyn.

'There you are. I told you there's nothing to worry about. We want to find the vicar, don't we?'

Jefferson lowered his head. 'I didn't mean to sound so defensive, it's just—'

'My fault entirely,' interrupted Riley. 'This is hard for you and getting my wires crossed with the sergeant hasn't helped. Why don't you nip home and have a rest? If I need to speak to you again, I'll be in touch. You have my word that as soon as we hear anything, Lyn or Anthony will be in touch.'

Jefferson nodded and turned toward the open doorway. He hesitated before turning back to the inspector. 'Clive Greenacre.'

'Sorry,' replied Riley.

'You asked if the vicar had—'

'Argued with anyone?' said Riley.

'You said unpleasantness, not argued,' retorted Jefferson

An awkward silence fell.

'It's alright, Ian, we're all on the same side. Inspector Riley wasn't trying to catch you out.'

The two men exchanged stilted smiles as the tension slipped away.

'What can you tell us about Mr Greenacre, Ian?'

Jefferson pondered for a moment. 'Clive Greenacre lost his wife several months ago, after a long illness. They were both devout Christians. I don't know why, but Clive got it into his head that the vicar could have saved her. From what I've heard of her last illness, the poor lady was beyond anyone's help. He's taken several verbal pot-shots at the vicar since her death.'

'Did you witness any incidents?'

'Not directly,' responded Jefferson, 'but I heard shouting in the church one day. He was as white as a sheet and shaking when we met. I calmed him down eventually but got little sense out of him.'

I didn't expect this, thought Lyn.

The inspector moved closer to Jefferson while checking the man's body language to ensure he didn't spook him again. 'Did the vicar suggest at any point if Mr Greenacre had threatened him?'

'No, but he looked scared. That was a couple of months ago. He's not mentioned the matter since.'

Jefferson looked across to Lyn. 'Can I go now?'

Riley answered. 'Of course, and again, thank you for your help today.'

Jefferson slipped through the doorway as if he'd never been in the vestry at all.

In less than thirty seconds, the three people in the room left while talking about Jefferson's revelations.

'Can I trust you two to follow up on the Greenacre lead while I sort this DNA job out? That's if Division will allow me to test half the village at such an early stage in the investigation.'

'Of course you can,' replied Ant in a bright tone, which caused Riley to scrunch his nose and slide a finger across the deep furrows on the inspector's forehead. 'Something tells me I'm going to regret letting you two loose. Oh, and while I remember. Don't forget to go to the police station and give my sergeant a written statement about what you were doing before the vicar went missing. I've an administration audit coming up and I don't want the pen-pushers finding any holes in my investigation file.'

'Righty ho,' replied Ant, his voice as bright as before. This only made Riley even more uneasy.

Now in the church's chancellery, Lyn scanned the space. 'Where did Ian disappear to? That's a neat trick. We were only a few seconds behind.'

Chapter Five

RIDDLE ME THIS

LYN never tired of catching a first glimpse of Stanton Hall. The long, winding driveway through the estate provided a wide vista of flat grasslands, punctuated with stands of deciduous trees. Deer roamed as free as their ancestors had 400 years previously. Ten minutes later, Lyn's favourite spot on the estate came into view. Capability Brown's landscaping trick. This involved a slow turn around a man-made hill to reveal the medieval half-timbered building in all its glory.

This place is so beautiful, thought Lyn.

She set a leisurely pace for her MINI as it reached the summit of the rolling hill. 'Look at that,' Lyn exclaimed as she gazed down on the hall and made for a large gravel space in front of the hall dominated by an ornate stone fountain.

Ant placed his palms on the dashboard as if pushing the vehicle. 'For pity's sake, woman, can't this thing go any faster? We'll miss afternoon tea.'

'Don't "woman" me, you old grump. Anything's better

than that leaking excuse for a motor vehicle you insist on driving. Jennifer does nicely, thank you—and at least it keeps the rain out.'

'Jennifer?' exclaimed Ant. 'I thought it was Doris?'

'"It," as you so rudely call Jennifer, used to be Doris. I decided she needed an image update, which is more than you can say for your heap of old iron.'

The exchange of pithy put-downs continued until Lyn brought the compact car to a stop outside the towering double doors of the hall. Michael, the family's young butler, stood waiting for the dispute to end and the new arrivals to exit the MINI and climb the steps to his position.

'Well, are we just going to sit here and knock lumps out of one another? Or get in to say hello to your parents before they finish afternoon tea and retire for their nap?'

Lyn's ultimatum caused Ant to look up at Michael. The butler gave a slight nod from the shoulders to acknowledge the Earl of Stanton's son. 'I know the look,' said Ant. 'He's not impressed. Best get out and make my peace with him.'

Ant repeatedly tutted while trying to open the door and almost fell on the driveway. 'This stupid—'

'Don't start again,' chided his fiance.

He brushed gravel dust from the left knee of his trousers and pulled himself up to adopt a military bearing.

'You're not in the army now, well, perhaps technically you are, but anyway, relax. You look silly,' said Lyn as she turned to Michael and winked. The butler failed to move a muscle and instead made an announcement; 'The Earl and countess await you in the red drawing room, Sir, Madam. They've been there for some time'

He's not happy with us at all, thought Lyn.

'You see, I told you,' whispered Ant as the pair ascended the steps wearing a look of embarrassed submission.

'Ah, yes. About the time, Michael. Are we that late?'

The butler made no reply. Instead, the immaculately suited retainer half-turned and gestured. 'You know the way?'

'Blimey, we are in his bad-books,' muttered Lyn.

'Keep your head down. He'll come around,' Ant whispered as they walked towards the drawing room.

Lyn pondered the daunting inevitability of the pair stepping into the boots of Ant's parents in due course. *If I go through with the wedding, will we cope with it all? I love his parents, but is Ant expecting too much of me?*

She didn't have long to ponder the matter as Ant opened the gold-gilded doors to the spacious room and stood aside. 'You first.'

They greeted the Earl and Countess with smiles as they entered the lavish room and sat in Georgian-style armchairs. 'There you both are, at last. We'd almost given up on you, hadn't we, Anne?'

'Oh, you are a silly man, Gerald,' replied the countess. 'Stop making such a fuss.' She held out a hand of greeting. 'Now, come here both of you and give me a kiss.'

Lyn couldn't help but notice how frail they were becoming. *Their health scares haven't half taken a toll. They both look so much older than their years.*

'That's it,' smiled the countess as first Lyn, then Ant, stooped to plant a loving kiss on her cheeks. 'Now, will you have something to eat? There's plenty on the side.'

'Now, what have you two been up to?' said the Earl.

'Oh, nothing much,' replied Ant as he made for the food.

Lyn noticed the Earl winking at her. 'Your mother and I don't believe a word of it. I see we shall have to, as usual, rely on our prospective daughter-in-law to spill the beans.'

'I will, so long as that son of yours saves me the last of that Victoria sponge and pours me a nice cup of coffee.'

'Consider it done,' replied the Earl as he gave his son a playfully stern look.

'I get the picture. Three against one, eh?' said Ant as he dutifully poured his fiance's drink into a fine bone China cup.

'Don't forget the cake. I know you.'

'As if,' replied Ant, placing the last slice of the sponge, jam, and cream delight onto an octagonal side plate.

Lyn sat on the Earl's chair, holding his hand, and recounted the events of the past day and a half.

Gerald patted Lyn's hand. 'Well, in my experience, I'd say the vicar either scarpered, for whatever reason, and wants the police to believe someone's got to him, or—'

"And it's the 'or' that we're investigating," Ant interrupted, cake in mouth, earning a disapproving look from his mother.

The Earl looked up at Lyn who remained perched on his chair arm, holding his hand. 'You said the vicar has a fancy woman?'

'Well, a woman scorned and all that,' offered Lady Anne, who then delicately separated a small corner of her Victoria sponge with a petite silver fork.

'I agree with your mother. There's nothing worse if you ask me.'

The room fell silent for a second until gentle laughter filled the large space.

'And you are an expert in such matters, are you?' said Lyn as the other two joined in teasing the Earl.

'Oh yes,' replied Ant's mother. 'And you would know because…?'

Gerald blushed, realising what he'd said. 'Of course, I

can't speak personally since your mother is a paragon of good grace and patience with me.'

'Excellent recovery, Dad, but you should stop digging before that hole gets too deep.'

Lyn gave the Earl an affectionate kiss on his forehead before getting up to refill her coffee. 'Anyone else want one?'

'Not for me, and thank you for moving the conversation on,' replied the Earl, while chuckling about the predicament he'd got himself in to. 'Will you stay for dinner?' he asked, just as the butler came in to confirm dining arrangements.

'If it's not too much trouble for the staff,' replied Lyn as she first checked with Ant, then looked over at Michael.

'I shall arrange matters with the cook,' replied the butler. 'I'm advised that we've taken delivery of fresh Cromer Crab, if your ladyship finds that acceptable?'

'How wonderful,' replied the countess. 'And please pass on to Mavis our thanks. Crab sounds just the thing.'

Michael withdrew from the grand room and closed the door with the deftest of touches, while Ant wandered over to his father.

'Might I have a quiet word, Dad?'

The Earl's knitted brow deepened as he nodded, suggesting they retire to the deep, floor to ceiling bay window.

'I wonder what those two are up to?' whispered Lyn to Ant's mother in a conspiratorial tone.

The countess smiled as she reached out to touch Lyn's arm. 'Best leave them to it.'

That worries me, thought Lyn as she looked at the two men, admiring a display of Delftware on one side of the great window.

'Much as I enjoy the company of my parents,' started

Ant, 'I can't help wondering if dinner was the sole reason for asking us over, Dad?'

The Earl exchanged a serious look with his wife, who'd momentarily averted her gaze from Lyn.

'Is something wrong?' said Lyn in a concerned tone. 'Forgive me for saying, but I get the distinct impression something is troubling both of you?' She alternated her gaze between Ant's mother and father. 'Come on, out with it. Whatever the matter is, we'll deal with it.'

After several seconds of strained silence, the Earl took hold of Ant's arm and guided him back to Lyn and the countess. 'Much as we love having you both over, you're right, son, there's a rather delicate matter we wish to discuss with you.'

Heavens, one of them is seriously ill. thought Lyn as she glanced at Ant's worried face.

'Ah, I know what both of you are thinking, and the answer is no. Neither of us is poorly, at least not in the sense that either of you may be thinking. However, we've decided something that's been taxing us for some time. When you became engaged, matters came into much sharper focus, because that decision will affect both of you.'

'Mum, Dad, what are you trying to say?' said Ant as he crossed the few yards to stand at Lyn's side.

His parents exchanged glances again. 'What your mother is trying to say is that, although our health has got no worse recently, we feel the time's right to hand over the baton, so to speak.'

Lady Stanton took up the conversation. 'I can see you are both shocked and believe us. We ask this of you with no small feeling of guilt, even selfishness—but we're both tired of the responsibility of running the estate. There, I've said it.'

Lord Stanton reached out to hold his wife's hand and shared a look of unshakeable love.

'I know you'd hoped for the first few years of your married life to be a time to build a life together, outside wider family responsibilities. The thing is, Anne and I wish to enjoy the time left to us, while in relatively good health. We've thought long and hard about this, but as your mother said, we're tired, and that is only going to get worse. The last thing we want is for both of you to have your lives thrown up in the air at short notice, when something happens to one of us.'

'But—'

'I'm sorry, Anthony, please allow me to finish. That's what happened to your mother and me when your grandfather died. We swore then that if we ever had children, we'd do all in our power not to allow history to repeat itself. I hope you'll accept that it's better to plan for a handover now, rather than wait for the inevitable?'

The room fell into a solemn silence. Only the regularity of a long-case clock counting away the seconds gave any sense of time passing.

Lyn moved from Ant to kneel to one side of the countess' armchair. 'But I'm not sure I—'

'My darling,' began Ant's mother. 'You spent most of your younger years in and around this house. You know better than most how much work is involved in keeping this place and the estate solvent. But there's more to it than that. Do you understand what I'm saying?'

Lyn choked up as she gazed at the rich hand-woven carpet, then at Ant. 'Duty?'

'That's right,' replied the countess. 'Oh, I know it sounds an outdated way of looking at the world. I suppose in the olden days we'd have called the responsibility of those with land to those who depended upon the family as noblesse oblige. Today that's sounds presumptuous, even patronising perhaps. Still, many villagers depend on us for employment and wider wellbeing. Don't misunderstand, I don't believe anyone is due deference from another person, no matter the situation. Still, we cannot escape our responsibilities—and nor should we.'

The Earl moved to behind his wife's chair, bent forward and placed a gentle kiss on her forehead. Anne raised a hand to cup her husband's fond embrace.

Ant gestured for Lyn to stand and accept his offer of a cuddle. 'Are you OK?' he whispered.

Lyn nodded while wiping a tear from her cheek. 'I'm sorry for getting upset. It's just, well, it's—'

'No need,' interrupted the Earl. 'It's not as if we're disappearing from the face of the earth. We'll be here for both of you. But as of the day of your union, we shall defer to you two on all matters concerning the estate. Don't worry, we'll be moving to Mill Cottage, so we won't be under your feet.'

I don't think I'm ready for this, or am I being selfish? I assumed we'd have a couple of years together before taking over things. And what about my career? Will they expect me to give that up? thought Lyn.

Lyn noticed the countess giving her an intense look. It was as if her future mother-in-law had read her mind.

Oh, no. Anne knows what I'm thinking. What do I say now?

'Come here, my dear,' whispered the countess in a soft voice. 'Let the men get on with their talk. There's something I want to share with you.'

Lyn uncoupled herself from Ant's embrace, causing her intended to check if anything was wrong. His mother's reassuring smile toward his fiance told him all he needed to know.

'I, too, shuddered at what was being asked of me when Gerald proposed. I knew, of course, that joining the family would shape the rest of my life. However, like you, I expected some breathing space to adapt to married life. Unlike you, I didn't have the added complication of a successful career of my own.'

'Am I being too self-centred, Anne?'

The countess reached out for Lyn's hand. 'Not at all, my dear. After all, why should you have to give up everything you've worked for? Even in the early seventies, women expected to give everything up for their husbands. The way they always had—but listen to me, it wasn't right then, and to be sure, isn't in today's world. Stick by your guns and don't allow your marriage to cost you your career. It's different for them,' she continued, pointing at her husband and son, deep in conversation. 'They are a logical breed. Something either is or is not to be done. Men often cannot see the nuance of life. Instead, we thrive on the grey areas that so confuse them.'

There's more to Anne than I've given her credit for. She's happy to stay in the background, yet her influence on the family is immense. I wonder whether that has been through design, or necessity. If it's the latter, I can't live with that.

Before Lyn could respond, the countess raised her voice a little as she called over to her husband. 'That's enough family business for one day, my darling. Time for our afternoon nap before dressing for dinner.'

'Dress?' said Ant. 'I thought we were to have an informal supper. Neither Lyn nor I have—'

'Don't panic, Anthony,' responded the countess with a

loving smile. 'An informal supper it shall be. I doubt the crab will notice the difference, so come as you are, both of you.'

She turned to Lyn and winked. 'Grey. You see what I mean?'

How clever you are, thought Lyn.

Anthony and his father frowned at each other, then the countess.

'Oh, never mind, you two. Come along Gerald. Let's leave these two to their own devices, shall we?'

As the Earl helped his wife out of her chair, Ant opened the ornate doors to allow them to pass through, arms entwined. He then joined Lyn by the open fireplace.

'Oh, and regards the vicar,' said the countess as she turned back to look at Ant and Lyn. 'I suspect men and women in his position often find themselves pulled first in one direction, then in the other. As a man of God, he'll try to please everyone. Such an approach inevitably leads to resentment on the one part and anger among those inflicting undeliverable demands upon him. The question is, who has the greater imperative and is prepared to take what they believe is theirs by right? To solve your riddle, find that person.'

A stillness descended on the room as Ant and Lyn sat side by side on the fireplace fender seat, pondering the meaning of the countess's words.

'What mum is saying is—'

'Your mother is suggesting whoever has the most to gain, or lose from whatever led to the vicar's disappearance, is the one responsible for him vanishing.'

'Why did you interrupt me? That's what I was going to say,' responded Ant in an indignant tone.

Lyn moved sideways into her fiance so that he almost

overbalanced onto the hearth. 'Great minds think alike, yes?' she said.

Ant gripped the green leather upholstery of the fender seat to steady himself. 'Or perhaps fools seldom differ?'

They exchanged a peck on the cheek as Ant made as if to push Lyn backwards.

'Don't you dare,' she said.

'Oh, I see,' responded Ant, laughing. 'It's OK for you to almost push me into the fire, but not the other way around?'

Lyn jumped to her feet to evade his playful grasp. 'The difference is, I knew the fire was out. I doubt you'd have checked first.'

Ant looked over his shoulder at the richly sculpted fireplace. 'I suppose you're right,' he giggled.

At that moment, the young butler entered the room without making a sound, other than a discreet cough, to announce his presence.

'Is everything OK, Michael?' asked Lyn.

'If I may, there is a call for Lord Stanton.'

'Me?' questioned Ant as he realised the butler held his mobile. 'I wondered where I put that.'

'I found it on the hall table, sir. It rang, whereupon I answered it to avoid the noise disturbing his Lord and Ladyship. It has a distinctive ring tone, does it not?'

Lyn shook her head at Ant. 'Have you still got that silly cow mooing at the top of its voice as your ringtone?'

Ant blushed.

'Michael, I don't know whether I'm marrying a grown-up man or a court jester. Do you see?'

The butler's facial expression remained inscrutable. 'Should I say you are engaged, sir?'

Ant frowned. 'I am engaged... oh, I see what you did there, Michael, very droll.'

The butler moved not a muscle. 'Very well, sir.' He lifted the mobile to his ear. 'Lord Stanton will speak to you now.'

Handing the phone to Ant, the butler announced the call. 'Your colleague, Fitch, sir. He intoned he had something important to tell you.'

Lyn almost beat Ant to the mobile, failing at the last second because of a quick sidestep by her fiance.

'Fitch? That you? It's Ant here.'

Lyn listened intently as Michael withdrew, leaving the two of them impatient to hear Fitch's important news.

Come on, tell me what's going on, thought Lyn.

'Right, we'll come straight over. Don't move. Lover's Lane, you say?'

Lyn waited for Ant to close the call and let her in on the urgent news. For a short while, he stood, looking into the empty fire.

'Well, are you going to tell me or not? What's going on?'

Ant slowly turned to face his fiance. 'Someone has spotted the vicar.'

Chapter Six

ON THE SCENT

FRIDAY MORNINGS in Stanton Parva are a slow-paced affair, except this one since it was the first Friday of the month, which is market day. Instead of the usual village rhythm, people from miles around crowded the narrow high street.

'I hate it when this lot turns up', said Phyllis Abbot to her life companion, Betty Fothergill.

'Well, if you want my—'

'Yes, I know,' interrupted Phyllis. 'You think it's a good thing for the village? Well, I'm telling you that strangers bring trouble. Remember last month when it poured down?'

Betty looked confused. 'Are you saying the incomers made it rain?'

Phyllis gave Betty one of her withering looks. 'Rain? what are you talking about? What I mean is … oh, never mind. Now let's get over to the cheese stall before the second homers from London swipe all the Norfolk White Lady. I love a nice slice of brie.'

Ant and Lyn were deep in conversation as they exited the police station after giving their statements.

'Blimey, it's busy today. Where do they all come from?' said Lyn as she navigated the worn stone steps of the Victorian building.

Ant gave the neat rows of canvass covered market stalls a nonchalant glance as he, too, trod carefully to avoid tripping. 'I expect it's been the same since Henry VIII gave permission to hold a cattle market in the village. It seems to me the only thing that's changed is they don't sell cows anymore — not walking and mooing ones, anyway.'

'You'd know it for a fact, do you?' said Lyn in a weary tone.

'Yep,' replied her fiance, 'We have the original charter in our archives up at the hall. It's signed in his own hand. He had a tiny signature for such a big bloke, you know.'

Lyn shook her head. 'I don't know why I bother. Anyway, that nugget of information won't do anything to get us back in the inspector's good books after dragging him out last night. Didn't you think it odd that Fitch mentioned the vicar and Lover's Lane in the same sentence?'

'How was I to know the couple we... well, stumbled across, had been to a fancy-dress party earlier?' replied Ant.

'Perhaps the giveaway was the illuminated habit, and the red leg garter the young woman wore was a bit of a clue.'

The inspector's loud voice startled the pair as he pushed his way between them without acknowledging them.

Lyn thought it was better not to respond. The look she gave Ant made sure he didn't either. Hardly had the inspector put ten yards between them when two familiar figures approached.

'Ah, Phyllis, Betty,' said Lyn in as breezy a tone as

possible after the telling off they'd both just endured in the inspector's office. 'Did you buy much at the market? It's busy, isn't it?'

Please, Phyllis, be gentle with us for once, thought Lyn.

'Busy... Busy? It's a disgrace. I'd only allow locals in if I had my way. What say, you, Betty?'

Her long-suffering companion attempted a reply but knew full well Phyllis would cut her off mid-sentence. 'Well, what I think is—'

'Yes, well, we all know what you think. But I say keep it local. Isn't that so, My Lord?'

Betty gave Lyn a wearisome look as they both concentrated on Ant.

'Indeed, Lord Stanton. I should love to hear your thoughts on the subject,' said Lyn in the most earnest tone she could muster without giggling.

Ant, still befuddled by Phyllis' over-formal address, narrowed his eyes at his fiancé, before turning his attention back to the elderly lady. 'Mrs Abbott, I understand what you are saying. However—'

'I'm so glad you agree with me, My Lord. Perhaps you might have a word with the powers that be? I'm sure your family keeps influence over those who make such silly decisions?'

Give me strength, thought Lyn.

'Well, er...' began Ant.

'Oh, yes, I'm sure the earl and his son here will sort out those stuffy bureaucrats at County Hall in Norwich,' said Lyn.

'And speaking of influence,' said Phyllis, without acknowledging Lyn's contribution at all. 'Have they found our dear vicar yet?' She pointed at the police station.

Enough of this, thought Lyn.

'We can't say—'

'I only ask because of your close working relationship with the police. It's only to be expected, of course. You know, the landed gentry and that kind of thing. I remember my grandfather always—'

Do I exist? thought Lyn as she shrugged her shoulders at being ignored.

'Yes, Phyllis. My grandfather emphasised the importance of aiding the police. I'm sure you'd agree that's the way to go?'

Impressive, thought Lyn as she offered her intended a congratulatory smile.

'Oh, oh yes, Your Lordship, I only meant—'

'I know what you meant, Mrs Abbott. It's so good to know we agree that everyone deserves an equal chance in life. By the way, may I call you Phyllis?'

That's stumped her, thought Lyn.

'Oh... er... that's, I mean, of course. And can I call you—'

'Anthony. Yes, of course you may. Let's make it our little secret, shall we?'

I don't believe what I'm hearing, thought Lyn.

The two elderly ladies swapped embarrassed glances as Phyllis made off, gesturing with the long, slim index finger of her right hand that Betty should follow suit.

Ant waved the ladies off with a cheery smile. 'You two go safely now, do you hear?'

'Oi, Little Lord Fauntleroy, that's enough of that,' began Lyn. 'Your head's big enough without buttering up the likes of Phyllis Abbott. You may think you got the best of that encounter. However, by lunchtime she'll have told half the village she's had it on the best authority that you're a communist.'

'What are you talking about?' replied Ant, giving Lyn a puzzled look.

'It's no use you looking at me like that. I heard the words myself. You said everyone is the same. In Phyllis-talk, that means you're about to divide the Stanton Estate up equally among the villagers.'

Ant looked confounded and scratched his forehead. 'Don't be silly. She won't... will she?' His pained expression told Lyn she had him on the hook.

'She will. And to convince them, she'll tell anyone who'll listen that she heard the news from the very top. As proof, Phyllis will crow that you've given her special permission to address you as Anthony.'

Before her fiance could respond, the inspector's voice boomed out again. 'Still here? Haven't you anything better to do than gossip and make my police station look untidy? He pointed a finger at first one, then the other, as he narrowed his eyes. I haven't forgotten last night, by the way.'

Riley held out his arms in a V-shape as if mimicking a snow plough to prise them apart for a second time as he ascended the solid steps. In a repeat performance of ten minutes earlier, he chose not to favour either with eye contact.

'This is ridiculous!' He turned to confront the inspector. However, Riley vanished into the building without looking back, leaving Ant facing a closed door.

'The world's gone bonkers,' stuttered Ant, as he gazed down at the bustling market. 'Peter takes the huff over an innocent mistake. Now you tell me I've turned the Stanton Estate into a commune. He hesitated for a few seconds, his eyes closed, and head tilted upward as if seeking divine intervention. 'She won't, will—'

'Of course not, you silly man. But she'll tell all comers

that she's now your special friend. Your father may have his views on a woman scorned, but I have a prophecy for you. 'Yea, and the imaginings of Phyllis did become truth to the multitude.'

Ant shook his head again. 'I don't know who's daftest, you or Phyllis.'

'Who's daft?' The desk sergeant's authoritative voice stopped Ant in his tracks as the policeman's rounded face appeared through the partially opened entrance to the station.

'I'm not saying. It will only depress young Anthony here.' She pointed a finger at her companion while lifting her eyebrows to stress the point.

The desk sergeant eyed both up before shrugging his shoulders. 'Now that sounds like a domestic to me, and my inspector says you're making the front of his police station look untidy. Please, will you move along?'

'He said, "please?"' spluttered Lyn.

'Not exactly,' responded the sergeant in an awkward tone. 'I'm giving you the polite version … if you know what I mean. Anyway, you'd be doing me a favour if you both did one. The last thing I need on my plate today is the inspector getting into one of his moods. You know how petty he gets and to cap it all, I've run out of his favourite biscuits, and he'll be calling for his mug of tea in ten minutes.'

Lyn thrust a forefinger upwards and took the exaggerated stance of a Victorian character actor from a second-rate touring company. 'And shall the force of good be thwarted by the wicked absence of a chocolate digestive? For all the world knows good cannot triumph over evil without tea and biscuits.' She held her majestic pose as if waiting for applause. Instead, an old couple passing by suggested Lyn didn't give up her day job, and what would her pupils think of their headteacher acting so foolishly? Deflated, Lyn gave up, her mood further deflated by the confounded look the sergeant and Ant gave her.

'Is she all right, do you think?'

'Dunno,' replied Ant, 'But it's the second time in five minutes she's done that.'

Both men continued to stare at Lyn.

'Best move on before she does it again, don't you think? Folks will think she's busking… or gone gaga, neither of which is a good look in front of a constabulary building,' said the sergeant, nodding his head in the opposite direction of the market throng.

'I am here, you know,' said Lyn in an indignant tone.

'That's the problem,' replied the desk sergeant, as he pointed a finger in the direction they should both take.

'It's alright for you,' moaned Ant. 'I'm stuck with her all day. Perhaps a glass of lemonade in the Wherry Arms will fix the problem.'

Ant took Lyn by the hand and pulled her away from the police station steps.

'Good idea,' replied the sergeant. That gives me just enough time to buy a packet of his flaming biscuits before he yelps for his tea.

The two men exchanged knowing looks as the sergeant peeled to the right, while Ant continued to guide Lyn towards the pub.

As they entered the Wherry Arms, Lyn looked at Ant and burst into laughter.

'You are crackers when you want to be,' said Ant, as he followed her through the narrow double doors.

'It doesn't do to be too predictable,' replied Lyn with a wide smile. 'Anyway, that's the reason you love me!'

'I don't know about that, and I wouldn't like to be you at

your next assembly. The children are bound to ask if you are feeling better.'

Lyn giggled as she waved at the pub owner, Jed. 'It's his round and mine's a large white wine.'

'And a pint of Bodger pale ale for your better half?'

'No,' replied Lyn. 'He's having a glass of lemonade because he's got some driving to do.'

Ant gave Lyn a hurt sort of look. 'What are you up to?'

'Not being predictable. Now get your wallet out and pay the man.'

'That'll make a change,' chipped in Jed as he finished pouring Lyn's wine.

'It's in your back trouser pocket,' shouted Lyn as she pointed at her fiance's rear. 'Don't think you're getting out of paying by pretending you've left your wallet at home again.'

Jed roared with laughter. 'She's got your number, mate. That'll be £27.50 and it's OK, I accept card payment, as you well know.'

'£27.50? She's having wine, not champagne?'

'Now there's a thought,' said Lyn.

'Think yourself lucky I haven't added any interest to your tab, Anthony Stanton. You may be son to the lord of the manor, but in here you pay like everyone else... ah, a debit card. That'll do the job.'

Jed pulled the card from Ant's fingers before he placed it next to the reader. 'What's wrong with everyone today? I wish I'd stayed in bed.'

A ripple of laughter spread around the bar as half-a-dozen of Jed's other regulars joined in the fun.

'It's a dud,' said Jed. 'Have you not been paying your bills? All you lot are the same,' laughed Jed as he held Ant's card out for all to see.

'It is not,' pleaded Ant in a hurt tone.

The bar broke into a riotous laugh as Jed handed the card back to Ant.

'Here, take it, you daft devil. It's so easy to reel you in. Go on, sit, while I bring your drinks over to you.'

Ant looked forlornly at his debit card and shook it, as if cash might emerge from the thin plastic. 'Hilarious,' he muttered as he shuffled over to the small round table already occupied by Lyn.

'Nothing wrong with a laugh, Ant,' said Jed as he placed their drinks on the hammered copper tabletop and left the pair after winking an eye at Lyn.

'Suppose not,' moaned Ant in a muted tone as he placed the wallet back into his pocket and gave Lyn one of his little-boy-lost looks. It didn't take long before they exchanged a knowing smile.

The following twenty minutes involved a lively banter with the other regulars until the church clock rang twelve times to denote noon. Conversation stopped as thoughts turned to the missing vicar.

'Do you think the police will find the reverend?' asked an elderly man, to no one in particular.

Jed answered the call. 'It's not been that long, so there's every hope. Isn't that right, Anthony?'

Mention of his name woke Ant from his thoughts. 'You're spot on, Jed. The inspector knows what he's doing.' The room fell silent again as Ant and Lyn exchanged concerned looks.

'Well, that's brought us up short,' said Lyn in a quiet tone, before looking into her half-empty wineglass for something more meaningful to say.

As the seconds passed, the hubbub around the bar returned as old friends got on with their gossip.

At the bar, Jed continued to clean and place pint glasses on shelves that had fulfilled the same job for centuries.

'I've got an idea,' said Lyn. 'What about if we split up? I'll walk over to Cynthia Hake's place while you take a trip out to Clive Greenacre's cottage. That way, we can cover more ground.'

Ant smiled, 'So that's what the lemonade stunt was about.' He wiggled a finger at Lyn. 'OK, I'll go with that. Talk about being manoeuvred into position or what?'

Lyn winked at her fiance. 'Come on, let's get going.'

———

THE SHORT WALK to Cynthia Hake's home should only have taken ten minutes. However, as Lyn walked down the busy high street, items on several market stalls caught her interest. This, together with villagers wishing to pass the time of day, meant the journey took more than twice that.

She lingered as she passed the buttercross on the small village green at the bottom of the street. Memories flooded back of the hours she'd spent as a young teenager idling her time away, mucking about on its stone steps with her friends.

It seemed we didn't have a care in the world, like the young ones messing around on it now.

A quick glance at her wristwatch brought Lyn back to the task at hand.

Crikey, I'd better get a move on.

Cynthia's cottage was one of the older buildings in the village. Small, squat with walls built of poor-quality bricks, long ago covered in a reddish-pink wash. The old timers said the colour was determined by the amount of oxblood mixed into the whitewash. Lyn consoled herself, knowing that no such practice continued into modern times. She marvelled at the perfect proportions of the little building and chocolate box cottage garden.

After closing the waist high wooden gate behind her, Lyn strolled the twenty feet that brought her to a weather-beaten door. She knocked. No answer.

Bother, I've missed her. Perhaps she's working today?

A second heavy tap on the door brought more luck. Lyn sensed movement through the small bullseye glass that broke up the solid elevation of the old door.

The door seemed to open of its own accord until Lyn caught sight of Cynthia's hand grasping the door's edge.

'Thank heavens I've caught you,' said Lyn brightly as the cottage owner's small, round face and shoulder length black hair came into view.

She doesn't look pleased to see me. Then again, after that little to do at the cafe, I can understand. She's probably still embarrassed.

'Ah... Lyn. It's you. I... er. About the other day, I, er—'

'You don't need to apologise for anything, Cynthia. In fact, I just popped around to check you were alright? I've told Anthony before that he can sound pushy, even when he doesn't mean to. You know what men are like, right?'

Cynthia offered a weak smile as she opened the door wide. 'That's kind of you. Do come in'.

Lyn could tell the woman remained pensive as she showed her into the small living room of the old cottage. A rush- carpet covered most of the stone slabs that made up the floor. Despite Cynthia's efforts to soften the interior, the stone fireplace, and furniture gave the room an austere look.

'Goodness me,' commented Lyn, 'I bet this place could tell some tales. It must be one of the oldest cottages in the village?'

Her question seemed to put Cynthia more at ease as she offered her guest a seat. 'Dad once told me it's been here since the 1600s. Can you imagine that? He said it was originally part of a saddlery, but no one knows. All I know is that the roof leaks and the old pigsty in the back garden is a danger to man and beast, falling to bits as it is.'

Lyn smiled. 'I know what you mean. The old schoolhouse has one as well. I guess everyone kept some sort of livestock in the old days.'

The two women exchanged awkward glances as the conversation dried up.

'Tea?' blurted Cynthia. 'I was about to make myself a cup when you knocked.'

'An offer I can't refuse,' replied Lyn, without believing Cynthia's comment for one second.

As her host moved into the tiny kitchen, Lyn gazed around the room.

The place hasn't seen a decorator in years, certainly not since her mother passed on twenty years ago. thought Lyn.

The thought struck her that the only family photographs on display were those of Cynthia's father, either alone or with his daughter. The mother's been erased from sight.

How odd, thought Lyn. They always seemed to be such a happy family. I guess no one knows what goes on behind a family's front door.

The thought saddened Lyn as it brought to the fore her own unhappy childhood.

Who am I to talk? she thought.

Cynthia's timid call from the kitchen interrupted Lyn's unhappy train of thought. 'No milk and one sugar?'

'The other way around, if you don't mind,' replied Lyn.

A few seconds later, Cynthia re-entered the living room

carrying a small tray with two delicate cups and saucers. 'So much for me being a server who's supposed to remember these things.'

Lyn took her drink and placed it on a small coffee table. 'Not to worry. You must serve hundreds of people each day. It must be impossible to remember every detail?'

'Well, we certainly see many people during the tourist season, that's for sure.'

Lyn took a sip of her tea before setting the cup and saucer in her lap. 'I bet you do. A bit like our vicar. You know, seeing just a trickle of people though the week, then they all come at once on a Sunday.'

She watched for Cynthia's reaction. Other than a quizzical glance, that was it.

Oops, that was clumsy of me, thought Lyn.

Several seconds passed before Lyn tried again. 'I suppose that was too abstract of me, but you saying you saw most customers over a relatively short period reminded me of the church. I don't know why... except, of course, we're all worried about him.'

The women mirrored each other's actions by blowing over the top of their teacups before taking a sip.

'I know everyone's talking about the reverend. It's out of character, isn't it? I've not spoken to him for weeks, but all the same, you can't help being worried, can you?' commented Cynthia.

That's interesting, thought Lyn.

'Do you still do that amateur sleuthing thing? You know, helping the police and so on? What do you think has happened to the vicar?'

Even more interesting, thought Lyn.

'It's slow going, Cynthia, and of course, I can't say too much. What I know is that something caused the vicar to vanish. We just don't know the why yet... but we'll get to the truth of it, mark my words.'

Still no reaction, thought Lyn. Perhaps she knows nothing and we're barking up the wrong tree? Time to push my luck.

'Cynthia, someone saw you arguing with the vicar on Tuesday evening outside the church.'

If that doesn't provoke a response, I don't know what will, thought Lyn.

Her instincts proved right as she observed Cynthia's demeanour stiffen.

Lyn's host got to her feet and strolled the few feet to the open stone hearth. Placing her cup and saucer on the overmantle, she half-turned towards her guest. 'Then whoever said that to the police is mistaken. Much as I'd like to help, I was at home all evening. I like to watch the new Miss Marple series on the BBC each Tuesday evening. I don't know about you, but I haven't managed the trick of being in two places at the same time.'

She's coming out fighting, that's for sure, thought Lyn.

'I love Miss Marple,' said Lyn with a controlled smile. 'Such a clever sleuth. You know, she comes across as kind, and keeps her cool until the end, when she ruthlessly uncovers the killer. Such fun.'

Cynthia pointed a finger at her guest. 'I see now who you model yourself on. It sounds fun?'

'Not when someone's life is in danger, or already taken,' replied Lyn with grim determination etched on her face. Realising how she might look, Lyn changed tack. 'If only I was half as smart as that lady. Anyway, I'd better get going. I've taken enough of your time already.'

'But you haven't finished your tea?' replied Cynthia, pointed to Lyn's half-empty cup.

Lyn got to her feet and made for the front door. 'No, no. You've been so kind and I have a habit of hogging people's time. It must be the teacher in me.'

As Cynthia passed Lyn to open the front door without making further comment, her guest caught a hint of the woman's perfume. 'I love that. Is it "Amore Amore"?'

'How clever of you! It's an exclusive perfume,' replied Cynthia, sniffing an upturned wrist as if to remind herself of the complex aroma. 'An old Christmas present from my father, bless his soul.'

Chapter Seven

I HEAR YOU

AFTER TWO HOURS of fruitless searching for Clive Greenacre, Ant pulled the open-topped Morgan sports car off the narrow roadway onto a strip of grass. He was careful not to drift too far to the left in case he ended up in the deep drainage ditch that, like many rural roads in Norfolk, bounded each side of the routeway.

Five villagers passed him in and around the village that I know of, yet no one spoke to the man. How strange is that for what's supposed to be a close community?

Before he sank further into failed despair, Ant noticed a large, mud-spattered yellow recovery wagon rapidly closing the distance between the two vehicles.

That's all I need, he thought, knowing he'd have to spend the next ten minutes being ribbed by Fitch.

'For goodness' sake, turn off the engine, will you? I'm choking down here.'

Ant waved a hand in front of his face to waft away the cloud of diesel fumes being pulled forward from the rear of the huge lorry on a strong tailwind.

Fitch cupped a hand to his left ear as if unable to understand his friend's plea. It was only when Ant pointed to the rear of the wagon that Fitch raised a thumb and turned off the ignition.

'You knew what I meant, fool. It's a strange bloke who derives pleasure from almost suffocating his best friend. What, with the price of fuel now, that little exhibition must have cost you a fiver.'

Fitch's smile told Ant that the cost had been worth his friend's helpless reaction.

'What are you up to, anyway? Have you nothing better to do than lurk about in the middle of nowhere? I thought you were looking for the vicar, 'cos you won't find him here - unless you know something I don't?'

Ant thumped his chest and gave a throaty cough by way of reminding his friend he'd almost done for him. 'Hilarious, I don't think,' started Ant. 'If you must know, I'm on what's turning into a wild goose chase to track down Clive Greenacre. Plenty of people have seen him this morning, but would you believe not one of them spoke to the man?'

'I can't say I blame them,' replied Fitch, as he looked down on Ant from his lofty driving position.

'What do you mean?'

'Well, it seems every time anyone attempts to pass the day with Clive, all they get is a surly growl as he hurries past. I'm told he's still not got over his wife's passing. If anything, the longer things go on, the angrier he's getting.'

The words cut into Ant like a knife.

I remember that feeling. It felt like no one understood the pain I was going through over my brother. I hated everyone and the more they tried to sympathise, the more I hated them.

'Ant… Ant, are you… Oh Lord, that was crass of me. I didn't mean to…'

Fitch watched as his friend stared blankly into the distance, his hands gripping the small steering wheel of the sports car, lost in his own thoughts.

'Listen, Ant. What I meant was—.'

'It's fine,' replied his friend after what seemed like an age. 'I know what you meant. It's just sometimes… well, never mind that.

He released his grip on the Morgan's steering wheel and looked up at Fitch. 'The thing is, Lyn is busy talking to Cynthia Hake to probe if she knows anything about the vicar's disappearance, and I'm supposed to be doing the same with Greenacre, except I can't find him.'

Fitch laughed. 'Well, hanging about here won't solve your problem - but I can.'

'What do you mean?'

'I saw Clive not fifteen minutes ago at the church Lych Gate. He was heading into the graveyard. I don't think you need to be Sherlock Holmes to work out why here's there, do you?'

Ant's eyes lit up, and in a second he'd fired up the throaty engine of the Morgan, 'Are you going to move that lump of a machine so I can get going or what?'

Fitch feigned a hurt look. 'So that's the thanks I get for finding your invisible man, is it? And another thing. Don't call Miriam a 'lump'. She has feelings, you know. She'll remember that the next time you want that pile of scrap you're driving towing back to the garage. There are some things one shouldn't take for granted. And Miriam is certainly one of them.' Fitch extended his arm out of the open window and made as if to stroke the driver's door panel with an open palm.

The two men exchanged warm smiles as Fitch pulled the heavy wagon forward just enough to allow Ant to speed up through the resulting opening and disappear down the road in a puff of dust kicked up from the road edge.

———

TEN MINUTES LATER, Ant stood at the ancient Lych Gate, scanning the churchyard for anyone tending a grave. The task was even more difficult, given the sheer number of headstones that stood at precarious angles within the church's ancient enclosure.

I suppose it's only natural how full this place is since they've been committing souls to the ground for over 700 years, thought Ant as he surveyed the lumps and hollows caused by graves sinking over time, only to be topped up with the next claimant interred in the family plot.

It wasn't long before he caught sight of a man's head periodically bobbing up amongst the labyrinth of time-worn headstones. Ant took care not to disturb any of the flowers left on graves as he deftly stepped between graves.

I guess the untended ones don't have a family left to visit them, thought Ant as he viewed the pitiful state of several plots.

His plan to cause as little disturbance as possible failed as the man he'd seen tending a well-kept grave jumped in shock as Ant's voice pierced the quiet.

'Oh, you gave me a turn there,' said the man in an agitated but gentle tone. 'I'm in a world of my own when I'm tending to mother's flowers and such-like. Can I help at all?'

The man continued to pluck at a bunch of flowers he held to weed out any straggly ends as he spoke.

Mother? thought Ant as he smiled at the elderly gentle-man. *Looks like I've got the wrong man.*

'Oh, dear. I'm so sorry to have disturbed you. I thought you were someone else and—'

A sudden crashing sound from inside the church startled both men.

'What on earth was that do you think?'

The man tending the grave gave Ant a worried glance. 'There was another bang a few minutes ago. I assumed the diocese have called the builders in to tackle the damp. They've been making that racket all the time I've been here, so whatever they're doing, it seems to involve knocking stuff about.'

No one's mentioned the vicar arranging repair work as far as I can remember, thought Ant. *I think it's time I found out what's going on. Something isn't right here.*

'Do you think we should see what's happening?' commented the man.

'You stay here. I'll check what's going on. I'm sure it's something and nothing, but better safe than sorry, eh?'

Ant turned and walked the short distance to the main entrance of the old church. As he cautiously pushed on the door to gain access, a screeching sound filled the air. What on earth is going on?

This time Ant knew he'd found his man. With a comb-over like that and a hunched gait, he has to be Greenacre. He's getting on in years, but looking at the mess in here, he's not short of energy.

As Ant approached, the angry man upended a dark-stained oak cupboard resting against a wall. Glass flower vases crashed into a thousand glinting shards as the old piece of furniture landed on its front face with a thunderous crash, the sound of which bounced around the hard stone surfaces of the building.

The man caught sight of Ant and advanced as if about to attack.

'Are you sure this is a good idea, Clive?'

Using his first name stopped Greenacre in his tracks. 'I know who you are, but how do you know my name? I'm nobody. Not any more.'

'That's not true, Clive. I know what it's like to lose someone close to you.'

'You, with all your privileges? What do you know about loss? Your type is fireproof. Nothing touches you.'

Greenacre took a step back and turned to his left. He grabbed the end of a pew and lifted the heavy seat, all the time glaring at Ant.

'That's nonsense and you know it,' barked Ant, his patience tested as he placed a hand firmly over Clive's. 'And you can put that down.'

Greenacre attempted to remove Ant's firm hold without success.

'Get off me. What do you know of my loss? You don't understand,' replied Greenacre, as he crumpled into a sobbing heap, resting against the upturned cupboard. 'We'd been married fifty-two years and then one day, she's gone. He could have saved her but did nothing.'

Ant wasted no time in firing back. 'And I had an older brother until a few years ago. One afternoon, he offered me a lift in his new car. I said I wasn't interested, but was envious, really. I never saw him alive again. Now all I've got to look at is a stone in the graveyard and wonder what might have been... just like you, Clive. As for money and land? That won't bring my brother back, will it?'

I know what it's like to be angry. To pick on someone to blame for the loss - even the person who died. Don't dare tell me I don't understand, thought Ant.

Greenacre scowled at his unwanted companion. 'And now I'm expected to feel sorry for the likes of you, am I? You say you know loss? But you still have your money, don't you? So, what do you do when your tenants can't pay their rent? You chuck 'em out, that's what.'

The accusation stopped Ant in his tracks. Where did that come from?

'Don't look at me like that, ' thundered Greenacre. 'I've let things slip since my wife died and what do you do? You send me a letter threatening to evict me unless I bring my rent up to date.'

What? thought Ant.

'Evict? What are you talking about, man? To the best of my knowledge, my family hasn't repossessed a single property from a private tenant in my father's lifetime.'

Greenacre sneered. 'Then you'd better have a word with your land agent. He's the one who sent the letter, and don't tell me he signed it without first getting your permission. He only does what your father and you tell him to do.'

Greenacre turned from Ant with a look of disgust while waving a hand dismissively.

'And when you turn to the church for help, what do they do, eh? They offer to say a prayer. What good is that when your wife is dying? Oh, the vicar was full of good intentions and spouted sanctimonious platitudes. None of it saved my Margaret. And now he won't leave me alone. He talks to me, you know, even when I can't see him. He's a devil, that's what he is. And you're just the same. Leave me alone, all of you, before I do something I'll regret.'

Greenacre held his hands to his ears, as if attempting to block an unwanted sound.

Clive is conflating the vicar's apparent actions with what he says my family has done to him. He needs help. The man's a ticking bomb.

'What about the damage? Do you think this mess solves anything?'

Ant knew Greenacre had heard his question but fell quiet to let him answer in his own time. After a short while, the man shuffled away from his unwanted company until he took up position, leaning against the great pulpit. Pulling his arms into his body and half crouching as if attempting to occupy as little space as possible as the oak-panelled pulpit towered above him. Greenacre fixed his gaze onto the worn clay floor tiles and hummed quietly to himself.

I'm losing him, thought Ant.

'How can I help?' he offered in a quiet, serious tone. 'And you have my word. There will be no eviction. I promise I'll sort that out as soon as I'm back at Stanton Hall.'

Eventually, Clive stopped his tuneless drone, lifted his head and engaged Ant. 'All I've done is shift a load of tat in a building that's outlived its purpose... that's if it ever truly had a purpose.' Greenacre's tone was sombre, as if he'd given up all hope of ever finding joy in life again.

What a desperately sad place he's in, but was he angry enough to have hurt the reverend? thought Ant.

'As for helping, you can't. I don't care what you do to me. All I wanted was for the vicar to save my wife.' Greenacre looked around the space. 'Every Sunday for forty-years we came here. We lived our lives according to the teachings of the church. And for what? I'll tell you for what, so the last words my Margaret had the privilege of hearing were those of the vicar spouting on about eternal life. Well, I'm not bothered about the afterlife. I just want her back with me.'

Ant moved a few feet nearer to Greenacre. 'You know that—'

'Don't dare say it.'

'I just—'

'Just nothing,' snarled Greenacre. 'I'm glad the vicar's gone. That's what I say and good riddance to the evil man.'

Perhaps he knows more about the reverend's disappearance than he's letting on? thought Ant.

Just then, Greenacre put his hands back over his ears and shrieked as he ran for the church doors, knocking Ant sideways as he brushed past. 'He's trying to drive me mad. Tell the vicar to stop talking. I know what he's up to and it won't wash. It's his fault Margaret isn't with me anymore.'

The ancient wooden door crashed into a Perspex-fronted collection box as Greenacre flung the heavy construction open and made his escape. Now Ant stood alone in a space he had his own hangups about.

I don't want to believe it, but I think we may have our man.

Chapter Eight

THE EMPTY ROOM

WHAT WILL *Peter Riley will make of Mr Greenacre's antics,* thought Ant as he stepped from the church and looked up at the heavy clouds.

I'm in for a right soaking.

As he walked along the high street to meet Lyn at the buttercross, a rainstorm swept through the village centre.

Thank heavens the old thing still has its roof, even if it's open-sided. He sprinted across the road, his feet slapping on the wet stones, before bounding up the steps into the historic meeting place.

'You look like a drowned rat. Here, take this. It's your steak pie. If nothing else, it'll warm your insides. I'm glad I got them before this lot started.' 'Good call,' replied Ant. 'I didn't expect the weather to turn, so I left my coat at your place. 'It's nice to see you're on time for once.' Lyn made as if to take the pie back from her companion. 'Don't be so cheeky, you. Next time, I'll let you starve. Anyway, it gives you a sort of rugged appearance. Or do I mean bedraggled?'

Ant stepped back, just in time to feel the droplets from the leaking gutter hit the nape of his neck. He wiped away the rainwater and shielded his lunch from the weather.

'Careful,' said Lyn as she stifled a giggle at her fiancé's close call. 'I know what you're like if you miss a meal, so keep that pie dry. That way, we both get to have a stress-free afternoon.'

She knows me too well, does this one, thought Ant as he smiled at her while raising the pie to his mouth, ready to take a hearty bite. The scene fell silent as he munched on his lunch, and Lyn looked around the near deserted high street, pondering the rapidity of the squall's departure. 'Don't we have the craziest weather? No wonder we can't wait to get away to warmer climes for our holidays.'

She didn't expect an answer from Ant. He was too busy chomping on what remained of his lunch, but she noticed he did glance at the damp stone slabs of the pathway and nodded in agreement.

After a couple of minutes, and the pie dispatched, Ant turned his full attention to Lyn. 'That has to be one of the best lunches I've had in ages. Very satisfying. That's more than I can say for my run in with Clive Greenacre.'

'Ah, you found him, then?'

'More like I came across him after a tip-off from Fitch. By the time I got to him, he was ripping the church to bits one pew at a time.'

Lyn's shocked expression said it all. 'That bad? What do you reckon, anger at losing his wife?'

Ant looked unseeing across the village green while telling Lyn about the rest of his encounter with the unhappy widower. 'I can't decide if grief has driven him loopy, or guilt has set in for what he's done to the vicar. I'm not sure if he's involved or not.'

'For now, we don't have a choice but to assume he is involved,' responded Lyn. 'You need to bring Peter Riley up to speed and let him decide. The last thing we want is the inspector stumbling across something we already know. We both know how prickly he is about that type of thing.'

'I do,' replied Ant. Mention of the inspector made him reflect on how far their relationship had come. I know Lyn thinks I should try harder with him, and I misjudged him at first. It's hard to put aside the feelings about how they handled my brother's car accident. That was well before Peter Riley arrived in the village, but it's so hard to let go of that sort of anger. Ant knew the effect on his mental state dwelling on such negative thoughts about the death of his brother. He made a joke of how easy it was to upset the inspector before asking Lyn how she'd got on with Cynthia Hake.

'I'm not sure I got much further than your run in with Greenacre. Except I discovered she uses the same perfume as we picked up on the letters. It's a promising lead, don't you think?'

'That depends,' replied Lyn. 'The problem is, Amore, Amore, isn't that exclusive? I can hear Peter Riley telling us that pinning the perfume theory on Cynthia wouldn't hold up in court.' She hesitated. 'There was one other thing, though. Cynthia is adamant that she didn't meet the Vicar on Tuesday evening because she was watching her favourite TV programme.'

'But Bootsy was adamant on that, wasn't he? Either way, something isn't right.'

'I agree,' replied Lyn. 'What's next?'

'A bit of target practice.'

'What?'

'Watch this,' replied Ant, as he scrunched up the paper

bag his lunch arrived in. He took careful aim and tossed the projectile at an open-topped waste bin four feet from the buttercross. His efforts came to nothing as the paper ball bounced off the rim of the waste bin and landed in a rain puddle.

'Hmm, I hope you pick that up? I don't want you setting a terrible example to the children, since I'm forever telling them to clean up after themselves.'

'But it's soaking now,' protested Ant.

Lyn gave him her best headteacher look, which was enough to send him on his way to retrieve the paper and drop it in the bin.

'Anyway, you're no better a shot than you were when we were children.'

'Get away with you,' he responded, while drying his wet hand with a handkerchief. 'Three days out of five. I beat you.'

'Anthony Stanton, most times you'd cheat by putting me off when it was my turn, in fact—'

Tina, her secretary, interrupted Lyn's gentle attack, approaching from the village green on the far side of the buttercross. 'Do you two do nothing else but bicker? And you intend to get hitched? Heaven help you both, that's all I can say.'

Lyn turned to give Tina a welcoming smile. 'I thought that was a prerequisite for a long and happy marriage?'

Tina raised an eyebrow. 'If that's the case, you're in for the longest marriage in recorded history.

What are those two on about? thought Ant, whose confusion has not gone unnoticed by his intended.

'Don't worry. All you need to do is say is, "yes dear", when I ask you to do something. It's simple. Isn't that so, Tina?'

Noticing Tina hesitating, Lyn asked the secretary if everything was well at the school.

'To be honest, I've been ringing around trying to get hold of you - your mobile isn't answering.'

Lyn frowned as she reached into a pocket for her phone. 'Oops, I must have switched it to silent when we called in at the police station earlier.'

'Thank goodness for that. I was getting worried. Then I remembered you told me of your childhood haunt, and that was my last shot. It worked. So, no harm done.'

'Trouble?' asked Lyn.

'Not so much trouble, but you know what they say. Attack being the best form of defence.'

Lyn sighed. 'That means either the Simpsons or Jones' are on their way to see me.'

Tina groaned. 'It's Mr and Mrs Jones. They're not happy.'

'When are those two ever happy concerning their daughter's life at school?' responded Lyn in an exasperated tone. 'What's the issue now? The dinners, another fight with Jasper Longman, or the nose-picking letter I sent?'

Tina rolled her eyes and gave a dismissive shake of her head. 'Violin.'

Lyn frowned. 'I knew it. That girl makes noises which defy earthly explanation. Get this, the peripatetic teacher we bring in to teach her has threatened to leave if her parents insist the child continues with her studies. It seems the din is risking her wellbeing? The question is, what to do about it?'

'I can think of one or two ideas, both of which would get me sacked,' giggled Tina.

'You and me both,' responded Lyn as the two women exchanged conspiratorial glances.

As Lyn moved away from the buttercross, Ant interjected with a suggestion.

'You could always suggest that she take up the keyboard. The girl can plug in earphones and distract herself, avoiding a collective nervous breakdown in the village.'

'Do we still have that old thing, Tina?'

'Er, I think so. We put it in the storeroom in the first place because one child broke the speakers, meaning they can only hear it through the headphones.'

Lyn turned to Anthony with a beaming smile. 'You're a genius! ' 'Yes dear,' responded Ant, wearing a deadpan expression.

———

NOW WHAT DO I DO? thought Ant as he watched Lyn and the school secretary walk across the village green, ready to do battle with the Jones'. I know, the Wherry Arms.

In minutes, he swept through the open door to see Jed looking downcast.

'You look as if you've lost a pound and found a penny. What's up with you?'

Jed gazed around the empty bar. 'At this rate, I'd make more money by shutting up shop and busking on my penny whistle. It's always the same on market Friday. All my regulars will be at the home brewery tent swigging the cheap stuff.'

The bar owner continued to grumble under his breath as he lifted a pint glass from a timber shelf above the bar. 'A pint of Fen Bodger, is it?' Ant laughed. 'Sorry to make things worse for you, but I'm driving, so it'll have to be half. I didn't know you played the penny whistle?'

'I don't,' replied Jed in a morose tone as he reached up

to the shelf to replace the empty pint glass with its smaller half-pint cousin. 'I expect they'd pay me to give it a rest. If you keep ordering half pints, I'll have no other choice.'

Jed sighed as he pulled the beer pump handle towards his ample stomach and watched Ant's glass fill to the official weights and measures mark.

As he slid the drink across the bar and into Ant's open palm, his mood lifted. 'I tell you what, why don't I sell you a dozen bottles of Fen Bodger to take with you and top up for the other half-pint you're not buying now?'

Ant let out a loud baritone laugh. 'Playing the sympathy card, eh? You're a born salesman, Jed. Go on then.'

Jed's grin spread to a smile as he reached under the bar for two six packs of beer.

Just then, Detective Inspector Peter Riley crossed the pub's threshold and strolled into the bar. 'Quiet in here today, isn't it?'

Ant looked over his shoulder and smiled at the policeman. 'Don't rub it in. Poor Jed's already down in the dumps, and if you're not careful, he'll have flogged you some bottles to take away before you have the chance to say, "You're nicked".'

Jed leaned over the bar to whisper into Ant's ear. 'Why does he always make me feel guilty about something or other? It's not just him, they all have the same effect on me.'

'Call me cynical,' whispered Ant, 'but it seems to me you have a serious case of GCS.'

'GCS? What's that, then?'

'Guilty Conscience Syndrome.'

'There no such thing, you've just made that up.'

'Then you've nothing to feel guilty about, have you?'

Jed stepped back and dried a glass with a hand towel while winking at Ant. The beginnings of a wry smile crossed the bar owner's face as he turned his attention to Riley. 'It's good to see you, Inspector Riley. Off duty, are you? Fancy a pint on the house?'

'No wonder your profits are dropping through the floor if you're giving the stuff away,' laughed Ant.

The detective frowned. 'No such luck… I'm sure you're not attempting to bribe an officer of the law with free alcohol, are you?' 'Cheers', said Ant as he held up his half-pint. You deserved that, Jed.'

'Me? Bribe a policeman? I've heard nothing so daft in all my life… but if the inspector is up for a couple of bottles to take home, who's to know, eh?'

Ant shook his head. 'You're incorrigible, you are.'

'I'll take that as a compliment… er, what does it mean?'

Riley wasted no time in taking over the conversation. 'It means you're a lost cause, because you can't change your ways, Jed.'

The barman smiled as if proud of the label. 'It's no bad thing to be consistent, is it?'

'That depends on the context,' replied Riley. 'For example, those beers you've just sold to Anthony. I don't see a UK duty paid stamp anywhere. A mistake I'm sure… but if you'd like me to undertake further tests I'll—'

'No need for that, Inspector Riley. I'll just put these away and check my stock list against the brewery's invoice after we close.' With that, Jed removed the two cartons of beer and placed them back behind the bar, then busied himself re-washing several already clean glasses.

Riley and Ant exchanged amused glances at Jed's discomfort, making their focus on the bar owner obvious. This made their host even more uncomfortable.

The inspector turned his attention to Ant. 'I saw the car outside and assumed you'd nipped in for a quick one.'

Never off duty, thought Ant.

'As you can see, Peter. Just a swift half. Are you going to breathalyse me?'

Riley laughed. 'Not on this occasion.' His smile vanished. 'The thing is, I want to run something past you'. The inspector glanced around the deserted bar and pointed to a table in the far corner of the small room. 'Old habits die hard, eh, Peter?' said Ant as the inspector opted for the far seat.

'A sensible copper always sits with his back to the wall. You know how it is,' replied Riley, while allowing his gaze to wander from one spot to another in mock emphasis of his point.

'If you say so, Peter, although I have to say things look safe around here for the moment. That's if you exclude the filthy look Jed is giving you.'

The two men watched Jed in amusement as he muttered and slung the tea towel over his shoulder before shuffling from the bar to his quarters.

Riley played with a pen he'd taken from his pocket. 'The one person who isn't safe is the vicar. It's been two days since he vanished.' Ant picked up his beer from the copper-topped circular table and swished the remains of his beer around the glass. 'You look and sound worried.'

Riley frowned as he continued to fumble with his pen. 'To be honest, I am. We can discount any madcap idea of the reverend stealing away in the middle of the night.'

Ant nodded. 'I agree. Any news yet with the DNA sample from the document chest?'

'At least that's one positive bit of news I have for you. Yes, we got a clean sample. The task now is to identify his closest relative, to confirm a match.'

'You're that sure it's his, are you?'

'Yes. I don't doubt we'll get a match.'

'Let's hope you're right, Peter. Any news on fingerprints from the envelopes?'

'Early days,' responded Riley, 'All I can say is of those we got a clean print, none match our records, so whoever touched those envelopes are strangers to the police.'

Ant picked up his half-pint glass and drank the rest of his beer before returning the container to the table. 'A crime of passion?'

Riley rubbed his chin between two fingers. 'That may not be as far-fetched as you think.'

'I can't see it, Peter. Lyn says she's never known him to show the slightest interest in women.'

'Then why keep the letters?' said Riley.

'Oh, I don't know, vanity? Before we get carried away with the vicar's love life, there are a couple of things you need to know about Clive Greenacre and Cynthia Hake.'

Riley rested back in his chair and listened intently. 'So, besides the vicar doing a runner, or whatever, we have a female parishioner who may have the hots for him. Also, a widower who blames the man for not keeping his wife alive.' Ant's smooth forehead morphed into several deep furrows. 'It's getting complicated, that's for sure.'

The inspector held up a finger as if to question his companion. 'Don't you think we can discount Bootsy's testimony about seeing the vicar arguing with Ms. Hake? After all, he's not known to be a paragon of virtue, is he? Maybe he's just covering his tracks?'

'Then you pick your choice and take your chance?'

Riley laughed. 'Anthony, that's not an objective way in which to carry out a police investigation, is it?'

The two men exchanged a quizzical look.

'That's my point, Peter. What is it we're supposed to be investigating? Kidnap or murder?'

The inspector turned his head to gaze from the vintage bay window onto the windswept High Street. 'If it's the former, experience suggests time is running out, especially since we've not heard a word from the supposed kidnapper. No, my money is on the latter. Only the felon knows what they're up to, and if more victims will follow in the days to come.'

Chapter Nine

AN URGENT CALL

'THAT'S something else you're going to have to get used to,'
said Lyn as she pointed to the sink in the kitchen of her
beloved home, The Old School House.

Ant looked blankly in the direction his fiance pointed.

'See, you don't have a clue what I'm talking about, have
you? In fact, I'm certain you don't recognise them?'

Ant looked over to the far side of the kitchen, then back
to Lyn. He waited, then frowned.

'They're called dirty dishes.'

His frown remained.

Lyn's eyes narrowed as she took a slow step towards her
intended.

'You either don't understand what I'm saying or are
even more entitled than I've given you credit for. Which is
it? And be careful how you answer my little lord-a-leaping.'

Ant made as if he was about to respond when he
paused, looked towards the stacked dishes and pans on the
draining board and gave Lyn a look of triumph.

'But it's an automatic?'

'What is?'

'The dishwasher. It's an automatic?'

'What are you talking about, man?' Lyn gave Ant a look of incredulity. 'Please explain how the automatic dishwasher program works to open the door, grab the dirty dishes, stack them, and switch itself on.'

Ant looked at the dishwasher, before turning to his fiance. 'Now you're just being sarcastic... everyone knows—'

At that point, the ringing of the front doorbell interrupted the terse exchange.

'I hope we're not too early,' said Fitch as he stood at the open door with girlfriend, Sophie, by his side. 'Ant invited us last week. He told you, didn't he?'

Lyn tried to hide her surprise.

'I knew it,' huffed Fitch.

'And I told you to ring before we left to make sure it was still on,' said Sophie. 'You know your mate has a memory like a sieve?'

The two women exchanged a look of exasperation.

'Not to worry, I've been thinking about ordering food in. Indian or Chinese?' said Lyn.

'Chinese. Definitely. Isn't that right, my little oily rag?' said Sophie as she glanced at her boyfriend with a look that invited agreement.

'Er, definitely,' spluttered Fitch as Lyn gestured for her guests to step into the hallway of the Victorian cottage.

No sooner had the four friends reached the kitchen when the doorbell rang out again.

Lyn gave Ant a suspicious glance.

'What?' said her fiance.

'I'll "what" you,' she remarked. 'How many more invitations have you forgotten to tell me about?'

She shook her head as she left the kitchen and sauntered to the front door and opened it to be confronted by Detective Inspector Peter Riley. 'I'm just about to order a takeaway. Come on, everyone's in the kitchen'.

The detective still wore a confused look as he held a hand up to acknowledge the greeting offered by his new friends. 'There's been some mistake,' chuckled Riley.

'You mean I didn't invite you over for dinner?' Ants befuddled look-caused the others to smile.

'Er, much as I appreciate the thought, but no, you didn't. In fact, I caught sight of your Morgan and Fitch's pickup … is this a bad time?'

'No, no. Not at all, Peter,' said Ant, wearing a self-satisfied grin. 'In fact, you've just given me a "get out of jail" card, so to speak.'

Riley glanced at Lyn, who continued to scrutinise the man she expected to marry with a pitiful look.

'Don't worry. The man is having one of his ever more frequent pre-senior moments. To be perfectly honest, I'll be astonished if he remembers to turn up for our wedding at all.'

The kitchen erupted into laughter as Ant wore a vacant look. 'Any way,' continued Lyn, 'If it's not dinner, to what do we owe the honour?'

Riley gave Sophie an anxious look. ' I wanted to discuss the case, but…'

Lyn caught on immediately. 'Oh, don't worry about Sophie. She and Fitch got together at the Christmas Party up at Stanton Hall. The girl is one of us now, poor thing.'

'She's also a midwife,' chipped in Fitch, 'So she'll come in handy for these two in a year or two. Isn't that right, Ant?'

Sophie gave Fitch's side a playful dig.

Meanwhile, Ant's cheeks reddened.

'Not if he carries on like he has been these last few weeks,' laughed Lyn.

The mood quietened as Riley prepared to speak. 'The thing is,' he said hesitantly.

'Listen, I don't mind stepping into the other room while you lot discuss police stuff,' said Sophie, pointing to the open kitchen door.

'Don't be daft,' said Lyn. 'You were crazy enough to get tangled with an oily rag.'

'Oh dear', murmured Riley.

'Don't worry, Peter, that's what Sophie calls Fitch. It's a sign of affection, you know.'

She watched as the two lovebirds exchanged a knowing glance.

'Think of Sophie as an extra pair of hands to help with our investigations. Being a midwife, they're very safe, you know.'

Riley winced. 'Er, yes. I see.'

The detective took his time to compose himself as he looked at each of them.

I'd love to know what's going through Peter's mind, thought Lyn.

Riley tried to hide his embarrassment and steered the conversation back to the case. 'Oh yes, I see. An extra pair of hands. Yes, excellent.'

Poor Peter, thought Lyn, he doesn't know what's hit him.

'Well, it's about the scent analysis from the envelopes. Here I must be careful because the results are yet to be verified. As things stand, the police lab has confirmed it is Amore, Amore, as you predicted Lyn.'

'Didn't you say Cynthia wore the same perfume when you called in on her?' asked Ant.

"Yes, I did," replied Lyn, switching on the coffee perco-lator and getting five mugs from a cupboard. She also grabbed a packet of biscuits from a tin on the worktop.

'It sounds like we have our prime suspect,' announced Fitch, in a confident tone.

A moment of silence fell across the kitchen as the group digested the consequences of Fitch's assertion.

Sophie soon broke the silence as she helped Lyn with preparations for the coffee. 'But would she be so daft as to leave such a strong clue?'

Riley shook his head. 'She didn't expect the reverend to keep the letters or realise others would notice her perfume.'

As Lyn handed a coffee mug to each of her guests, she pointed to the milk, sugar, and biscuits on the kitchen table. 'Help yourselves,' she said, before turning to the inspector. 'I agree with Sophie. If I had sent those letters, there's no way I'd have used the same perfume as I normally wear.'

Fitch picked up his drink and took a sip from the steaming mug. 'What if she's being set up? You know, by a love rival or something?'

Sophie prodded her boyfriend, forcing him to adjust his balance so as not to spill his drink. 'You've been watching too many episodes of Rosemary and Thyme. I've told you before about binge watching those old TV shows.'

'And let's not forget,' said Riley. 'Cynthia Hake denies meeting the vicar on Tuesday evening. Perhaps Fitch's theory may not be too far-fetched after all?'

A second moment of reflection set in as the house guests made a grab for the digestives.

'Like it or not,' began Ant, as he dunked the biscuit into his steaming drink. 'Bootsy says he saw her with the vicar on Tuesday. They were arguing and I doubt it was about the vicar's most recent sermon.'

'But can we be sure he's telling the truth and not just covering his own tracks?' said Lyn. 'What if he heard them arguing about the letters? Let's say the vicar warned Cynthia he'd kept them and threatened to show them to the police unless she left him alone? What if Bootsy spotted an opportunity to blackmail both by stealing the letters from the vestry and playing one against the other? They both have a lot to lose if those letters come out. Oh, that's a tragedy.'

Four pairs of eyes fell on Ant as his words sank in.

'I suppose that's one way of looking at it,' said Riley. 'As you say, whatever went on the other night, lives are being ruined.'

Everyone except Ant nodded, who, instead, looked forlornly into his mug. 'No, I don't mean that. My choccy biccy. It's gone soggy and fallen into my coffee.'

'Serves you right,' said Lyn. 'How many times have I told you what a filthy habit dunking biscuits is? And now you see what happens.'

Fitch did his best to cover up the fact that he, too, was attempting to fish the remains of a chocolate digestive from his mug.

'And you're just as bad,' said Lyn in her best head-teacher tone of voice.

The two men blew their fingertips to cool them down after being immersed in the hot liquid as Lyn and Sophie offered an exasperated glance.

Several seconds passed before the two men satisfied themselves that efforts to rescue further remains were futile.

'That's gross,' exclaimed Lyn as she watched both men half-drank, half-chewed the mottled contents of their mugs.

Just then, the inspector's mobile interrupted the ongoing slurping sounds his two male associates were making.

It must be serious, thought Lyn.

Eventually, the inspector thanked the person on the other end of the line.

'Police business?' spluttered Ant as he wiped all traces of biscuit crumb from his mouth. Riley hesitated to answer as he continued to look at the now blank screen of his mobile.

'Is everything ok?' asked Lyn. 'You seem nonplussed. Was it news about a case?'

Please, not the vicar? thought Lyn.

The inspector shook his head as he placed the mobile into his jacket pocket. 'To be truthful, I'm not sure whether it's good or bad news.'

The others looked at the detective, unsure what to say.

'Do you need to go? ' asked Lyn, sensing Riley's tense body language.

'Yes, I should. Cynthia Hake has apparently just walked into the police station and told my desk sergeant that she wants to bring charges against the vicar.'

———

'WHERE IS SHE?' asked the detective inspector as he stepped into the small reception area of the police station. '

'Interview room one, Sir,' responded the sergeant. 'And she's brought someone with her.' Riley gave the desk sergeant a curious look.

'Do we know who?'

'It's a vicar.'

'The vicar?' responded the inspector in a tone of consternation.

'No, sir. A vicar. Not the vicar, if you know what I mean.'

Riley narrowed his eyes. 'What are you talking about, man?'

The desk sergeant looked as baffled as his superior. 'Truth be told, Sir, I'm confused myself, what with all these vicars, like.'

'Never mind which vicar it is. Let's get on with it.'

The desk sergeant nodded as his superior swept past him.

After a brief pause, Inspector Riley confidently took his seat at the work-worn oak desk. 'Ms Hake. How pleasant to see you. I understand the matter is urgent?'

Cynthia wore a pensive look as she half-turned to her left.

The inspector took up the challenge. 'And you are?' he asked in an inquisitive tone.

The stranger smiled. I'm Alison King. But everyone calls me Ali.'

Riley purposely took his time to respond. Instead, he turned his attention on Cynthia Hake, who failed to meet his eyeline before returning his attention to the unexpected guest.

'Evening, Reverend King. And you can call me, inspector. Everyone does.'

Ali immediately broke into a deep, throaty laughter, which Riley thought incongruous for a person occupying such a small, slim frame.

'So that's how it's going to be, is it? That's a pity because Peter is such a nice name. He's one of the twelve apostles, you know. Although he redeemed himself, he didn't do himself any favours when he denied the existence of Our Lord not once, but three times.'

Riley tried hard not to react as he racked his brain about the trials and tribulations of Saint Peter.

'Tell me, inspector,' she continued. 'Do you think it's possible to get over the death of someone close to one? I don't know, let's say a family member. I see it all the time in my ministry. You know, the process individuals go through. Loss, despair, confusion, and anger. Are you still angry, inspector?'

Riley gripped the chair arms so tightly that the knuckles of both hands turned white.

'St. Peter must have gone through those emotions. That comforts me. You know, remaining angry for a while, because it will all work one way or another in the end. I want you to know it will pass for you, too.'

Riley struggled to remain in control of his emotions. 'For someone who's new to the area, or at least, I presume you are. Since I've not come across you before, you appear to know a great deal about people's personal lives. Some might call that presumptuous.'

The pair fixed their gaze on one another, each leaning forward a little.

'Detective Inspector Riley, we seem to have got off on the wrong foot. You're correct, I am a newcomer, but it's a small place and part of my ministry is to get to know how a place ticks. I intended no offence. Like you, my job seems to dominate my every waking minute. I apologise if I caused you distress. That wasn't my intention.' Ali offered a penitent smile as she sat back in her chair and made sure Cynthia hadn't been upset by the exchange.

There I go again, jumping in and thinking the worst of people. Perhaps she's right. The job affects everything I do, thought Riley.

'Reverend, I,' He paused for a few seconds. 'Perhaps I, too, should apologise. As you hint, we are victims of our vocation. As you suggest, let's start afresh. I take it you are here to speak for Ms Hake. Or am I the presumptuous one now?'

A gentle smile spread across Ali's petite features. 'Sort of. Cynthia asked me along to provide support... and to speak on her behalf when necessary. She's never been in a police station?

"Not once," replied Ali, comforting her friend.

The detective fixed his gaze on Cynthia. 'Are you alright to carry on? I'm sorry for the little spat. Your companion and I understand each other better now.'

The shy woman looked at Riley from beneath a long fringe, as if peeking from behind the stage curtains to see what the audience looked like before her entrance. 'Yes. I'm fine. I... I just don't like people arguing. It reminds me too much of—'. She paused.

'I understand,' said Riley in a soft, understanding tone.

A pause followed as Ali and Riley waited for Cynthia to explain why she'd ask to see the detective.

'It's OK, Cyn. Nobody is judging you. Why don't you explain to Peter why you're here?'

Riley chose not to react to Ali's use of his first name.

Better let that one be, thought Riley.

Cynthia placed her hands, one over the other, in her lap and sat ramrod straight in her chair. 'I've known Ali for a couple of months, and after explaining to her the dreadfulness of recent events, she suggested I speak to you.'

'That's true, Peter. I told Cyn that it's best to seek help when something's bothering you, so here we are.'

Why do some people always have to shorten first names? Lyn is just the same with Anthony, thought Riley.

'Reverend Morton's been...' Cynthia caught her breath as tears flowed.

'Take your time, Cyn. There's no rush. Is there, Peter?' Ali looked at the detective for support.

I'm wondering who's in charge here, thought Riley.

'Reverend Morton has been harassing me for over a year now. He's always making me feel uncomfortable when I'm around him. No one sees what he does or says. He's clever that way.' Cynthia wept as she fell quiet and fixed her gaze on the desktop.

Riley retrieved a pen from an inside pocket and nervously twisted the top to reveal a gold nib in response to Cynthia Hake's outburst.

'Has he—'

'No.'

'Then...'

'It's the way he, you know, sort of looks at me and touches my hair. I hate it and before you say anything, no, I haven't encouraged him to act like that.'

Riley sat ramrod straight. 'No, no. I'm sure that's the case. Let me assure you that the police take these matters seriously. We'll follow every lead to expose any man who engages in actions such as you describe. I know from long experience how you must be feeling.'

Ali entered the exchange. 'Peter, I know the authorities mean well, but all too often say, "Oh, well, there's not enough evidence to make an arrest". Also, and I mean no disrespect, how can you understand how a woman feels?'

Riley knew he made a mistake using the form of words he'd chosen. He adjusted his fountain pen nib and placed it precisely parallel to the table edge. 'You're right, er, Alison. I can't understand how Ms Hake feels. However, I can bring the resources I have to bear on the matter. You have my assurance that when the Reverend Morton reappears, we will investigate the matter.'

'Does that give you at least some reassurance, Cyn? Remember, Peter knows I'll be on his case if he shows any sign of slacking off.'

I bet you will, thought Riley.

To the detective's great relief, just at that moment, the desk sergeant barged in. 'Yes,' said Riley. 'I told you I wasn't to be interrupted, Sergeant.'

The police officer gave his superior a quizzical look about an order he'd never received. 'Er, well, there's a call you need to take, inspector. It's urgent, otherwise I wouldn't have—'

Riley thanked his lucky stars. 'Very well,' he replied in a gruff tone, which sounded none too convincing. 'By exception, I will take the call. Please, I need—.'

'Don't worry, Peter. We've covered everything. Isn't that right, Cyn?'

Her nervous looking companion offered a tense smile as both women got to their feet.

The desk sergeant guided the two women from the interview room. 'I'll put the call through now, Inspector,' he said as he shut the half-glazed door.

Riley retraced his way to his chair. He gathered his thoughts on how the meeting had gone. Ali could be a genuine friend in regard to the disappearance of the Reverend Morton. If anyone can get the locals to talk, she can. But what to think about Ms Hake's allegation? I've never heard the slightest hint of the man acting other than one expects those of his vocation to behave. And what about Ms Hake? Hasn't she just proven her motive for harming the vicar?

The sudden ringing of the old-fashioned black telephone that sat on a corner of the desk broke Riley's train of thought. He picked up the heavy receiver. 'Evening. I understand the matter is urgent?' He listened to the caller with growing incredulity. 'Are you certain?'

Chapter Ten

THE BOATING LIFE

THE EARL OF STANTON'S vintage wherry, "Field Surfer", looked resplendent in the early morning sun. Horsey Staithe provided the perfect mooring point.

Although some way from Stanton Hall, the Staithe provided the perfect jumping off point to explore the Norfolk Broads.

Ant stayed busy tidying the deck of Field Surfer while tourists admired the timber-clad water pump that looked like a windmill. However, instead of grinding grain into flour, the mill's single purpose was to drain the boggy land to allow livestock and arable farming to thrive.

Horsey wind pump stood as a rare survivor, where once it was one of hundreds, they fulfilled a vital job. Now, tourists marvelled at the many ruins in various states of decay which dotted the landscape for miles around.

As Ant coiled a long length of ship's rope between his right hand and elbow, a voice disturbed his peace.

'At least you didn't make me trek all the way over here

last night, but what's so urgent that it can't wait until after the weekend? You are aware it's Friday, aren't you? I intended to get away for a few hours and wanted an early start, to avoid the tourist traffic on the A47 this afternoon.'

Ant smiled as he laid the coiled rope in its allotted position on the deck. Noticing a young couple passing the wherry on the narrow cinder path that wove its way parallel to the calm waterway, he offered a cheery wave. 'You're right, we should get a move on,' replied Ant. He held out a hand to help his unsteady visitor half-hop, half-stumble, across the narrow gap between land and water.

Riley did his best to disguise his unease at being afloat, even though the wherry was yet to awaken from its slumber. He surveyed the rural scene nervously and settled his gaze on the grasslands stretching into the distance on either side of the old vessel.

At length, he mustered the courage to let go of the mast and, holding tight onto a guy rope with one hand, he wiped his forehead with the other. 'Where's your better half?' asked Riley to distract himself.

Ant purposely adjusted the rope the inspector had adopted as his own. This caused the policeman to trip forward as the hemp took up the tension. 'Hilarious,' sputtered the flustered inspector. 'What do you do for an encore? Make me walk the plank?'

Ant roared with laughter as another passer-by smiled at the comic scene. 'Peter, would I do that to you? As for Lyn, we're not joined at the hip, you know. In fact, she's given me special permission to come out today on account that I've got a policeman to look out for me.' Ant maintained a serious tone.

Riley looked shocked. 'That bad, eh?'

Ant glanced at the deck and nodded. After a few

seconds, his shoulders heaved. 'For a detective inspector, you are gullible sometimes. Of course, she didn't. In fact, she's busy with the children. It seems it's "One Earth Day". Did you know that?'

Riley finally gained the courage to let go of the guy rope and instead shuffled uneasily from one foot to the other. 'No, I did not,' he replied. 'As for Lyn, how am I supposed to know what she allows you to get up to? That's how married women are with their husbands, isn't it?'

'We're not married yet.'

'Take that as a warning, then.'

Ant smiled and shook his head. 'This talk of what marriage is like will have me, not you, walking the plank.'

The inspector sniffed the air confidently, but then the sail hit his cheek.

'Ah, perfect weather for sailing, a light breeze, and just look at that sun. Neptune is with us, Peter.'

The inspector steadied himself while continuing to rub his cheek. 'Let's get on with it, shall we?' he said in an irritated tone while giving the skipper a withering glance.

Within ten minutes, they were on their way and leaving the narrow waterway to reach a wider part of Stanton Broad.

He's getting his sea legs, thought Ant.

The pair fell silent as the wherry effortlessly sliced through the mirror-like surface of the water.

'Are there many of these old boats left?' enquired Riley in a calm, contented tone.

'Only a few,' replied Ant in an equally calm tone. 'Dad found her derelict in an old boating shed belonging to a family friend years ago. He asked if he could buy her. Six weeks later, a lorry arrived at the Hall with what looked like a heap of broken timber. I gather my mother was none too pleased. It took him years to rebuild her. Lyn and I used to have great fun sailing her. At first with dad and as we got older, just the two of us. She was as bossy as she is now, I can tell you.'

Ant kept a confident hand on the tiller as the vessel made progress into the wider stretch of broad.

'I can see why your father gave her such an evocative name,' said the inspector. He whispered, as if paying due reverence in a place of worship.

Ant hesitated in answering. Instead, he took in the rural landscape of lush riverbanks, a chorus of wildlife and the huge Norfolk sky.

'What I mean is, looking at the sail from a distance, you'd have no clue there was a body of water here. As your dad so eloquently described the optical illusion, it's as if the boat is gliding over grassland.' Riley shielded his eyes from the strengthening sun as he glimpsed the half-demolished remains of a brick-built water mill. 'Your childhoods must have been idyllic.'

Ant frowned. 'You'd think so, wouldn't you? Lyn had a hard time with her parents arguing all the time. She told me she couldn't wait to leave the village.'

'I thought you were close growing up together?'

'We were until I left the junior school. After that, my parents sent me to a public school, and we lost touch. That and losing my brother. I guess we each got too caught up in our own worlds. Lyn went to university, and I joined the army.'

The inspector smiled.

'Something funny?' said Ant.

'Not at all. It's just you mention the army. It reminded me of my time in the Royal Navy.'

'Royal Navy?' Ant let out a throaty laugh. 'You drained

of colour when I helped you aboard Field Surfer. How the heck did you manage on the high seas?'

It was Riley's turn to laugh. 'You're right. I never got over my seasickness. Then again, Lord Nelson was the same, and it didn't stop him from getting one or two excellent results against the French. He was born and brought up a few miles from here, you know.'

Ant raised his eyebrows. 'Yes, coming from Norfolk, I kind of knew that. Anyway, speaking of Nelson, did you run away to sea as soon as you could?'

Riley shook his head. 'Nelson didn't do a runner from his family. Like him, I had a relative who put a word in for me. My childhood was a happy one. A loving family. A father in the police service who rose to the rank of sergeant. He never looked for a promotion after that. He was happy. Things changed after mum died. They always do, don't they?'

Ant looked in a reflective mood. 'How did it affect you?'

Peter Riley shrugged his shoulders. 'I'd just joined the police and buried myself in my career. Looking back, I should have been kinder to dad. He quickly shrank into a shadow of his former self. He took early retirement and spent most of his time fishing. I found it impossible to get through to him. I suppose I stopped trying, so it's just Christmas cards now, and the occasional awkward visit.'

'It's difficult losing someone close to you, isn't it?' 'Your brother?'

'Yes,' replied Ant in a remorseful tone.

'I guess,' responded Riley. 'I still feel guilty about it all. You know, things left unsaid and all that.'

Ant steered the wherry toward the bank, aiming for a rickety wood staging. 'We have more in common than anyone would think, then?' Riley gave his compatriot a wistful glance and braced himself for the impact.

'Don't be such a baby. We won't sink.'

Before Riley could react, Ant tied the wherry to the staging. He took a moment to steady himself against the side-to-side movement of the near-derelict wooden construction.

'I'm not so much worried about the boat,' said Riley as he accepted Ant's offer of a hand. 'It's more about this lot collapsing from under us.'

'Come on, it's safe enough,' commented Ant just as a wooden plank made a loud cracking sound.

'As you say, Anthony, quite safe,' replied the hesitant policeman as both men scrambled onto the grassy bank.

They watched as the staging continued to sway until at last it came to a contented rest.

'Hmm,' commented Riley. 'And we are here because?'

'Look behind you,' replied Ant as he trudged through the sodden undergrowth.

'Look at what? All I see is a half-demolished wreck of a building. Don't tell me you gave me a restless night's sleep and an early start to look at Saint Peter's church,' replied Ant. 'A fine old building, isn't it? The place has loads of history, you know!'

The inspector looked at his soggy shoes, then at Ant. 'I'm billing you for my footwear. Now what's all this about, Anthony? I don't want to sound ungrateful for the sight-seeing trip, but we have a vicar to find, remember?'

'You an old cynic, Peter. Follow me and all shall become clear.'

It took a few minutes to reach the broken-down build-ing, despite its proximity to Field Surfer.

All manner of clandestine obstacles lay in wait for the

two urban explorers as they followed the faint marks of an ancient trail.

Ant squeezed through the half- open door, which hung off its top hinge. Riley followed, his eyes darting from place to place as he took in the decrepit condition of the place.

Yet, among the broken roof tiles and scorched interior that gave a clue to how the church met its unseemly demise, stood a large cross. The iron icon rested on a stone altar, its top obscured by the detritus of fallen roof timber and vegetation blown in by the cruel wind.

'The church served the hamlet of St. Peter's on the Water,' said Ant.

Riley took several delicate steps to the centre of the once grand building, taking care to avoid the perils at his feet. 'Don't tell me, it's now called St. Peter's in the water?'

Ant shook his head on hearing the well-worn jest. 'Not exactly. A fire destroyed most of the building caused by lightning. The thatched roofs did the rest.'

'Why didn't they rebuild?' enquired the inspector as he looked up at the glimpses of sunshine through several openings in the roof.

'The high water-table,' replied Ant succinctly. 'You experienced it for yourself when you told me I owed you a pair of shoes. The land around here falls gently away from the Broad-hence all the old watermills. It got to the stage that they couldn't drain the water quickly enough. No good for arable crops either.'

Riley kicked aside several broken tiles so as not to impede his progress. 'Then they just abandoned the place?'

'They rebuilt the hamlet a mile or so across the fields on drier land.'

'Leaving the church high and dry.' Riley again laughed at his own joke. At that point, a small fragment of burnt roof timber floated down and kissed his shoulder on its way to add to the charcoal-littered floor.

'That's what you get for telling rubbish jokes.'

'Hilarious, I don't think,' responded the inspector as he dusted himself down.

After a pause, Riley stretched out his arms and looked from side to side. 'And all this has what to do with our missing vicar?'

Ant considered the point well made, given how much of Riley's time he'd already taken. 'Have a look at this.' He pointed to the altar. 'My father tells me the locals still hold an annual service here on the anniversary of the storm that destroyed the hamlet.'

The inspector followed Ant's carefully chosen footsteps until the pair stood side by side at one end of the decaying altar.

'And?' responded Riley without showing much interest.

'It's the tradition for the vicar of Stanton Parva to take the service.'

The detective realised the connection at once. 'You mean ... when did the most recent service take place?' Riley quickly lifted his police notebook from an inside pocket of his jacket.

Ant smiled at Riley's renewed fervour. 'Last week.'

Just then, a second, much larger piece of burnt timber fell from the roof, missing Ant by a few inches.

Both men tensed as a cloud of dust enveloped the bedraggled building.

'I suggest you show me whatever it is you've dragged me here to see, before this place collapses with us in it.'

'You may have a point there,' replied Ant. 'Just bear with me for a couple of minutes.'

'A couple of minutes? On your head be it.' Riley paused for a second. 'But it won't just be your head, will it?'

Ant let out a belly-laugh, before checking himself for making so much noise. 'Now that's funny. Why aren't you laughing?'

Riley pointed to the ruined roof without bothering to look up, which made Ant laugh more.

As dust continued to fall, like the aftershocks of an earthquake, the men patted themselves down. The action went some way to remove the worst of the detritus from their hair and clothes.

After calming down and collecting his thoughts, Ant pointed to a patch of floor behind the altar. 'That's what I wanted to show you.'

Riley moved in front of his companion and squinted at where Ant had pointed. It took several seconds for the detective to latch on. When he did, his body language stiffened. 'Broken glass? You bring me all the way out here, almost get me drowned, then risk me being pole-axed from a collapsing roof, and you get excited about half-a-dozen bits of glass. Are you mad, or just daft?'

Each time Riley raised his voice, a sprinkling of dust descended from the shattered roof. As the inspector reached a crescendo, a loud crack ricocheted around the ruin. The development even alarmed Ant as he put a finger to his lips to suggest Riley quieten down.

'It's not just any old bit of glass. Did you notice the fake silver top over there?'

Riley took the hint. After noticing the object, he retrieved a handkerchief, crouched down, and carefully rescued the top without touching it or the glass shards. The inspector stood and scrutinised the screw cap, taking care not to cut himself on the sharp-edged remains of the bottle.

'It's not so much the bottle, as what it once contained,' said Ant, encouraging the inspector to sniff the small object in his handkerchief covered hand.

Riley did as instructed, inhaling several times though his nose as if testing wine for its vintage. 'Perfume! said Riley before turning the item to check for a brand name on the silvered top. How interesting.'

'Let me guess, Amore, Amore,' said Ant.

The inspector looked at his friend. 'Something tells me you have more to reveal, or you wouldn't have insisted I look. One thing, though. Who told you it was here?'

Ant gently took the linen-covered object from his companion to give it his own close inspection. 'I can understand you being sceptical. A cynic might say it's too convenient that the same scent we found in the letters turns up here, and that it's me who alerted the police. However, there's a much more mundane explanation.'

Riley glanced at the bottle-top. 'And that would be?'

Ant handed back the bottle-top, which Riley transferred into a clear cellophane evidence bag, a supply of which he always carried with him.

'My father runs the committee that monitors the condition of the church and reports his findings to the diocese. He carried out an inspection a few days after this year's service. It's still consecrated ground.'

Riley huffed. 'What, and he just came across a discarded bottle and thought, "Oh, this might be important to the police. I must tell my amateur sleuth son to tell them". Come on, Anthony, I wasn't born yesterday.'

Ant lost his patience. 'No, you don't understand. Dad didn't think twice about the bottle. He finds all sorts of things in what is an abandoned shell. In fact, he tells me he didn't notice it until he felt something crack under his foot.

The reason he mentioned it to me was nothing to do with finding a discarded bottle. It was the overpowering aroma that the broken bottle released. Mum gave him some gyp when he came home, I can tell you. I was with her in the kitchen having a cuppa when he walked in, and he reeked of the stuff. She made him take his shoes off and put them outside. That's how he came to tell us what had happened. You see. No conspiracy theories or two plus two making five.'

I'm not sure he believes me, thought Ant.

'I'll accept your explanation, for now. You'll expect me to check out if your father knew or has had any contact with Cynthia Hake.'

———

'I'VE TOLD YOU BEFORE, it needs a new starter motor,' said Fitch, as he and Ant lent over the engine of the vintage Morgan sports. 'There's only so many times I can fix this thing. Now, what do you want me to do, and there's a clue in me telling you I'm not wasting any more time patching it up?'

'And you know what? Peter Riley didn't half give me a hard time about dad finding that bottle.'

Fitch let out a heavy sigh. 'Are you still going on about that? You haven't heard a word I've said, have you?'

Ant looked surprised. 'Yes, I have. You said she needs new fuel lines.'

'That rather proves my point, Lord, I don't have a clue, Stanton. That said, it might be a good idea to renew them along with the starter motor, but that's not the point. Is this what getting married does to a bloke? If so, I don't think I'll bother.'

Instead of attempting an answer, Ant looked like a young boy having had his last sweet pinched in the playground.

'I can see I'll get no sense out of you until you've got Peter's comments out of your system so, come on, let's have it.'

Before Ant could say anything, a Stanton Hall staff member arrived on a buggy and parked just a couple of feet away from Ant and Fitch. 'His Lordship said I'd find you here.'

'He spends more time with me trying to fix this heap of rubbish than he spends with Lyn these days. I wonder if he's trying to tell her something?'

The estate worker laughed, while Ant gave his best friend a filthy look.

'Hilarious, I don't think,' said Ant. He turned to the young man on the buggy. 'Never mind this one, he's in love. She calls him her oily rag. It tells you who's boss in that relationship, doesn't it?'

This time, it was Fitch who adopted a strained look.

'Listen,' said the young man in a light-hearted tone. 'I'm not getting in the middle of you two. I've got my own girl problems. Anthony's dad just needs to know if you signed the purchase order for them new fence posts for the top field on Home Farm?'

'I did indeed, and if my memory serves me right, they're stored in the new barn,' replied Ant.

Mission complete, the young man started the buggy and sped away, barely missing the butcher's assistant on his bicycle.

'I don't get you aristocrats,' said Fitch with half an eye on the young butcher to make sure he'd survived his ordeal.

'How can you call that wreck, "New Barn", when it's' over 300 years old?'

'Simple, because the old barn is 520 years old.'

Fitch shook his head as he handed his friend the grubby remains of the Morgan's starter motor. 'That thing looks older than either of your barns. Let me order a new one. I'm a mechanic, not an antiques dealer.'

As Ant took the damaged starter motor, he dropped the heavy metal object onto the concrete surface of the yard near the front left-hand corner of the Morgan.

'Well, if it wasn't broken before, it sure is now', said Fitch with a wry smile.

Ant stooped to retrieve the black-painted component, before noticing a hair-line crack in the headlight glass. He quickly lost interest in the starter motor.

'We have to find out who was at the memorial service at St. Peter's,' said Ant excitedly as he handed the starter motor back to his friend.

'What?' replied an astonished Fitch. 'You're not with it at all, are you?'

'Yes, I am, you were talking about... er.'

'You make my point for me.'

'It's all about who attended. Don't you understand?' said Ant. 'Once I can prove that to Peter Riley, it'll all make sense.'

'Well, I'm glad it makes sense to somebody, because you're living proof that all toffs are eccentric, or bonkers. In your case, it's both.'

Ant wasn't listening. 'I need your Land Rover. You can have it back tomorrow.'

'Oh, can I? Thank you so much,' replied Fitch. However, his voice became lost by the clattering sound of the vehicle coming hesitantly to life. Ant revved the engine to within an inch of its life, causing a cloud of bluish-grey smoke to escape from the exhaust pipe.

Fitch got ready for the noxious mixture as Ant imitated the driving skills of his estate worker and sped towards the garage exit.

Looking over his shoulder to a mist-enveloped Fitch, Ant shouted at the top of his voice. 'It's all about the old church. Don't you get it?'

Chapter Eleven

SECRETS

THE EAGER HUBBUB of children rushing out of school, ready for the weekend, reminded Ant of his own time at Stanton Primary. It all seemed a long time ago now as the realities of adulthood hung heavily on his mind.

After a bit, the chaos in the yard calmed down when he saw Lyn waving to the last of the kids leaving the premises. In the background, the caretaker rattled an enormous set of keys to encourage the headteacher to vacate the premises so that he could lock-up.

'I presume your Morgan is in the garage again since you've purloined Fitch's Land Rover. Does he know you've taken it?'

'Of course he does,' said Ant in a fake hurt tone as he revved the rattling diesel engine.

'Hm,' replied Lyn. 'If memory serves me correctly, he rang the police last time. Something about teaching you a lesson?'

Ant frowned. 'Fitch was out of order there. I thought the police were heavy-handed, pulling me over like that. I swear Peter Riley had a hand in the constable cuffing me and keeping me in the back of his patrol car so long. He knew who I was, you know.'

Lyn laughed as she clambered into the bone-shaking vehicle and slammed the door closed. 'I know, I know. You've never shut up about it since it happened. Anyway, what have you been up to? You look flushed.'

Ant fought with the clutch and gearstick to force the Land Rover into first gear, then moved off, leaving a cloud of smoke behind them. He briefed his companion about visiting St. Peter's with the inspector. He also outlined the suspicions he had about Cynthia Hake.

Lyn probed her companion about the perfume bottle his father had found. 'What do you mean, how do I know it fell from somewhere? Think about it. The only reason it's been trodden underfoot is that it fell from somewhere. That stuff is expensive. Either it fell from Cynthia's handbag, or she put the bottle on the altar, and it got knocked off. As you mentioned, there were bits of the roof falling on Peter Riley and you. What if a piece of timber, or tile, fell and hit the bottle? It's at least possible, isn't it?'

He thought for a moment while continuing to battle with the obstinate gears of the rickety vehicle. 'None of this makes sense unless Cynthia Hake attended that service, and that worries me.'

Lyn hung on for dear life as the Land Rover lurched from one side to the other and paid scant regard for the bumps and hollows of the road's surface. 'That's easy to prove.'

'Oh, is it, Sherlock?'

'It is, and don't dismiss what I have to say, or I'll let you fathom it yourself. 'Watch out, we'll be in a ditch!' yelled Lyn.

Ant swerved left to avoid a roe deer that came through a hedge gap. The startled animal sprang like a gazelle as it crossed from right to left.

'Hang on, there's at least one more to come. That was a male, so I imagine his lady- friend isn't far behind.'

No sooner had Lyn made her prediction than a second, smaller deer made a run for it. 'Lovely animals, but they cause so many road accidents, which they normally come off worst. Daft things!'

He looked at the rear-view mirror to check for following traffic. In the absence of any, he kept the Land Rover stationary while he allowed his heart rate to settle and gathered his thoughts. He glanced across to check Lyn was ok.

'Don't worry about me,' she said. 'It's only what I expect from a drive in the country with you behind the wheel. Come on, let's get going. By the way. Where are we going?'

'Not so quick,' replied Ant, as he let the clutch slip to allow the Land Rover to move off. 'You're not getting off that lightly. Why are you so confident you can find out who was at that service? It's not as if you can ask the vicar, is it?'

'Money,' responded Lyn with an edge of intrigue in her tone.

'Money? What are you talking about?'

Lyn smiled as she wagged a finger at Ant. 'And here's me thinking you must be clever because you worked for military intelligence.'

'Now you're just being obtuse,' replied Ant, trying not to let his frustration show.

Lyn took one of the cleaner rags from the dashboard and cleared a mud smear from the side window. 'I wonder how Fitch gets the inside of this thing so dirty.' She knew her delaying tactics infuriated her fiance, which gave her the greatest glee.

'Are you going to tell me, or keep up your little game until—'

'Until what, my little Lord Snooty?'

Perhaps I've pushed this as far as I dare, thought Lyn.

'Don't be so melodramatic. Think about it. What does any vicar ask his flock for as part of a service?'

Ant thought for a few seconds before his face lit up. 'Ah ha, money. You said money, before. You mean the church collection?'

'At last,' said Lyn, giving Ant a gentle stroke on his chin with her right palm. 'More than that, most regular church-goers do what? I mean, how do they give money?'

Ant thought about it for a second. 'Envelopes. Regular churchgoers give their donation in a small envelope.'

'Not only that,' responded Lyn. 'Each envelope's numbered, so that the church can keep track of who has donated what. All we need to do is speak to Ian Jefferson. One of his responsibilities in our church is to count and record the collection after every service. The vicar is bound to have asked him to do the same for the memorial service at St. Peter's. A numbered envelope can prove that she was there. If we don't find it, it probably means she didn't attend, which gives us an obvious line of enquiry. The problem is that she may have donated cash, or not at all, which is much more problematic for us, don't you think?'

Ant pulled onto a grass verge where the road widened. 'Either way, someone will have seen her. If not, and there's no envelope, there's a chance she didn't attend the service. Anyway, let's not speculate now. We'll be in a better position to decide what to do when we've seen Ian Jefferson. For now, we have something else to concentrate on.'

'So, I get to find out where you're taking me. I assume it's not lunch?' He hadn't even thought about that.

Cheapskate thought Lyn.

Ant looked sheepish. 'Er, not just yet.' Instead, he updated her about the inspector's acquaintance with Alison the previous evening. 'The upshot is that he thinks it might be a good idea if you have a few words with her. You know, girls together and all that, to find out more about her relationship with Cynthia Hake. Peter seems to think she might help with the investigation. The issue he's got is how much Cynthia appears to rely on her, so wants us to have a dig and see what comes up.'

Lyn scowled. 'Men, you never change.'

'What have I done now?'

'That's the trouble. You lot do it so often that you don't realise you're at it.'

'At what?' replied her confused companion.

'Being sexist, that's what. You automatically think, "Oh, they're both women, so Lyn can deal with it." Let me tell you, my little lord, you're on thin ice.'

'Stop there, Lyn. Who's being sexist now? What I mean is, given what we think that place exists for, there's no way Peter or I would get within half-a-mile of it.'

The verbal stand-off continued for several seconds as the pair glared at one another. Ant broke eye contact first. 'Look, I'm sorry if all that came out wrong. You, of all people, know what I feel about that sort of stuff. All I'm saying is that being a woman, you are far more likely to get into a place that is a women's refuge. That's all I meant.'

Lyn's demeanour softened. 'I didn't mean to bite, but we get fed up with it. I tell you what, let's start again.'

They knew when to walk away from an argument and were comfortable enough with each other not to sulk. Both instinctively leaned across and exchanged a tender kiss.

The weather mirrored their newfound cheerfulness as

the sun fought with the overhanging canopy of trees on both sides of the narrow road. Bright shafts of light penetrated the shade at every opportunity. Moving from dappled shade to bright sunshine, then back into the soft light, gave Lyn a sense of inner calm in her busy life.

We're so lucky to live in such a beautiful place, she thought. 'Come on, then. Fill me in on Alison King, and what she's doing up at, what did you call it, the mansion?'

Ant battled with the Land Rover's quirky steering and gear-change systems as he tried to remember the history of the Georgian building. 'Dad told me it used to belong to the Stanton Estate, and that grandad helped set up a charity during WWI and gifted the property to them. Not only that, but he also gave the charity an endowment to keep it running.'

'It sounds as if your grandfather was ahead of his time,' responded Lyn.

'Grandad castigated young men from affluent households who had relationships with female servants and then cut and ran.'

I don't know as much about Ant's family as I thought I did, thought Lyn. 'And then the war came?'

'You've got it. Most of the young men working on the estate volunteered to enlist from the beginning in 1914. A few had village sweethearts. Dad tells me that just like in WWII, things moved fast. Leave was intermittent and only lasted a few days. So many young men and women pledged themselves to each other and, I suppose in the heat of the moment, passion took over.'

Lyn adopted a serious, lonely expression. 'I know what you're about to say. Many of the boys never came back.' Ant sat back in the driver's seat as the Land Rover broke free of the tree canopy and headed into the bright sunshine.

The open vista of the Norfolk countryside lay before them as they made rapid progress towards their destination. 'It's a sobering thought, isn't it? And to make matters worse, the children born out of wedlock got stigmatised and labelled, "Base-born". To add insult to injury, those children were all in the prime of their young lives when the second World War came along twenty years later.'

Lyn shed a tear as she thought about the devastation wrought on so many local families. 'And we're still living with the consequences today.'

Ant nodded. 'Five minutes at a war memorial can be an emotional experience. Seeing the same surname two or even three times is a sobering sight.'

The conversation became muted for a short time until Ant commented on two elderly men arguing nearby. Each leaned on opposite sides of the same rickety gate as they gesticulated at one another. 'I tell you what, though, the country may have been turned upside down twice in forty-years, but some things never change. Just look at those two. You'd never think they were twins.'

Lyn smiled as she dabbed a tear from her cheek. 'I suppose it's reassuring. You know, nothing stays the same except those things we want to stay the same. Despite all the arguing they do, I bet they'd be lost without each other.'

As the vehicle rounded a long, gentle bend in the road, Ant caught sight of a dilapidated drive and brought the Land Rover to a halt.

'This is the place, is it? Where's the house?'

'That's what made its location so perfect,' said Ant. 'You can't see the place from the road. The mansion's a couple of hundred yards down the track. There's a couple of twists and turns, so you won't see the place until you're on top of it.'

Lyn was about to open the Land Rover door when she looked back at her fiance. 'Explain to me again what we're doing here? If it's about unmarried mothers, well, thank heavens, we don't need to hide them away from prying eyes anymore.'

'You're right. But domestic violence is still very much with us. Alison oversees the place, on behalf of a charity that took it over twenty years ago.'

'Why should you find anything if your grandfather gave the place away?' responded Lyn.

'Because he placed a couple of covenants in the deeds and bill of exchange, which was set at one old penny a year. He wanted to make sure they always used the place for the purpose he'd agreed with the original charity.'

Lyn gazed down the tree-lined driveway. 'I suppose that makes sense. But how come the house was transferred to a new charity?'

Ant rubbed his chin. 'That's a good point that I'm determined to understand. Dad should have been informed of any change in use. That said, it seems a good cause to me, so I don't want to make too much fuss.'

'Explain, please,' said Lyn.

'As you know, these places operate on a sort of "need to know" basis. It seems not even Peter knows what goes on here, or they would have recognised each other at the police station. He told me he'd never seen Alison before.'

Lyn slipped from the Land Rover. 'Then am I checking how busy they are, or who they work with?'

'That's a useful angle, but remember, Peter's keen to understand why Cynthia Hake is clinging so closely to her.'

Lyn frowned. 'I would have thought that's obvious given what's Cynthia accused our vicar with doing?'

'Do you believe that?'

'Of course not, but—'

'But what?' replied Ant.

Lyn thought for a moment. 'You win. I'll go in with an open mind and see what turns up. Ali was friendly enough when we met her in church, and Peter thinks she can help us. Perhaps she can give me more of an insight into what help she's been giving Cynthia.'

As Lyn climbed from the Land Rover and walked down the overgrown drive to the once grand house, she turned and blew her fiance a kiss.

———

LYN PRESSED the call button on an aged intercom box to one side of the paint-peeled front door, 'Hi, Ali. Sorry not to have given you a warning, but I was just passing. Any chance of a cup of tea? said Lyn in a clear, confident voice.

It took two attempts to raise a response, but eventually Lyn saw the outline of a figure in the hallway through the elaborate art deco stained-glass door panel. Alison King opened the door, revealing a long hallway with an impressive oak staircase.

'It's great to see you again so soon. Come on in and tell me what brings you all the way out here? You're one of the few people who's been able to find the house. Of course, that's the whole point of the place.'

Ali offered a warm smile as she showed her guest into an enormous space that once fulfilled the role of a morning room.

'Wow, what a room. It must have been one heck of a house to call home at one time.'

Ali looked around the large, perfectly proportioned space. 'You can say that again. But someone's loss is the charity's gain. Without this place, we'd be struggling to cope with all the referrals we get.'

'That bad? Is it rude of me to ask how many... eh—'

'We call our guests, "service users". A horrible name, I know, but that's what we must call them to keep the funds coming in.'

Lyn chuckled. 'You don't have to tell me about the bureaucracy. I drown in the stuff and wonder what happens to all that paper once I complete it and send it back. What would we do without computers to manage it all?'

'Computers?' replied Alison with a chuckle. 'I don't use them myself—far too technical for me.'

The two women passed the next few minutes talking about anything but the rules and regulations each had to comply with.

'Anyway, I promised you a cup of tea. Why don't you take a seat? I'll be back in a jiffy.'

Lyn thanked her host and chose a window seat over-looking the generous private grounds bordered with lofty trees underplanted with a range of overgrown bushes. Together, they formed an impenetrable barrier to those who might wish to see what went on in the mysterious building.

Ali soon returned carrying a tray with two brightly decorated mugs of tea, together with the usual accompaniments.

'Now,' began Ali. 'How can I help?'

Lyn took a mug from the plastic tray and thanked her host for her hospitality. 'To be frank, I need your help.'

Ali rested the tray on a tattered mahogany sideboard, collected her drink, and sat on the opposite end of the window seat. 'Happy to help if I can. Come on, tell me all about it.'

'I'm concerned about Cynthia Hake. A little bird tells me you're providing support. It's just that—'

'You don't need to explain, Lyn. I know Stanton Parva is a small place, and people see and hear things all the time. The question is, do they apply the correct interpretation?'

'You're telling me,' replied Lyn.

The pair mirrored each other by taking a sip of tea and taking a moment to glimpse the wild landscape that was once superbly attended flower beds.

'I guess I'm confused why Cynthia has become so close to you, rather than the more usual help available in the village. You know, the doctor, a best friend? I only ask because I'm concerned about her. She's behaving differently to anything I've seen in her before, and I've known her for several years now.'

Ali grimaced. 'I'm not sure Cyn being "close" to me is the right adjective. If anything, the time I'm giving her is taking me away from my principal work.' Ali motioned her arms about the room. 'This place. Our portfolio of services. Well, it's a lot for a small team to cover. But what can you do? It's my calling, just as yours is nurturing the next generation of grown-ups.'

Lyn remained quiet.

'Is there something wrong?' asked Ali.

'No, not at all. It's so quiet here. You said you had a small team?'

Ali smiled. 'Ah, I see. You're wondering where everyone is. Simple. A week of team building in Buckinghamshire, then a few days' training on health and safety.'

'Oh, let's not go there,' laughed Lyn. 'But your service users?'

Ali took a sip of her tea before returning the mug to the water-stained window sill. 'Another simple explanation.

We'll only begin taking referrals when some essential repairs to the gas and water supply are complete. Then there's all the fire safety stuff we need to install. It's costing the charity a fortune, I can tell you.'

Seems reasonable enough, thought Lyn.

'You must think me so nosy. I've always been the same, and it's got me into a scrape or two over the years.' Lyn raised her eyes to reinforce her point.

'Not at all. I get it and to be honest, I don't help myself by keeping a low profile. The fewer people know about what we do here, the better. You understand, don't you?'

'Of course, and full marks to you for helping women who must be desperate for help, not to say a safe place to stay. And that sort of brings me back to Cynthia. Did she ask to stay here?'

'She did, but as I've explained, we're just not ready.'

'How did she take it?'

'Not well, if I'm honest. I suppose that's why I give her so much time. I'm sure things will sort themselves out soon. They usually do, don't they?'

Lyn took another sip of her tea and caught sight of a grandfather clock standing in the far corner. 'Goodness me. Is that clock, right?'

Ali looked over at the clock. 'I'm tempted to say yes, twice a day, but I gave it a wind first thing this morning, so yes, it is. Why do you ask?'

'Because I'm about to be late in meeting my prospective parents-in-law. It's usually Ant and I'm always having a go at him. In return, he's always telling me not everybody's ruled by the school bell. Now he'll have something to tease the living daylight out of me.'

Both women stood and took a last look at the sun as it appeared to bounce across the tree canopy.

'Is he with you?'

'Yes, he's in the Land Rover, just outside the gates. To be honest, I told him to say there because of what you do here. He'll be miffed when I tell him you're yet to start, and he missed a nice brew.'

The new friends shared the joke as Ali showed Lyn out and waved goodbye.

'Don't be a stranger.'

'I won't,' replied Lyn.

'I tell you what. Why don't I give you my mobile number? That way, you've no excuse for not keeping in touch.' Alison looked around for a piece of paper and pen. Unable to find either object, she resorted to delving into her oversized handbag that hung over a nearby chair. After what seemed like an age, she proudly held up a ballpoint pen and a slip of paper. 'There you are. Don't forget to use it, will you?'

'I may take you up on your offer sooner than you think,' replied Lyn as she stuffed the folded slip into her jacket pocket.

As she neared the beaten-up vehicle, she caught the first glimpse of Ant. What a surprise. He's asleep. She slowed her pace and crept forward so as not to disturb her fiance as she quietly opened the passenger side door, she noticed two things. First, she'd left the window wound half-way-down. Second, the disorderly heap of grubby rags, food wrappings and documents that occupied the dashboard moved.

No wonder Sophie calls Fitch her oily rag, thought Lyn, before scuttling an irritated grey squirrel out of the vehicle.

Ant remained oblivious to the goings-on and continued to snore in a repeating pattern of snorts and throaty warbling.

'Oi, wake up my little Saint Francis of Assisi,' said Lyn,

while gently shaking Ant's shoulder. 'You've got half the wildlife of Norfolk clambering all over you.'

How can anyone make so much noise and stay asleep? thought Lyn. She shook his shoulder again. This time giving no thought for Ant's comfort.

'Come on, the Land Rover's on fire.'

The threat of imminent danger served only to raise a partially formed response, while Ant's eyes remained half-closed. 'Wha—'

'Fire!' shouted Lyn. This time the alert worked as her fiance threw open his door and sprang from the vehicle, only to stumble and fall onto a patch of shingle.

'Now I know why you toffs sleep in separate bedrooms. I can tell you now, that's one tradition we'll keep once we're wed.'

'What are you talking about, woman? Get away from the Land Rover, it's on…' Ant's voice tailed off as he got to his feet and rubbed gravel remnants from his palms. 'It's not on fire, is it?'

Lyn's face beamed at having caught him out. 'No, sleeping beauty, it's lucky for you your pockets are empty of the mints you usually carry, or you'd still have a family of squirrels rifling through them.'

'Squirrels? You're talking in riddles?'

'Too much to explain,' said Lyn, giving Ant a peck on the cheek.

'What was that for?'

'Are you complaining?'

'Er, no. it's just, well. Er, what was that about separate bedrooms? You don't snore, do you?'

Lyn erupted into laughter. 'Come on, you couldn't make it up. Right, let's get going.'

As Ant pulled the Land Rover off the opening of the

mansion's driveway, he still wore a puzzled look. 'Were you serious?'

'About the bedroom?'

'No,' replied Ant. 'The squirrels.'

They exchanged a serious look before Lyn realised he was joking.

'I see you've woken up.'

'You can't kid a kidder,'

'That's what your dad's old gardener used to say when we were kids, remember?' replied Lyn with a wistful look.

'You bet. He was a character, wasn't he? Remember when…,' Ant's voice tailed off.

'Remember what?'

He hesitated. 'Oh, it doesn't matter. A long time ago now. Listen, we'd better get back to the case. What did you find out from Alison?'

He's remembered something that he doesn't want to talk about, yet I must have been there from the way he phrased the sentence? Better let it go for now, thought Lyn.

'I don't know about her, but I tell you what, that house hasn't seen a coat of paint since Noah was a lad.'

'Anything else other than a condition report?'

Lyn gave her fiancé a stern look. 'Oi, while you were in the land of nod, I got some information from a woman I'd met for two minutes previously.'

'Did she open up to you?'

'I think she's legit. One thing she said was that Cynthia Hake is more of a work-in-progress than a friend.'

'Explain, please?'

Lyn briefed Ant on her conversation, including the fact that Cynthia had asked to stay at the mansion.

'That's interesting,' replied Ant.

Lyn scrunched her nose. 'Not as interesting as eating.

Don't forget. You promised me lunch and you're not getting out of it this time.'

With that, Ant slammed the clutch to the floor and grabbed the gear stick. 'You will do as you're told.'

Lyn shook her head. 'We'll see who's boss.'

The Land Rover protested at being disturbed by fighting Ant all the way. At last, he got the vehicle into third gear, having long ago given up on gears one and two.

Once underway, the pair fell into a comfortable silence as Ant guided the unruly Land Rover past a road sign for Stanton Parva. As the tree line thinned to expose a magnificent sea of yellow from the ripening fields of oilseed rape.

'It doesn't sound as if we're much further forward concerning the relationship between Alison and Cynthia, does it? Where the heck do we go from here?'

Where did that come from? It's not like him to sound so negative. thought Lyn.

'Hang on,' replied Lyn. 'We've discovered a lot. For instance, we now know Cynthia forced the pace with Alison. Are Alison's allegations against Reverend Morton valid, or is Cynthia using her as a distraction for something she did to the vicar?'

Ant looked over to Lyn. 'If your reasoning is anywhere near the truth, at least we know we're dealing with an arch manipulator.'

Chapter Twelve

GHOSTS

'ARE you still pondering about Alison, or is something else bothering you? I know that look. Come on, what is it?'

Lyn hesitated. 'No. Believe it or not, I was pondering all the bad habits I'll have to put up with once we're married.'

Ant let out a throaty laugh as, for once, the gearbox of the Land Rover did as it was told. 'I take it you don't just mean mine, although I can't think of any.'

His fiancé returned a look that could not be mistaken for agreement. 'Of course, I mean yours. Saying none come to mind rather proves my point. Well, what you see is what you get.'

The exchange fell into a few seconds of silence before both began laughing. Lyn knew the spell of light-heartedness couldn't put off something she'd been meaning to raise since they'd last seen his parents. To her surprise, Ant pre-empted the subject.

'Mum and dad gave me a shock when they talked about stepping away from the business side of things. What do you think about their decision?'

She turned her head to the left to take in the glorious sea of yellow swaying gently in a light breeze. The distraction also gave Lyn time to frame her answer. 'I love your parents too much to have said anything. But I'm not sure I'm ready to give up my teaching career. I worked so hard to get this headship, and—'

'I get it.' He glanced across to Lyn, whose eye line remained fixed on the endless carpet of iridescent yellow that stretched to the horizon. Ant pressed on. 'What are you saying?'

Still, she avoided eye contact. 'I'm not saying anything, except it was a shock to me, too. Anyway, you're the one who brought the subject up. One thing's for sure. Your parent's thoughts on the matter raise some questions.'

'You mean about us getting married?'

It's not fair, him putting me in a corner like this, thought Lyn.

The Land Rover picked up on the mood, as it reverted to type and played up again.

'Bother', shouted Ant as he fought with the clutch.

'What?' said Lyn as she left the peaceful landscape behind and turned her full attention to her angry companion.

'No, sorry, I—'

'Will you please stop saying you're sorry?'

Ant took his eyes off the narrow road, deep in thought.

'Watch out. You'll have us in the ditch. Can't we discuss this later? We have more important stuff to be getting on with, rather than—'

Straight away, she realised her words were likely to be misunderstood. Confirmation soon came.

'Than talking about whether we get married.'

Ant's outburst confused Lyn. Why am I not jumping up and down at him saying that? 'Don't be so stupid.'

'Am I being stupid, or saying it to you?'

Say something before things get out of hand, thought Lyn. Except she couldn't form the words.

Ant subconsciously slowed the Land Rover as he took in the magnitude of what had just happened. 'Then you are having second thoughts?'

'What?' shouted Lyn, surprised that she felt a mixture of anger and relief. Their face-off came to an abrupt halt as the driver of a farm tractor beeped his horn in a rhythmic display of frustration. Ant glanced at his rear-view mirror. He could see a long line of traffic had built up behind the mud-splattered tractor. Ant glanced back at his speedometer. It hovered around the fifteen-miles-an-hour mark.

'You'll have to pull over and let that lot pass,' said Lyn, thankful for a break in their tense exchanges.

Ant didn't wait long as he manoeuvred into a field entrance on his left, leaving room for traffic to pass the Land Rover.

They spent the few minutes with glum faces and holding an open-palmed hand up to signify an apology to each passing driver. And then all was quiet.

Both wound their window down in a coordinated effort to release the bad karma from the vehicle.

The only sounds to be heard were birdsong, the buzzing of honeybees and the swooshing melody of oilseed rape, each in perfect harmony, one with the other.

'I didn't mean to upset you, but sometimes you come out with such daft things. Of course, I still want to marry you,' said Lyn as she placed an open palm on his cheek.

'But you hesitated,' replied Ant, taking her hand in his. 'That tells me you—'

'It tells you I want to spend the rest of my life with you.'

'I'm sensing there's a "but" in there.'

Lyn pulled her hand from his. 'Oh, stop it. What on earth's got into you?' she straightened up in her seat and looked him square in the eye. 'Ok, let's have it out. They brought you up to own and run the Stanton Estate. I grew up in a council house. The way we view the world will always be different. It's nobody's fault, but there you have it.'

What have I said? thought Lyn. She touched her finance's arm. 'It's selfish of me to say that. I also miss your brother.'

At first, Ant failed to react as Lyn rested her head on his shoulder. Then he relented. 'I know you do. And you're right. Our backgrounds are different. But you know it didn't make one jot of difference to our friendship growing up together, and you know how much mum and dad love you.'

Lyn lifted her head from Ant's shoulder and stared at him. Before she could speak, Ant continued. 'I had everything planned out for a career in the army before Greg died. You know, him the heir and me the spare. I never minded the tag, and all the jokes about it among mum and dad's circle of friends. In fact, I knew it meant I was free to do what I wanted. But now—'

'Now you have a duty to your parents to keep things going.'

Ant returned her intense gaze. 'You know I wouldn't stand in your way if you chose another path. My parents love you too much to guilt-trip you into marrying me. You know that much, don't you?'

'But you can't leave them, or the estate, can you?'

A half-smile spread across Ant's face. 'You know the answer to that.'

Lyn eased herself away from her finance and returned his smile. 'And do you seriously think I'd leave you to run things on your own? You're not safe to be let loose without someone watching your back. I suppose that "someone" had better be me.'

Ant's smile broadened into a beaming grin. 'I promise you we'll work things out. There's no way I'd expect you to give up the one thing I know you love - almost as much as you do, me.'

That little boy smile gets me every time, thought Lyn.

'Come on. I've got your favourite pizza in the freezer back at mine.' As the pair giggled like young lovers, Lyn noticed something from the corner of her eye.

'Stop.'

He reacted in an instant. Less than six feet in front of the Land Rover stood Phyllis, clutching a straw shopping basket tight to her chest, her eyes clamped shut.

Ant sprang from the vehicle and apologised to the terrified villager. 'I'm so sorry, Phyllis. I don't know what I was thinking of.'

Lyn leapt from the Land Rover to offer what comfort she could. The elderly lady opened first one eye, and then the other, while continuing to clasp the shopping bag as if it were a suit of armour.

'I know what came over you. You're all the same, you young ones. Too much of the "Lovey-dovey" stuff, if you ask me.'

I suppose being called a "young one" is a sort of compliment to a thirty - something couple, thought Lyn.

'Can we give you a lift to compensate for my friend half-scaring you to death?' she asked.

Ant, trying on his guilty look with little success. 'Young man,' retorted Phyllis, 'Apprentice Lord of the Manor you may be, but you've almost lifted me to heaven once already today. At the risk of tempting providence, I'll rely on my legs. They've served me well for almost eighty-five years, so I'm sure they'll last me out now. Don't you?'

She's still got pluck, thought Lyn.

'What happened to her being my new best friend?' mumbled Ant.

'I wouldn't push my luck if I were you,' replied Lyn in a hushed tone.

'Anyway, almost being killed twice this week by reckless drivers rather makes my point, don't you think? I'll bid you both a good day,' said Phyllis.

As the elderly lady walked away, paying no attention to other traffic on the road, Lyn realised what Phyllis said.

'Twice? You mean his lordship here has a competitor for being the worst driver in Stanton Parva?'

Neither Ant nor Phyllis appeared to see the funny side of Lyn's remark.

'If you mean that fool, Ian Jefferson, yes, Anthony has stiff competition.'

The mention of Jefferson's name alerted her erstwhile friends. As Phyllis once more turned to her front and continue walking, Lyn couldn't let the matter drop.

'When did you say Ian almost ran you over?'

Phyllis turned, her look making clear her irritation at the continuing toing and froing.

'I didn't. However, if you must know, it was on Tuesday morning. The silly man was arguing with the vicar. A vulgar man if you ask me, talking to the reverend like that. Anyway, he stormed off, that Jefferson man, I mean, and almost ran me over. He didn't even apologise, the beastly man. Then again, what can you expect from someone who dips his chocolate biscuits in his tea at my coffee mornings? The man leaves a terrible mess. And people ask me why I never got married.'

Lyn couldn't help but glance at Ant, given his habit of doing the same thing. 'What?' whispered Ant with a hurt look. Lyn chuckled at her fiancé's embarrassment and turned back to Phyllis. 'Are you sure about the day? You know, Monday, not Tuesday?' Phyllis tutted. 'I may be old, but I'm not senile, dear. If I said it was Tuesday, then it was Tuesday. But I tell you what, it wasn't the only argument got into on Tuesday. I happened to be passing the church again that evening. Bless me if he wasn't arguing again. This time with a woman. I couldn't see her, mind you, no matter how I tried. But I know a woman's voice when I hear it.' With that, Phyllis turned on her heels and walked off into the distance.

I hope I've got her spark if I live that long, thought Lyn.

Ant broke the silence. 'Are you thinking what I'm thinking?'

Lyn set aside her silent musing. 'If you mean Ian Jefferson's got some explaining to do, then yes, I am. Perhaps we should put the pizza on hold for thirty minutes while we have a chat with the man?'

'And now we have a mysterious woman to find. One day, two lively encounters, then he vanishes. What's going on?'

———

IAN JEFFERSON'S cottage formed one of three Victorian residencies built for farm workers. The modest red-brick houses stood in a row down a narrow track on the outskirts of Stanton Parva. 'It doesn't look as though he's at home,' commented Lyn, as her companion brought the Land Rover to a jerky stop, its gearbox resisting until the last second.

'Hmm, you could be right. All three cottages look abandoned. What a miserable place to live.'

Lyn scoured the dismal scene, where daylight struggled to penetrate the overgrown tree canopy.

'Still, it's an excellent location to get up to no good and keep under the radar, I suppose,' replied Ant.

Just then, the door to number three, Fletcher's Row, opened to allow a flustered-looking Ian Jefferson to tumble out onto a narrow garden path.

'It seems our luck is in after all,' said Ant as he pointed to the scruffily dressed Jefferson as he hung on tight to an old leather briefcase.

Seizing their opportunity, the pair left Fitch's Land Rover behind and paced towards their quarry.

'Hi, Ian. It looks as though we've just caught you in time?'

Jefferson appeared caught off-guard as he struggled to lock the front door, while turning his head to see who was calling him. 'Oh, er, well, you've caught me at an awkward moment. I'm late for a meeting. You know, church business.' Jefferson thought for a moment. 'It's just that, what with the vicar missing, there's so much to do, and--.' His words faded as he broke down.

Lyn hurried up the short pathway that divided Jefferson's unkempt garden in two. 'I know, Ian. We're all worried sick about him, so it must be doubly so for you. Everyone in the village knows how close you are, and how hard you work for the church.'

Jefferson gave Lyn a brief, forced smile before fiddling with the lock on his briefcase. 'You say that, but people don't understand. They think I'm milking the vicar's disappearance for sympathy. You know, some villagers I've known all my life have been outright nasty to me.

Why are they being like that? I have done nothing wrong.'

What an odd thing to say. thought Lyn.

'How awful,' said Ant. 'Anyone in particular?'

Jefferson continued to fidget with his briefcase. 'I'm not one to tell tales. Everyone knows that.'

'If you say so,' said Ant, which earned a visual ticking off from Lyn for over-acting.

'To be honest, that Cynthia Hake woman has been horrible to me.'

'Cynthia?' queried Lyn.

Jefferson left his briefcase alone, gave Lyn a hurt look, and shook his head. 'I hardly know the woman, so why is she being nasty?'

Lyn moved closer to Jefferson and placed a hand on his arm. 'Have you argued or done anything you can think of that may have upset her?'

Jefferson shook his head again. 'As I say, I don't know her that well. The vicar said I should turn the other cheek. But it's hard sometimes, isn't it? It's alright for the vicar. He's paid to say things like that. And it's his calling.'

Ant stepped forward. 'Talking about the vicar. Lyn told me she'd asked you when you last saw him. You said Tuesday. Is that right?'

Jefferson looked nonplussed. 'Er, let me see. Yes. I said it was Tuesday. Why do you ask?'

Come on, clever clogs, get yourself out of that one, thought Lyn as she gave her other-half a knowing smile.

Her companion was equal to the task. 'Oh, nothing. We're just helping the police to tidy up a few loose ends. It's just that...' Ant's voice tailed off as a tactic to engage Jefferson's curiosity.

'Just what?'

'Well, how should I put this? Best to speak plainly, I guess.' He studied Jefferson for any reaction to his line of conversation. 'Someone saw you arguing with the vicar by the church entrance on Tuesday morning. Then he vanishes over the next twenty-four hours.'

Jefferson looked distinctly uncomfortable.

We're going to lose him if Ant carries on like this, thought Lyn.

'We weren't arguing. Far from it. The vicar told me how excited at being chosen to represent the diocese at a gathering with the Archbishop at Lambeth Palace. He was very animated about the whole thing. Perhaps that's what this person you speak of saw?'

'There you are. That explains it all. There's nothing to worry about, Ian. All Anthony is trying to say, if a little clumsily, is that we want to clear up a misunderstanding. You'll understand the need to do that, right?'

Lyn's warm smile settled Jefferson down enough to re-engage him in the conversation.

'I see. Well, it was Monday. Now. If we're finished, I need to get on and please forgive me for rushing off.'

'Of course, Ian,' said Lyn as she observed the man scowling at Ant as he passed his visitors and scurried down the narrow garden path. Lyn turned to Ant. 'You're too blunt for your own good sometimes. I thought he was about to shut up just then. But well done for getting yourself out of a hole.'

Ant gave Lyn a perplexed look. 'So, is that a telling off, or a compliment?'

'Don't push your luck, matey.'

Ant smiled, rather than pursuing the point, and as they clambered back into the rickety Land Rover, both pondered on what had just taken place.

'What do you think, then?' asked Lyn.

'He's an awful actor, that's what. Did you pick up on his body language? You know, if he wasn't fiddling with his briefcase, he was picking at his ear. Anything but look at us.'

'I did,' replied Lyn as she struggled to push her seat belt home. 'The question is, is that how he normally behaves when he feels under pressure, or is he hiding something from us?'

'What, you mean working with the vicar to engineer his disappearance, then frame Cynthia Hake? It sounds too far-fetched to me,' replied Ant as he turned the ignition key to fire the engine into a smoky life.

'You know, after the goings-on of the last few days, anything is possible with this case. Sort of more Agatha Christie than Agatha Christie.'

Ant was too busy fighting with the gearstick to pick up on Lyn's quip and remembering the promise of pizza at her place.

A few minutes later saw the pair sitting in the Land Rover outside The Old Schoolhouse, Lyn's hard earned and cherished home. She turned to Ant after waving to the mother of one of her pupils as she passed the stationary vehicle. 'Let's agree on something before we go in.'

'You have me intrigued,' replied a surprised Ant.

Lyn playfully nudged his left arm. 'No, I'm being serious. Let's agree not to talk about the case this evening. Time is running out to find the vicar, but we must brief Peter Riley first.'

Ant exited the Land Rover without speaking, rounded the bonnet and opened Lyn's door. 'That sounds like a fantastic idea. Have you any Fen Bodger Ale in to go with the pizza?'

Lyn returned his broad smile. 'If you remember, Jed

guilt-tripped you into buying a shed load of the stuff, so, yes, I can make that happen.'

The pair spent the rest of the evening watching TV and abiding by their pact to avoid talking about the case. Then Ant's mobile rang.

Lyn looked at the Art Deco timepiece on the fire mantle. 'It's five-past- ten, for goodness' sake. Who's calling you this late?'

Ant didn't answer. Instead, he listened to the caller with growing anxiety. 'Is your mum or dad ill?' asked Lyn as she watched the colour drain from Ant's cheeks.

'Thank you. We'll meet you in thirty minutes,' said Ant solemnly as he ended the call.

'What on earth is the matter? You look as though you've seen a ghost.'

Ant remained seated without answering for several seconds, before getting up and standing by the fire-hearth. 'We have,' replied Ant, as he played with a box of matches on the fire mantle.

'We?'

'Yes, we,' replied Ant, still fiddling with the matches. 'That was Peter Riley. They found Ian Jefferson dead in his house fifteen minutes ago.'

Lyn's shock matched Ant's. 'But when we last saw —'

'And that's the problem,' said Ant, as his mood darkened. 'It's possible we were the last people to see Ian Jefferson alive.'

Chapter Thirteen

A SHARP LESSON

OUTSIDE IAN JEFFERSON'S COTTAGE, the police were efficiently cordoning off a section the pathway with police tape. Officers, several in white scenes of crime coveralls, mask, and gloves, carried equipment in and out of the busy property.

'They've brought the full works,' said Ant as he pulled up as near to Ian's house as the police would allow. 'It brings it home to you, doesn't it when you see the resources they bring to bear when the police need to, that's for sure?'

As the pair clambered from the Land Rover, a police constable took several brisk steps forward. 'I can't allow you to cross the police line.'

An authoritative voice called out from behind the young police offer. 'That's alright, let them through, they're with me.'

'Sir,' snapped the bobby without needing to confirm the owner of the command, as she stretched to lift the tape high enough for Ant to duck underneath.

'Thank you, officer,' said Lyn in a quiet tone, which she thought was fitting, given the sombre nature of their visit.

'I wish I could say it's nice to see you both again, but this is a rum-do. We received a call just over an hour ago. They didn't give their name. Just said we ought to get over here urgently, and that there'd been an accident. That's when we found him.'

'It's crazy, Peter,' said Lyn. 'I can't believe we were talking to Ian a few hours ago.' she looked across to Ant. His posture confirmed he remained as confused about events as herself.

'Can we get into the house? Is he still in there?' asked Ant.

The detective half-turned to scan the front elevation of the property, then nodded. They're almost done with their preliminary work, but you'll need to wear this garb. 'I've got a couple of spares in the boot of my car.'

Now suitably attired to enter the crime scene, a police officer noted their names and entry time on his record sheet.

'You mentioned speaking to our victim earlier this evening?' said Riley.

All three stood in line a few feet from where Ian Jefferson sat, as if asleep sitting up on his faux-leather sofa.

After a few seconds of silence as each took in the sad scene, Ant briefed the detective on his and Lyn's hurried discussion with Jefferson.

After digesting Ant's update, Riley moved nearer to the body and bent forward to inspect the dead man's face. 'Well, he won't be talking to anyone now. That's for sure. The question is, who was he rushing off to meet? You say he mentioned church business?'

'That's what he said,' replied Lyn. 'But I know for a fact it couldn't have been the parochial committee, or Parish council, because they meet on the first Monday and Tuesday of the month.'

Riley thought for a moment. 'A spot of counselling with a parishioner on behalf of our absent clergyman?'

Lyn shook her head as she glanced at Jefferson's inanimate body. 'I shouldn't judge, especially the dead, but I don't think Ian had the skills for that sort of thing. The word is he had some troubles. The vicar mentioned to me some time ago that Ian took up much of his time.'

'What do you mean?' asked Riley.

Lyn looked back at the corpse. 'We all have demons, but it seems Ian had more than his fair share. The vicar didn't tell me what the nature of Ian's burdens was. He left me with the impression that he'd become weary with the support Ian expected him to provide at the drop of a hat.'

It was then that Riley and Lyn noticed Ant inspecting the front door.

'No sign of a forced entry, then?' Lyn feigned surprise that Ant hadn't appeared to have listened to her disclosure but let the matter pass.

'Scenes of crime checked the back, and it's the same,' responded Riley. 'Most murders involve the victim knowing and trusting the killer.'

That's not the first time Peter mentioned that. It makes you wonder who you can trust, thought Lyn.

The detective walked the few paces required to join Ant. 'I doubt you'll find anything my team didn't come across.'

'It's got to be worth checking, hasn't it?'

'Well, now you've done that, I suppose you want to check the back door?'

Riley smiled as he followed Ant into the kitchen.

Lyn, now alone with Ian Jefferson's corpse, scanned the living room. Poor Ian, he must have been skint. It doesn't look as though this room's seen a lick of paint or new wallpaper since Adam was a lad. She concentrated her gaze at the dilapidated picture rail that ran around all four walls of the chilly space.

Not one family picture. Just religious stuff, she thought.

An ancient radio rested on a mahogany sideboard in front of the single window. This limited the already scarce source of natural light entering the soulless room.

Who has coconut matting these days? Either Ian was a keen saver, or he didn't have two pennies to rub together, thought Lyn.

Just then, the two men returned from the kitchen and stood at Ian Jefferson's rear, behind the decaying sofa.

'There's not a mark on him,' said Lyn as she looked at Jefferson, then the other two. 'It's as if he's asleep, poor man.'

Riley bent forward. 'Come and look at this.'

The two of them huddled on either side of the detective.

'What do you see?' said Riley.

Ant and Lyn looked bemused as they tried to spot what Riley alluded to.

'Just there,' said the detective.

Lyn inspected where Riley pointed. 'Is that what I think it is? Sorry, that made little sense. What I mean is, well, drugs?'

'My guess is heroin, although we won't know for sure until the toxicology report is ready.'

'Are you seriously telling me our church-loving friend here was a junkie?' said Ant.

Lyn flashed her fiance a severe look. 'Don't be cold-hearted. I don't suppose anyone willingly becomes hooked on drugs. That's if Ian was taking narcotics.'

Ant looked chastened as he busied himself with picking imaginary fluff from his coveralls.

'But it may explain the state of the place,' said Lyn.

'What do you mean,' replied a still embarrassed Ant, without making eye contact.

'Tell me, what do you see?' Lyn wafted her hands around to emphasise her point. 'Ian never married. He will have inherited this place from his parents. Plus, he'd have had his state pension, any savings he'd built up and his stipend from the church. Yet no one has spent a penny on this place. I bet the food cupboards are empty, too.'

Her speculation caused Ant to step into the kitchen before reappearing a few seconds later. 'Not even enough to feed a mouse.'

'I guess whatever money he had, went to feed his habit,' said Lyn.

Riley moved from behind the sofa and knelt on the left of Jefferson's outstretched legs. 'Let's see what we can find,' said the detective, uncovering Ian Jefferson's elbow. 'There's our proof.' He pointed to a line of puncture marks, some old, others more recent.

'Poor soul,' said Lyn as she peeked over Riley's shoulder to view clear evidence of a long-standing addiction.

Ant joined his two friends. 'Why change from injecting his arm to the neck?'

'It's not just his neck. The needle penetrated his right jugular vein,' said Riley. 'He mainlined, which takes some doing. One false move and you'd exsanguinate within a minute.' 'Exsang... what?' exclaimed Ant.

'Bleed out,' said Lyn. 'You were in the forces and saw action, didn't you?' Ant's face stiffened. 'Yes, and some things are better forgotten.'

Peter Riley and Lyn exchanged knowing looks.

'I'm sorry. I—'

'It's okay, Lyn. Anyway, let's get on with it, shall we?' replied Ant with grim determination etched on his face. 'Anyway, those marks confirm Ian was right-handed. You know, injecting into his left arm.'

'You're correct,' responded Riley, keen to move on. 'Which makes the injection into the right jugular even more curious.'

'What do you mean?' said Lyn.

Riley unzipped his coveralls and took out a pen from an inside pocket of his jacket and simulated an attempt to inject himself. 'Am I anywhere near my jugular vein?'

Lyn compared the location of the pen tip to the detective's vein. 'Er, no.'

The detective placed the pen back into his pocket. 'It's hard enough for any right-handed person to control a hypodermic needle with their left hand when you're right-handed. Imagine attempting to inject a drug that can kill into one of the body's major arteries without seeing what you're doing? It's a recipe for disaster.'

'He could have used a hand-mirror?' said Ant.

Riley gestured with his hand. 'Do you see anything nearby that he might have used?'

'What about the wall mirror over the fireplace?' suggested Lyn.

Riley shook his head. 'Mr Jefferson would never have made it back to the sofa after injecting into his jugular vein. If he'd successfully scored, he'd have slumped into a heap within a few feet of the mirror. If he got it wrong and bled out, this place would have looked like a battlefield hospital on a bad day. Yet here we have a man who exhibits having received a perfect injection to a life-threatening site, all the time sitting on a sofa as if listening to Radio Four.'

They stood in silence until Ant filled the void.

'That just leaves murder, then. But why? What's the motive?'

'Let's not get ahead of ourselves,' said the detective. 'There's also the matter of means and opportunity and the lab confirming if anything sinister is in Mr Jefferson's blood-stream. Knowing my luck, the mark on his neck will be an insect bite and he'll of died from natural causes. The latter outcome would make my life much easier. Either way, we'll just have to wait.'

The sound of an old mantle clock announced its tired chime striking the hour, before returning to an irregular beat counting out each minute.

'No wonder Mr Jefferson told you he was late for his meeting. I doubt the clock has kept time in decades,' announced Riley.

His associates appeared too caught up in the emotions of the sad scene to acknowledge the detective's musing.

'I know I sounded off at you, Ant. When you talked about Ian being an addict, you have a point. But how does this get to happen?' said Lyn in a flat tone.

Riley gave up his talk about the mantle clock and moved back to stand closer to Jefferson's inanimate body. 'It would surprise you. All it takes is a bit of the stuff and you're hooked. Who knows what led to him starting? Perhaps trauma of some sort, either physical or emotional. One thing will be for sure, to begin with, the drugs will have given Mr Jefferson an immediate feeling of his troubles floating away. Before long, whatever he injected took on a life of its own. Relief is no longer the focus, instead, the craving for the high and the desire to stop withdrawal become the priority. It's called chasing the dragon.'

Lyn let out a tired sigh. 'Do you think it began with prescription drugs? Perhaps his doctor can tell us?'

Riley shook his head. 'Even if it did, it'll have no bearing on this chap's ultimate demise. Anyway, the doctor is unlikely to tell us. You know, patient confidentiality and all that.'

'You could force the doctor,' interjected Ant.

'If you mean dragging them to court, that's certainly one route, but there's the fall-out it will cause with the local medical professionals. It's just not worth it.'

Lyn noticed a small photograph in a silver frame on the windowsill.

Ian was happy once, she thought.

'Who is it?' asked Ant.

She recovered the frame and inspected the back out of habit, hoping to find the name of the young lady linking arms with an equally young Ian Jefferson. 'A lovely couple, don't you think?' said Lyn as she held the fading photograph for the others to view.

'I'd say he's about sixteen in this picture. The same for his young lady,' said Ant.

Before Lyn returned the silver frame to its long-established spot, she took the trouble to wipe aside a layer of aged dust and flaked window paint. 'There, that's better,' said Lyn as she stood back, before moving closer to the picture to make one last change to its position.

'Do you think she could have anything to do with how his life turned out?' said Ant, addressing his question to Riley.

'Who's to say, Anthony? If the image served as a

constant reminder of love lost, then perhaps it does. It's interesting that he kept the image, while, as Lyn pointed out, no other images of people, whether family or friends, exist. I don't want to read too much into it, but apparently, Mr Jefferson couldn't bear to have the photo on full and open display. Yet neither could he contemplate being completely without a reminder of someone he was once close to.'

Blimey, I didn't think Peter had such a sensitive side, thought Lyn.

The mantle clock continued with its burdensome task of counting away each second, as a reminder that time continued to pass.

'So, we're sure it's murder?' Lyn's change of gear caught both men off-guard.

Riley recovered first. 'We've already established that Mr Jefferson had been lucky to—'

'Lucky?' interrupted Ant.

'Let me finish. Yes, lucky to have hit his jugular vein with no means to check visually where he was injecting, and with his weaker hand to boot. If this gentleman did indeed inject himself, which I do not believe.'

'Then to repeat. It's murder, then?' responded Ant.

Riley frowned. 'Let's not jump to that conclusion just yet. That said, I have a riddle for you. What is it you don't see?'

'What?' exclaimed Ant.

'Just stick with me for a few seconds. What isn't here?'

Ant scratched his temple as he scanned the room.

'That's a double negative, Peter. What do you mean?' said Lyn.

Riley looked confused by his companion's grammatical challenge and failed to respond. Ant let out a muted laugh.

I've got it. 'Stop thinking like an English teacher. Peter's right.'

'You're as bad as him,' responded Lyn in an exasperated tone. Stop being obdurate and... oh, yes, I see. No drugs paraphernalia.'

'Exactly,' exclaimed Riley, clearly enjoying the moment. Mr Jefferson either injected drugs himself or someone else did for him.'

Lynn gasped as she gazed down at the body. It's unbelievable that someone would intentionally inject a lethal overdose into another person.

'Are you ok?' asked Ant.

Lyn failed to answer.

Ant didn't push the point.

Riley, who'd turned away momentarily to give the pair some space posed a question. 'But was it murder?' His assertion confused his companions.

'What do you mean?' said Ant. 'We've established a third-party injected Ian. What other evidence do you need?'

Riley held up a finger as though instructing a class at a police college on the finer points of investigative techniques. 'Hm. Well, we can hypothesise that someone who the man knew and trusted injected him. Evidence for this is the lack of forced entry. It's safe to assume the victim allowed the other person to enter.'

Lyn moved nearer to the body. 'It's true that Ian would have to have remained still while the needle penetrated his vein. But why take the risk of using one of the most important veins in his body, instead of his arm?'

The detective's friends looked for an answer. 'Assuming he was desperate enough, injecting into his jugular vein would be about the quickest way of getting the stuff into his bloodstream. If your craving's got to such a point, you'll hold still when you're told to.'

'But to let another addict anywhere near your neck with a shared needle and heaven knows what in the syringe?' questioned Lyn.

Riley smiled. 'Hang on, you're making several assumptions there. Look again at the way Mr Jefferson is sitting. He's comfortable. Also, notice the cushions on either side of him. They're undisturbed. Someone might have staged the scene, or Mr Jefferson might have willingly accepted the injection.'

'And medical training?' asked Ant.

'Almost certainly,' replied Riley. 'Which, of course, is a handy skill to possess in the circumstances we see here.'

Lyn gave the inspector a troubled glance. 'Now who's getting ahead of themselves?'

'Like it or not,' responded Riley as he pointed at Jefferson's body. 'What we see here is no accident, which makes it murder in my book. The person responsible knew what they were doing, and how to cover their tracks.'

Lyn shook her head.

'Still not convinced?' asked the detective.

'No, I don't mean that.'

'Now who's using double negatives?' said Ant, trying to lighten the mood.

'Oh, hilarious, I'm sure,' responded Lyn in an uncharacteristically sarcastic tone. 'What evidence is there that whoever administered the injection meant to kill Ian? What if they were a trusted friend? Perhaps even a fellow addict. That would explain their skill in using a needle?'

'Far-fetched, don't you think?' said Ant in a pensive tone. 'None of us were here when Ian received his fatal dose.'

Lyn gave both men a stern look. 'What if the friend miscalculated the dose? After all, if Ian was so desperate for his hit, the sudden flooding of his system with heroin may have tipped him over the edge?'

Riley rubbed his chin as he listened, then turned to Ant. 'And what do you think?'

'I suppose it's just about possible. We know Ian argued with someone. Perhaps he was shouting at this elusive friend to hurry, which caused his visitor to become flustered and get the dosage wrong?'

This time, Riley shook his head. 'If we'd have discovered our victim in a derelict squat, filled with used needles and other stuff, I might agree. I've seen the results of sharing what little drugs and kit addicts have. They cut the heroin with all sorts of stuff to make it go farther.'

'So, it's possible that's what happened here?' asked Ant.

The detective was quick to respond. 'Not a chance. The context couldn't have been more different. Look around you. This is a controlled scene. Yes, the house furnishings are old-fashioned, and it could do with a dust, but it's a clean and well-ordered home. Then there's Mr Jefferson himself. As we've each commented more than once this evening, does he look like someone who desperately fought for his life? Everything I see tells me this man did not intend, or expect, to die today.'

A stillness fell as the three friends mulled over the conversation and unsettling scene, as if hoping inspiration might appear from thin air.

'That telephone call,' said Ant.

'Yes?' replied Riley.

'The sergeant said it was a teenager, or a man with a high-pitched voice?'

'And your point is?'

'Why didn't he say it could have been a woman?'

The question flummoxed the inspector. After a brief delay, Riley formed his response. 'I suppose...' he hesitated. 'I suppose that was his gut reaction.'

'Not the basis for a sound investigation, though, is it?' commented Lyn.

The detective's cheeks flushed like an urchin caught scrumping apples. 'Why didn't I consider that?' mumbled the detective. 'It's such a basic variable to consider.' Riley snatched his police notebook from his jacket pocket and wrote notes at a furious pace.

'Don't be too hard on yourself,' said Ant in a quiet, supportive tone. 'You said earlier that whoever did this was no fool. Perhaps the sergeant fell into a trap set for the police. It's possible, isn't it?'

Ant's reasoning calmed the inspector as he finished writing and replaced the small black notebook back into his pocket.

'It's something I should have picked my sergeant up on straight away. There's no getting away from the fact that I made a basic mistake I wouldn't tolerate from a raw recruit.'

Lyn offered a comforting smile. 'I'm sure your team will confirm things to you one way or another after we analyse the call properly. You record all incoming phone calls, don't you?'

'And outgoing,' replied Riley.

'There you are, then. There is still hope. Meanwhile, that just leaves the matter of timing.' Lyn's intervention in moving the conversation on did the trick of refocusing Riley.

'Let's see. We think Mr Jefferson died sometime between five and six p.m.'

Lyn frowned. 'That's only about ninety minutes after Ant and I spoke to him?'

'You said he was in a hurry?'

'Yes, church business, he said.'

'My guess is that he needed to get away from you two so that he could meet his dealer,' began the detective. 'The question is, if, as I suspect, he desperately needed his fix, why and how did he end up sitting on that sofa as calm as a cucumber?'

Riley's reference to the victim's countenance triggered an automatic reaction for all three to look at the body. 'Perhaps we're overthinking this,' added the detective. 'What if he was telling the truth when he told you he was in a rush to complete some church business?'

'I feel there's a, but, coming, Peter?' said Lyn.

'There is. What if the pressure on his time wasn't to get to a meeting? Perhaps it was more about getting back home for a specific time, say, four-thirty p.m.?'

The penny dropped, causing Lyn to become animated. 'Whatever business he had must have been local because he took off on foot. As you say, perhaps we're concentrating too much on where he went, rather than who he was expecting back here?'

Just then, four scenes of crime personnel appeared at the front door in full protective wear.

'We'll have to let our ideas ruminate for a couple of hours. This lot are here to remove the body.'

The three friends watched as the team went about their grim business.

'The place feels soulless. Now they've taken Ian away, doesn't it?' said Lyn as she surveyed a room that looked as though nothing out of the ordinary had taken place that day.

Each of them took a last look at the small space as they made their way to the ill-maintained front door. Lyn went first, followed by Ant. Suddenly, Riley stopped in his tracks.

'Well, just look at that.'

His associates took a second or two to register the detective's comment.

'That is interesting,' added Riley.

Ant and Lyn re-entered the living room. 'You're mumbling, Peter,' said Lyn. 'What are you going on about?'

The detective dropped to his knees and bent forward in front of the sofa.

'Are you alright?' asked Ant, bemused by Riley's sudden collapse.

The detective twisted at an awkward angle to reach for a glove from his jacket and used his free hand eventually to slide the garment into position.

'Wouldn't it be easier if you stood?' suggested Lyn.

Riley smiled. 'If I move from this spot, I'll never find it again.'

'Find what?' exclaimed Ant.

The detective stopped talking, turned back to the sofa, and reached for something from underneath the aged furniture. 'Got you,' remarked Riley in a triumphant tone. He backed away from the sofa and scrambled to his feet.

'Why are you pretending to hold something between your finger and thumb?' teased Ant.

Riley retrieved a small evidence bag from the endless depths of his inside pocket. 'This is no illusion. Look what I've got.'

The detective handed the transparent bag to Lyn. Ant moved closer to see the find.

Lyn held the bag up to the light of the open front door. 'A broken needle?'

'I didn't take Ian for an embroidery man?' said Ant with a cheeky grin.

'I won't dignify that remark with an answer. You can see what it is, or at least, what it once formed part of.'

Lyn's telling off wasn't enough to dampen Ant's mood as he continued to grin at his own joke.

Riley ignored the exchange as he slipped into detective mode. 'I wonder what this little treasure will tell us. Come on, you two. There's lots to do.'

This time, Riley disregarded the convention of allowing his guests to exit the premises first as he marched through the front door.

'Sir, if I could ask if you have removed anything from the premises. For our records, you understand.'

Riley smiled at the nervous bobby. 'First class, constable. Here, please record this.'

He handed over the plastic bag, allowing the young police constable to complete the detail on his clipboard.

'How are you feeling, by the way? A body is never a nice thing to discover, I can tell you.'

'Better now, and thank you, Sir.'

'Good, good,' replied Riley. 'That's another rite of passage done with.'

'Yes, Sir,' said a now less nervous young officer.

Ant and Lyn put their coveralls in a police bag near the front door before going to Fitch's Land Rover. Riley followed suit.

'Let's meet up tomorrow for a thorough debrief,' suggested Riley. 'I'll bring you up to speed with anything that develops overnight. That said, we'll need to step things up a couple of paces. I'm getting anxious about our missing reverend.'

As Lyn wished Riley a good evening, she hesitated. 'Do

you think Ian Jefferson's death was an isolated incident, terrible though it is, or might there be a link to the vicar's disappearance?'

Riley hesitated. 'If you're right about a connection between the two incidents, this isn't so much an investigation about finding a missing vicar. It's tracking down and stop a multiple killer before they locate their next victim.'

Chapter Fourteen

WHO ARE YOU?

'I ASSUMED you'd decided not to bother coming, since you don't enjoy getting your hair wet,' shouted Ant.

Detective Inspector Riley was the target of his schoolboy taunt. 'I see you've left your ermine coat back at the Hall. Now, are you going to let me in?'

Lyn chuckled from the safety of the church porch, 'serves you right, he's got you there,' as she gave Ant a light push which threatened to expel him into the downpour.

No sooner had the three friends re-united than the inner entrance shot open. This gave Lyn a fright as she winced at the glancing blow inflicted by the heavy oak door catching her foot.

'Leave me alone. I'm done with you,' shrieked Clive as the tortured widower ran from the church.

Lyn limped to the entrance door. She poked her head out into the maelstrom, trying to catch sight of where Greenacre was heading for.

'The poor man. It's more by luck than judgement he got

across the graveyard without tripping and pole axing himself on a headstone.'

'Can you see where he's headed?' asked Ant.

Lyn's action of half-stepping outside the porch brought with it a further soaking.

'He's shot off into Brick Row,' said Lyn as she wiped the rain from her eyes to get a better view.

'His house is in the opposite direction, isn't it?' said Ant.

Lyn ducked back into the porch, wetting her colleagues as she did so.

'Yes, it is. Looking at the state of the man. I doubt Clive's paying much attention. There's nothing more we can do for him now. Let's move into the church so to get this coat off and sort my hair out... and if either of you smirks in the slightest, there'll be trouble.'

The two men took Lyn at her word, with Riley opening the inner door to allow her entry without making further comment.

'Teacher's pet,' whispered Ant as he passed Riley.

'I'm not the one obsessed with hair, am I? Is it because you're going thin on top?'

Ant ignored the riposte and checked the thickness of his crown by feeling the top of his head.

'Oi, you two,' began Lyn in a hushed tone. 'Can I remind you why we're here this morning? For a pair of blokes who hated the sight of each other not that long ago, you're behaving like twins going through the "terrible twos",'

The men exchanged blank looks.

'I give up. Let's change the subject, shall we? What are we going to do about poor Clive?'

Lyn's question ended the levity in an instant.

'Now you mentioned it, I've had my own concerns

about him. The last thing we need is for Mr Greenacre to become a serious suspect. What he said to the vicar about his wife's death doesn't help. Perhaps I can get one of our welfare people to have a word with him. They'll be able to refer him on to the support he needs.'

'I've seen that type of behaviour before. If I'm honest… been there myself,' replied Ant.

He's thinking about his time in the army, thought Lyn.

'Afghanistan?' said Riley.

'No one who's experienced the battlefield ever gets over what they've witnessed, and the trauma of loss. I reckon Greenacre is in the early stages of grief. I'm not sure there's too much difference between PTSD and what happens when you lose someone so close to you that you seem to think and feel for each other.'

Rainwater dripping into buckets created a melodic backdrop to the discussion.

Time to move the conversation on, before Ant's recollections get too much for him, thought Lyn.

'Like it or not, Clive accused the vicar of having a hand in his wife's death. And he's done his level best to trash the church,' said Lyn. She pointed to the evidence of the man's rage from one end of the place to the other.

The others followed suit, surveying the damage yet to be cleared away.

'Perhaps he's still feeling guilty about the damage he caused on consecrated ground?'

Ant walked to a pew nearby that remained upended. 'To Clive Greenacre, what he's experiencing is real. The line between reality and the imagined has merged in his mind. Such outbursts will often contain a grain of truth.'

The detective reflected on the point. 'My issue is, which truth are we talking about?'

Lyn picked up two small splinters of wood debris from the pew, placed it between them on the floor, and sat down. 'Peter, you suggested getting a police welfare officer to speak to Clive. That won't work. Why don't I try to get through to him?'

'I wish to be fair to Mr Greenacre, but—'

'Ow!' shouted Ant, obliging the other two to give their friend a concerned glance.

'What have you done?' said Lyn.

He raised his right hand to display a trickle of blood running down his damaged finger. 'There're bits of broken glass all over the place from Clive's antics.'

Having confirmed his wound was clean, Ant pinched the cut shut between two fingers to stem the flow.

'You've gone soft. I thought you'd have spat on the cut, then rubbed it on your jacket like we use,' said Lyn, without a trace of sympathy.

Riley remained muted throughout the exchange. 'As I was saying, I intend to be fair with the gentleman, and thank you for the offer, Lyn. I'll take you up on that. That said, I can't ignore his behaviour given recent events. I hope we can establish that has nothing to do with the vicar's disappearance, let alone any connection to Mr Jefferson's demise. I'm sure we agree there are matters concerning the widower I'd be failing in my duty if I didn't pursue.' The detective looked at each of his friends. He was keen to ensure they understood his professional responsibilities.

Ant concurred first with a crisp nod, followed by Lyn, who wore a sad expression as she spoke.

'Of course we do, Peter. It's just, well, I suppose everything's getting very real. What a wicked world we live in. Life can be so cruel.'

Ant strode over to his fiance, when a stream of water

droplets landed on the nape of his neck. 'What the...' He crouched, as if the roof itself was about to collapse. 'Something tells me the church needs more buckets!'

Moving beyond the liquids reach, Ant raised his eyes to the ornate timber ceiling and shook his fist at the errant stream of water.

The watery interlude at least improved the previous gloomy mood.

'I have an idea. Let's arrange a celebration for the day we find the vicar safe and well. We can donate any profit to the roof restoration fund,' said Lyn.

'It'll have to be a spectacular event to raise enough money for that lot,' Ant pointed to the ceiling and got a wet finger for his troubles.

'Watch out, or you'll catch for it again. That's what you get for being such a pessimist,' said Lyn in a triumphant tone.

'I shouldn't be so cocky. With a bit of luck, the moment you move, you'll get soaked for your troubles.'

'And I bet you're praying I do.'

Lyn stopped her light-hearted riposte as a muffled bang filled the church.

All three took a second to process the unusual sound. Ant couldn't help himself.

'You're always saying if only these walls could talk? Well, perhaps they want a chat with you?' Ant chuckled.

'I've told you before how daft it is to laugh at your own jokes. A gentleman doesn't smirk at things he doesn't understand,' replied Lyn in a disinterested tone.

Riley watched, content to let them get on with ribbing each other. Now he was keen to move on.

'Er, if we might just bring some focus, while we're here?'

His question had the desired effect.

'Sorry, Peter.'

'Me, too,' said Ant as the two of them covered the short distance to join Riley at the altar rail.

The detective gave a slight nod in acknowledgement that they'd returned to the matter at hand.

'It's time we reviewed progress on not one, but two cases. Do they warrant being treated as a separate incident? Or are they linked?'

'Excuse me?'

The sudden burst of sound from the back of the church caused the three friends to hunch their shoulders and turn in unison.

'Can we help?' said Lyn, her tone betraying the fact she remained unsettled by the sudden interruption.

'Who's he?' whispered Ant.

'I've no idea.'

'We're just carrying out a survey on the roof. You know, the leaks,' said Riley. The detective looked up at the exposed timbers.

His associates followed suit. The stranger did the same. Aside from the sound of dripping water, the church remained at peace with itself.

Peter assumed I was about to tell that bloke why we're here. What a cheek, thought Lyn as she continued to view the ceiling, waiting for the stranger, or Riley, to say something.

The newcomer broke the silence. 'Are you, now?'

Lyn observed the middle-aged man donning builders' overalls. In one hand, he clasped a folded flat-cap, and in the other, a clipboard. The only thing lacking was a pencil fixed behind his ear to have fulfilled Lyn's assessment of the archetypal construction contractor.

'That's right,' announced Riley in a confident tone.

The thin man with the clipboard gazed around the

church for several seconds before responding. 'That's not like the vicar. He's such a fair chap. He didn't tell me he'd got someone else to quote as well. And me after doing so much work for him at near cost- price. Anyway, which outfit are you from?'

The mention of the vicar galvanised their attention.

Riley stepped forward a few paces. 'Us? We're from Peterborough. We did a big job for the reverend at Saint Christopher's in Market Deeping, and he recommended our company.'

Well done, you. I'm not sure I could have got us out of that hole that quick, thought Lyn.

'A funny do if you ask me. I only met the vicar last week. Why didn't he mention that to me? I dunno, you can't rely on anyone these days, especially customers.'

The detective warmed to the theme. 'Spot on. Same here. We finished a contract the other week. Did everything as per our quotation and a lovely job too, if I say so myself. Anyway, this customer asked us to do some extra, so we did. Our final invoice included £800 for the extra work. He said that since it was such a large contract, we'd should throw in the additional work for nothing. Things got so bad we settled for £500 just to get off the job

The builder huffed as he walked towards Riley, the pair meeting half-way down the middle aisle.

'Same as me, do you—'

Lyn broke into their convivial conversation. 'Boss, if I can just remind you, we've got to be at that other job soon, and it's an hour's drive.'

Riley took the hint. 'What would I do without the lovely Sally keeping me on my toes, eh?' He gave the builder a broad smile. What he couldn't see was Lyn's scowl.

Condescending rubbish. Why do I bother? thought Lyn.

'Let it go. He's only playing a game with that bloke. You watch,' said Ant in a muted tone.

Lyn's shoulders relaxed as she turned to her fiancé. 'It still gets me going.'

Riley kept questioning the stranger, unaware of the conversation developing behind him.

'Last week, you say? He asked us to quote about six weeks ago. We've been so busy, it's only now we could make it. It's a fair old distance from Peterborough. Have you had to drive far?'

The builder sniffed while rubbing his nose. 'Just a bit. I'm based north of Boston.'

'Blimey, that is a fair old distance, isn't it? A 150-mile round trip? You must almost be in Lincolnshire.'

'Little Holland,' they call it. The only reason I do work here is because my parents lived in Stanton Parva during the war. They always had a soft spot for the village. I wasn't born until 1955 and we moved soon after, so I don't remember the place. Dad said to do what I could for the church. He was a builder like me, see.'

Riley allowed the man's words to sink in before responding. 'Nice touch, all credit to your dad. But I tell you what, we've had a heck of a job getting in contact with him to say we were coming down today. We left a telephone message in the hope he'd be here, but no luck. How about you?'

The builder shrugged his shoulders. 'Same here. The vicar was as clear as the church bell about being here to meet me today. Perhaps he forgot. To tell you the truth, he was distracted when I came to see him last week. When I arrived, he opened the vestry door, looking pasty. He tried to cover it up, but I know from his expression that he'd forgotten about our meeting.'

Riley mirrored the builder's frown. 'Don't you hate it

when that happens? You know, you've done someone a favour, only to find they've forgotten all about it. What, with the cost of diesel and all.'

The builder looked at his wristwatch, causing Riley to push on before he lost his man.

'To be honest, the least he could do was to apologise and give you an explanation.'

The builder shrugged his shoulders. 'He didn't seem with it at all. In fact, he kept calling me Ian. My name's Ken, by the way.'

Riley acknowledged by conjuring up a fake name for himself. 'Oh, and mine's ... er, Richard. Rick to my friends.'

'Nice to meet you. Anyway, I corrected him twice. In the end, I gave up and told him I'd call back when he was less busy. That's how I come to be wasting my time today, like you.'

While the two men were talking, Ant and Lyn had busied themselves repositioning several of the buckets to catch more water from the leaky roof. With that done, they sauntered up to where Riley and the stranger stood.

The builder looked at his watch again. 'I need to get moving, since it doesn't look as though the vicar's going to show up.'

'That makes four of us,' replied Riley. 'About the quote. Look, my company doesn't need the job. We're a big outfit and, to be honest, we have more work than we can handle as it is.'

'What, you mean collude on the pricing, so I get the job? Sorry, that's not right. I don't treat people like that.'

Riley offered a gentle smile. 'No, no. Not at all. Neither do we. But if our costing gets lost in the post and never arrives. Well, where's the harm? From the little time I spent with you this morning, you'll submit a fair quote. What do you say?'

After a moment's hesitation, the builder returned Riley's smile and extended his right hand. The two men shook as a mark of mutual respect.

As the builder turned to leave, the detective interrupted his progress. 'I tell you what, why don't we exchange business cards? Just in case we can help each other in the future?'

Both men reached for a pocket when Ant let out a loud cough.

Riley turned as his friend gesticulated not to hand over his card.

The detective understood it right away. 'Would you believe it? I've run out. Never mind. Let me have yours and I'll follow it up with an email.'

Riley accepted the builder's details without reacting to the man's confused gaze.

'See you,' said the detective as he waved off the builder, before turning around to face Ant and Lyn.

'That was a close call. Imagine his reaction had he got your card and realising he'd been talking to a copper!' said Lyn with a cheeky grin.

Riley wiped his brow. 'You're telling me. Do you know I got so far into my part that I believed it myself?'

Ant joined in the jovial exchange. 'Ever thought of amateur dramatics? They've got a couple of great outfits in Norwich, or there's one in Cromer.'

The detective gave an exaggerated wave with his finger: 'No, thank you, I have enough dealing with you two, without being exposed to even more divas.'

The laughter continued until new material for the

source of their amusement ran out, and the conversation became stilted.

'Have we done here?' asked Ant, hoping to make a quick getaway now the fun was over.

'Yes,' replied Riley.

Lyn coughed. 'Excuse me, isn't there the small matter of the village's current crime spree? We were discussing if our cases are linked, remember?'

Riley shut his eyes and plunged his hands into his trouser pockets. 'Sorry, Lyn. I'm ash—'

'Don't be too hard on yourself, Peter. I suppose you got that builder's details, so you can always get hold of him again. You know, if you need to?' said Lyn, trying to cheer the crest- fallen detective up.

'And let's not forget, we have a valuable insight into the vicar's mindset in the days running up to his disappearance. All we need to do now is to establish if his low mood was because of something, or someone, in particular.'

'What, you mean, like, Ian Jefferson?' asked Lyn.

'Just saying,' replied Ant.

They turned to the frowning detective. 'Thank you both for your kind words. I feel better about things now.'

'You're sure?' asked Lyn.

'Honest, and to prove I'm back in the land of the living, let me see if I can summarise where we are. Case one. We have a missing vicar who may or may not still be alive. Also, we are yet to discover what, or who, led to his alleged disappearance. However, thanks to our friendly builder, we now know something, or someone, upset him last week.'

'Perhaps the cross words he had with Cynthia Hake,' offered Lyn.

'A excellent point,' replied Riley. 'As for case two, we

have a dead man, but yet to determine if friend or foe injected the lethal close.'

'So, we're excluding the possibility of Ian self-administering the drugs?' chipped in Ant.

Riley took a deep breath. 'I hope I don't regret it, but yes. My working assumption excludes that possibility. Remember, someone reported raised voices to us, so we're certain Mr. Jefferson wasn't alone in the immediate period leading up to his death.'

'But we don't know if the other person was male or female,' said Lyn.

'Correct. A teenager or a man with a high-pitched voice. That's all we have to go on,' replied Riley.

'The other person in Ian's house could just have been a woman, you know. Why the certainty it was a man?'

The detective looked at Lyn to confirm a point well made.

Ant sat on the end of the nearest pew and scratched his forehead. 'Could the vicar have been the other person? Let's say that Ian had been pressuring him to get him more drugs. The reverend refuses but relents as the calls come thick and fast, with the man getting more desperate. He goes to the house. By now, Ian Jefferson is desperate and, in a rush to ease the man's pain, his rescuer miscalculates the dosage?'

Lyn shook her head. 'You're saying the vicar first of all vanishes. That Ian knew how to contact him. The reverend does the deed, then disappears again. A bit far-fetched?'

'I'm trying to help, Lyn.'

'Alright, alright,' said Riley. 'Let's take the temperature out of the debate. We're all feeling the pressure. It doesn't help to criticise—'

'All I said was—'

'I'm aware of that, Lyn. Just saying is we need to be careful how the other person will take what we sometimes say in the heat of the moment, yes?'

The detective's words worked to calm the situation.

'Now, although I agree, it seems unlikely the vicar is involved in Mr Greenacre's demise. We should let it rest on one side without discounting the possibility. I've been in this game long enough to know sometimes a line of investigation dismissed too soon turns out to break the case.'

His friends stopped glaring at each other until they restored normal relations.

'And on that note,' added Riley. 'I'll take a peep at the vestry to see if I missed anything earlier in the week. Another thing I've learned is that as investigations get more complicated, the risk of mistakes increase.'

As Riley paced back down the aisle to gain entry to the vestry, Lyn and Ant took a second look at the document chest. The pair poured over it for several minutes. Their goal was to identify anything that might provide a clue to what caused someone's fresh blood to be found around the ancient locking mechanism.

Lyn became distracted, a point Ant noticed.

'What's up?'

'Did you hear that?'

'Not again. Are the walls talking to you? That makes it twice in one day.'

'I'll thump you if you don't behave. I heard something.'

Within a few seconds, Riley emerged from the vestry.

'You look fed up. Didn't find anything?' asked Ant.

'Not a sausage.'

'But I heard a voice. Wasn't it you?'

'No?'

'Lyn, stop this, it's getting ridiculous. It might have been a book falling off a shelf, or, I don't know, kids playing outside?'

'What, in this weather? Now who's being ridiculous?'

'Come on, you two. Let's not start that up again. Once you're married, well, that's another thing altogether from the privacy of your own home, or should I say, a stately home in your case?'

The pair managed a forced smile as Riley placed himself between the hostile parties and led them towards the church entrance.

As they reached the door, Lyn turned around and gazed at the impressive interior of the building. 'I know what I heard. I don't care what you two think.'

No one answered. They had already left the ancient building. Lyn stood alone. She lingered for a moment, lost in thought.

What are you trying to tell us?

She gave the interior one last look before turning and leaving the church to its secrets.

Chapter Fifteen

IT'S NOT TRUE

A TRADITION that had developed over the years involved Lyn baking a cake each week for Lord and Lady Stanton. However, her schedule fell apart after recent events. She now rushed to get this week's Victoria sponge finished to deliver it in time for Saturday afternoon tea.

As Lyn checked the oven and prepared her dish, she was grateful Ant had occupied his time on estate business.

No sooner had she completed the task than her mobile rang. 'I thought you were—'

She expected to hear Ant's voice. Instead, to her surprise, Detective Inspector Riley's dulcet tone rang out.

'Oh, hi, Peter. Is it the pampered one you're looking for?' She listened to Riley's response with a growing sense of foreboding.

'Am I alone? Yes, but why do you ask? Is something wrong?' Her heart thumped. 'Meet you in an hour at the old saddlery on the Norwich Road? Yes, I can, but what's this all about, Peter? You're frightening me.'

Time seemed to stand still as Lyn took in what Riley

had to say and to digest the specific instruction, he gave her for the meeting.

Why is he insisting I don't tell Ant? And what did he mean by not wanting to meet at the police station in case someone saw them together?

'Peter, for heaven's sake, what's this all—'

Lyn slid the mobile from her ear and looked at the device, astonished that Peter had ended the call so abruptly.

She glanced around her tidy farm-house style kitchen in a daze, trying to make sense of the detective's disconcerting call.

The aroma of baking gave Lyn a break from her negative thoughts. She fixed her attention on a wall clock that had remained in the Old School House by its previous owner and headmaster of the institution she now led.

Another twenty minutes should do it. That gives me time to get it done.

The time flew as she prepared the jam and cream filling.

Mustn't forget to dust the top with icing sugar this time.

Within twenty minutes, the Victoria sponge rested in its cake tin, and Lyn was driving from the village to meet Peter Riley.

I feel guilty for not telling Ant. Why was Peter so insistent I shouldn't tell anyone? thought Lyn.

The drive to the old workshop saw her pass through some of the best countryside Norfolk offered. On this journey, she was oblivious to the broads to her left, filled with an armada of small boats hired by tourists. To her right, fields of rapeseed streaked over the level landscape as far as the eye could see.

As Lyn approached the abandoned saddlery, she saw the blue and white police tape blocking the entrance, just as the detective had promised.

She followed Peter Riley's instructions to the letter: remove the tape, drive in, then reattach it. Once done, drive to the rear of the ramshackle building where he would be waiting.

As she rounded a corner, Lyn could see that Peter Riley was already out of his car and pacing back and forth. She also noticed his downcast demeanour.

I don't like this, thought Lyn as she parked her MINI ten feet from the detective's vehicle.

'What on earth is this all about?'

Riley's response was equally curt and to the point. 'Has Anthony said any more about why he was late for your meeting at the church on Wednesday morning?'

'Late for church?' Lyn looked around the disorganised storage yard, as if some understanding of the detective's question might pop out of thin air. 'Oh, you mean at the church to see the vicar?'

'Yes. Has he mentioned it again?'

Lyn's emotions wavered between wanting to cry and throwing something at her police friend for putting doubt in her mind.

'You dragged me all the way out here just to ask me something you could have asked over the phone? What's got into you, Peter? You could have just asked me if Ant was with me. Or don't you trust me, either?'

Riley had a formal tone, almost icy, one that Lyn hadn't experienced before. Even in the early days. When he resented her and Ant involving themselves in investigations.

'I couldn't risk Anthony overhearing what I had to say. For that, I apologise and to answer your question, yes, I do trust you or I wouldn't be speaking to you now. However, sometimes an investigation throws up something so unexpected that it calls for careful handling. This is one such occasion. Has Anthony said anything?'

'No. Why should he? What is it you know I don't? Just tell me what's put you in such a spin?'

She watched as the detective passed his phone from hand to hand, his nervousness showing.

'There's no way of dressing this up, yet even at this late stage, I hope there's a simple explanation.'

'What are you talking about?' Lyn's intonation changed as she attempted to keep control of her emotions.

Riley thrust the mobile into his jacket pocket, then ran a hand through his hair. 'I want you to consider who Ant was late for? That's right, the reverend Morton. The same man who's vanished. You told me you heard noises from the vestry before Anthony arrived. You also mentioned he looked agitated and out of breath when he finally showed up.'

'But that was only because knowing he was late; he'd rushed from tending livestock with the vet. Why are you making so much of Ant being late? You know what his timekeeping is like?'

'The problem is, the meeting between Anthony and the vet never took place.'

'Yes, it did.'

'Who told you that?'

'Ant did.' Lyn fell silent as a torrent of thoughts tumbled through her mind.

'The vet told me the opposite. He checked the practice diary to see if any of the other vets visited. No one saw Anthony on Wednesday morning.'

Lyn could not keep her frustration in check a second longer. 'You had no right to go poking around Ant's business. What kind of friend are you, anyway?'

'One who is an officer of the law first, and friend second.'

The pair glared at each other as if waiting for the time-keeper's bell to sound at a boxing match. Lyn's blood was up. She could tell Peter Riley was ready to re-start the battle.

'Did you check up on me? Did you spy on Fitch? And what about Ant's elderly parents? Did you harass them?'

Riley didn't hesitate to fight back. 'Yes, Lyn. I, or one of my officers, spoke to anyone and everyone we thought might help with our enquiries. What did you expect the police to do? Wait for the answer, a culprit to drop into my lap?'

'You should have … you could… oh, I don't know. I've had enough of this. You are telling me the man I'm about to marry is a liar. Worse than that. He may have done the vicar harm. And what about Ian Jefferson's death? Are you suggesting he did that, too?'

The tears ran as Lyn crossed her arms, then lent against the decaying brick wall of the old saddlery workshop.

Riley stepped forward and eased her away from the soaking brickwork. He turned Lyn with one hand on each of her shoulders until they faced each other.

'I'm sorry for upsetting you. That was the last thing on my mind. But I hope you can understand we check every-thing we think might turn up leads. This time, Anthony's got himself caught up in that process. My sole reason for meeting you without him knowing is to determine if I'd put the wrong interpretation on Anthony's actions.'

Lyn's demeanour softened, in part because of the softer tone Riley had adopted. And the reassuring touch of another human being as she struggled to make sense of a development that might threaten the future, she thought secure.

'What happens now?' Lyn dabbed her eyes with a supply of tissues she always carried for the children's bumps and scrapes.

'Until Anthony can account for every minute of his movements on Wednesday morning ... and they check out, he cannot be involved in the investigation. You understand, I hope?'

Lyn took some time to respond before nodding her confirmation.

'Good, thank you for that,' said Riley, while maintaining eye contact with Lyn and offering a broken smile. 'On a more constructive note, my officers are carrying out a search of Cynthia Hake's place as I speak. We shall also attempt to interview Clive Greenacre. You said you'd like to be involved?'

Lyn played with the used tissue, rolling it into a ball, then in picking the delicate paper. 'Yes. I'll be there. If not me, then who? Everyone should have at least one friend they can rely on.'

Lyn noticed that the detective broke eye contact and appeared anxious when she spoke of "friends". His sudden vulnerability set her tears off again.

Riley closed the gap between them as if about to offer a hug.

Lyn turned away. 'No, don't be nice to me. I'll only cry all the more.'

A smile returned to the detective's features. 'I get it.' He retraced his steps before making his way to the police car. 'Four-o-clock,' he shouted.

'Sorry?' said Lyn.

'Clive Greenacre. Four pm at the station. Okay?'

'Oh, yes. Yes, I'll be there.'

As the detective drove off, he lowered the passenger side window. 'Don't forget to put the police tape back when you leave, will you?'

She didn't answer. Her thoughts had returned to Ant.

Lyn rushed to her MINI in the pouring rain and watched the droplets create tears on the windshield. She stared at the abandoned workshops, lost in thought about Riley's devastating news.

Ant has never told me a lie in all the time I've known him. Then again, how would I know? He's changed since he saw active service. I accept that. But to deceive me on purpose? That's not the same as the PTSD episodes he can't control. Telling a lie is the opposite. Why would he do that to me? All the time I waited for him in church, he was up to something. How can I marry a man who does that to his future wife? Or am I being unfair to Ant? Even selfish? We've had our rows.

Neither of us are the same people as before I went to university, and he joined up. Were we both being naive to think we could pick up from where we left off? What if the feelings he says he has for me aren't his, but the ones he thinks his parents expect him to show towards me? After all, they've already made clear what they want.

Once we're married, does that mean I'm expected to deliver a male heir nine months after cutting the cake? And now we've come to this, a detective inspector telling me my fiance's alibi is a tissue of lies? If he wasn't with the vet, where was he? Is that why he was out of breath when he arrived at the church? And why was he so agitated?

That's not the man I know and love. Could it be true that he's involved in the reverend Morton going missing? If that's the case, it's possible that he played a role in the death of Ian Jefferson as well. I can't marry someone like that.

Lyn's tears began to flow again. Lost in her thoughts, she was oblivious to the gentle tapping on the side window. The rattle grew more intense, and she turned to see two young boys attempting to shield themselves from the rain by pulling their jackets over their heads.

'Miss Blackthorn. It's you. Are you ok?'

Both boys recognised Lyn from their time at junior school. Now young teenagers, she still remembered the pair.

She started the engine and pressed the button to lower the side window.

'Timothy Laidlaw, and Robert Ploughman. I hope it's not you two who've been vandalising this place. The police have told me all about it. Now, from what I remember, the both of you were cheeky so-and-sos, but I never took you for bad lads? Out with it, what are you doing here, and in this weather, too?'

Both teenagers ignored Lyn's gentle rebuke.

'You've been crying, Miss,' said Robert.

'Has someone upset you, miss,' added Timothy. 'Tell us who did it, and we'll get 'em for you. Won't we Rob?'

'You bet we will.'

'No one's going after anyone. If you must know, I twisted my ankle crossing the yard... and you still haven't answered my question.'

The boys continued to ignore their old headteacher's questions.

'Ugh, I did that once,' said Robert, reaching down for his ankle to emphasise the point. 'It hurt. But I didn't cry, Miss. Honest.'

The honesty of the two youngsters lifted Lyn's mood.

Being around the children under her care always did. That care didn't end when they moved up to high school.

'Well, Robert Ploughman. That just goes to show what a sturdy chap you are.'

The teenager smiled as he accepted Lyne's gesture to climb into the backseat of the MINI. Timothy Laidlaw followed his best mate. He leaned over to his ex-headteacher in a conspiratorial fashion.

'He did cry, miss,' said Timothy in a hushed tone. Lyn gave the boy a generous smile as she winked at him. His admission was safe with her. The car's de-mister ran at full-blast to clear the condensation as the boys settled into their seats and fidgeted to fasten their seatbelts.

'Thanks for the lift. We were soaking,' said Robert as he looked around the small vehicle. 'But how are you going to drive if you've turned your ankle, miss?'

Timothy nudged his friend before Lyn could answer the conundrum. 'Oi, know it all. I thought you knew lots about cars?'

'Yep.' The boy noticed Lyn's sharp look. 'I mean, yes.'

'Then why didn't you notice it's an automatic?'

Robert looked at the centre console. 'Ah, that's because this is a 2020 model. All the ones before that had a manual gearbox.'

'That's rubbish,' said an uncertain Timothy. 'Isn't that so, Miss?'

Lyn gave Robert the sort of look that showed she knew what he was up to. 'Oh, it's no use asking me. I just drive the thing. Now, are we ready?'

The boys exchanged competitive glances as they sat back in their seats, before each looked out of their respective windows.

Lyn took the MINI up to speed, being cautious not to

damage her tyres on any sharp debris in the yard. 'I'll assume that's a yes,' she said.

The journey to the outskirts of Stanton Parva took less than fifteen minutes, during which conversation was sparse. Lyn saw via the rear-view mirror that the boys spent their time making sure their hair was just so, as it dried in the heat of the MINI's air conditioning.

Soon enough, Lyn pulled up at a request bus stop that had the added advantage of a covered timber shelter. As the boys unbuckled their seatbelts and reached for the door latches, Lyn held up a single finger and fixed the pair with a stern look.

Robert and Timothy froze, as if back in primary school, waiting for a dressing down.

'Don't think you're getting out of this car without telling me what the pair of you were doing at the old saddlery. Remember, Miss Blackthorn sees all and forgets nothing.'

The lads looked at each other as if caught scrumping for apples red-handed.

Robert gave in first. 'We were up there a couple of days ago... well, not at the place. We were just passing on our way to do some fishing at Stickleback Dip. Both of us watched a bloke loading his van. A right wreck it was, too.'

'Yeah, and when he saw us, he went mad and said if we mentioned anything to anyone, he knew where we lived and would come after us. Then he pointed at his shoes... well, whopping big boots they were, they looked daft on him. Anyway, he shouted that if we didn't want to feel the sharp end of them, we'd better scarper.'

'So we did, Miss,' said Robert. 'He was a right ugly bloke, too. We ran like stink. And to cap it all, we didn't catch any sticklebacks, either.'

Lyn's features eased. She knew the boys were telling the

truth. 'So why go back? You had no way of knowing if the man might also be there?'

The lads exchanged grins.

'Because we saw him at the top of Gallows Hill. His lorry had over-heated, with steam flying all over the place. We knew he'd be stuck there for hours.'

Lyn shook her head and pondered the likelihood of the tale being true. 'And you went back to the old saddlery because?'

A guilty looked displaced the boy's previous confident smile.

'To be honest, Miss, while Bootsy was warning us off, I saw an old pram,' said Robert.

'A Pram?'

'Yes, Miss. We've been looking for a set of wheels for the box cart we're building. That'll make it go like a—'

'Never mind,' interrupted Lyn, fearful where Timothy's comparison might end up.

A movement in the rear-view mirror caught her attention. 'Here's your bus. Now listen to me.' She reached into the dash for some loose change. 'Here's a pound for each of you. That's enough for your fare. Now promise me you won't go back to that place. If the police catch you, they'll assume you two have caused all the damage, and you'll be in a heap of trouble. Do you understand?'

The boys nodded in unison, knowing Lyn's tone meant she was serious.

As they left the MINI, Lyn called Robert back. 'How did you know the man's name was Bootsy?'

The boy thought for a second, then gave his pal a look to confirm it was OK to talk. 'When I told my dad what happened and described the bloke to him, he knew the fella straight away. He said his name was Bootsy, and to stay clear of him because he was trouble.'

Before she could ask the boy anything else, a beep of the bus horn shattered the quiet. In an instant, Robert had dashed into the shelter as the bus slowly closed in.

'Sorry,' mouthed Lyn as she waved to the driver, offering a smile. She looked to her front and pressed the accelerator while mulling over the new information.

I could kick myself. Why didn't I ask the boys which day this week they came across Bootsy? What if he wasn't in the village at all when he said he overheard an argument involving the vicar? Perhaps he heard the rumour and repeated it to Jed as if he'd been there—Or even to cover his tracks, knowing he'd been seen robbing stuff at the old saddlery?

Chapter Sixteen

DECISION

THE EXCITEMENT of garnering some new information did not last long. Soon, Lyn's thoughts returned to the devastating news Peter Riley had shared. Her mind raced with conflicting thoughts. Lyn's first reaction was to defend Ant's action. But how could she? The detective's evidence proved Ant had lied to her.

It's so out of character for him. I know he tells fibs sometimes to get information from people we're investigating. But he's never lied to me. Then again, how would I know?

By the time she pulled up next to Stanton Parva's church, Lyn was in floods of tears. Her choice of parking hadn't been a conscious decision. I'm sick of the sight of that place.

Yet there she remained, unsure what to do next. The answer came as a figure leaned forward, their face almost touching the rain-smeared window to her right. Lyn's instinct was to ignore the person's presence. Yet she knew that to be rude. As she turned to glimpse her unwanted visitor, Lyn recognised the familiar face.

'What's wrong?' Mouthed Fitch's girlfriend, Sophie.

Although she made no sound, Lyn knew what she was saying. At first, she turned away. The action of the door handle being pulled caused water to drip down the glass like streams into a stormy lake. Lyn turned to look at Sophie, this time making the full extent of her upset obvious. She watched Sophie and guessed she looked a mess. Lyn knew she always went blotchy when she cried and that it took ages for her complexion to return to normal.

Sophie gestured for Lyn to unlock the car door. Reluctantly, she obliged.

'Heavens, is it ever going to stop raining?'

Despite Sophie's comments on the weather, Lyn didn't react as Fitch's girlfriend rushed to get in the car to avoid the worst of the downpour. An awkward silence fell between the women, only broken by Lyn's crying and the sound of the windscreen wipers struggling against the rain.

'I tell you what,' began Sophie. 'Why don't we pop into the garage for a coffee? I'll wash the mugs out, promise.'

Lyn stared out the windshield, blinking each time the wiper-blade crossed her view.

'If you're worried about Fitch, he's out picking up some car parts for a job. You won't come across Ant, either, because the two daft lumps are together. Come on. What do you say? A free coffee has to be better than sitting here moping about, er, what is it you're upset about, anyway?'

Lyn pressed a button to put the car into drive mode and inched the small car forward. All without saying a word to her companion.

'Unless you're kidnapping me, I'll take that as a yes,'

said Sophie, taking care not to look at Lyn for fear of making her cry again.

It took less than a minute for the MINI to cover the distance from the church to Fitch's repair workshop. Lyn scanned the yard for any sign of the two men. She found a sheltered spot to park the car near Fitch's messy office building, glad that they were not around.

Soon after, the friends settled into the small, untidy space that Lyn remembered Fitch described as the beating heart of his work empire.

'Do you know,' said Sophie as she stood at a paint-splattered sink, washing out two mugs, 'I thought I could change him. You know, stuff like getting him to choose his socks from his drawers so they matched and doing this place up and keeping it tidy.'

Lyn didn't answer. Instead, she looked at her engagement ring, while twirling it around between her finger and thumb. Sophie took the hint and remained muted as she made a coffee, then handed over a mug, for which she apologised.

'It's only instant. I don't trust Fitch to clean the mugs, and I don't want to risk exposing our customers to a filthy coffee percolator.'

Lyn attempted a smile as she accepted the mug emblazoned with "Fitch's Auto Repairs". She had the smallest of sips before placing her drink on the grey- painted concrete floor. The women sat in silence, with only the rattling office door and the creaking of the kettle as it cooled, disturbing the quiet.

'Time for girl talk, don't you think?' Sophie waited for her friend to respond. Instead, Lyn remained lost in her own world. 'Look, Lyn. It won't be that long before the boys are back. Why not talk to me before the terrible-two get back? I'm worried you'll do something you'll regret if you don't let it out now. Come on. Nothing you say will leave this office. I promise you.'

Sophie's genuine concern touched something deep within. Lyn. She seemed to recognise that time was running out to repair her relationship with Ant. 'I can't marry him.' Lyn spoke with such anger that Sophie recoiled in her chair.

For a few seconds, Lyn stared at her companion. Eventually, Sophie responded to Lyn's unexpected outburst.

'Okay, now let's talk about that.' Sophie's muted tone and steady voice, together with her look of understanding, helped Lyn regain control. 'You're safe here. Come on, tell me what's happened. You never know, talking about it might help you decide what to do next.'

Over the following few minutes, Lyn explained, between tearful interludes, what she'd learned from Peter Riley.

'And what do you think about that? In your mind, is Ant guilty as charged? I mean, what motive has he got to harm our vicar?'

'You think he did it, don't you?' said Lyn, her breathing shallow as she sat rigid in her chair.

Sophie tensed. 'Of course not. Not for one second.' She half-turned to place her coffee on the cluttered desk, before turning her attention back to Lyn. 'The question you have to answer is, do you? After all, why else blurt out that you're not going to marry him? Why would you dump an innocent man? Maybe you're not ready to get wed, and Peter's nonsense is a convenient excuse to get out of it?'

Lyn bristled. 'Don't be ridiculous. Why would you say such a thing? I thought you were my friend?'

'I am. Only friends can say what I just said with no intent to be detrimental.'

'Well, you're doing a terrible job.'

'Like you,' replied Sophie, keeping her calm tone.

'And what's that supposed to mean?'

Sophie delayed her response and observed Lyn's nervous behaviour with the coffee cup. Lyn's frown deepened as she waited for her companion to respond.

'You need to get your head straight,' began Sophie. 'If you don't confront Ant about what the inspector said, you're giving up on a man you've grown up with. That tells me there's something else going on. So out with it. What is it that's getting to you?'

'I don't know what you're talking about. All I'm saying is, what if he met Reverend Morton early on Wednesday morning, well before I arrived? What if he got into an argument over the order of service for our wedding? I know it sounds daft, but the Stanton family insists on a particular way of doing things. It's been that way for hundreds of years. Perhaps the vicar put his foot down and Ant got angry?'

'What, over a marriage service?'

'Ant's PTSD can flair up out of nowhere, with no obvious trigger and once he goes off on one, he can be a handful. If he imagined he was back on a battlefield and needing to protect his soldiers, it doesn't bear thinking about who he thought the vicar was.'

'You mean the enemy?'

'Yes, I shudder to think what he's capable of if he had a complete breakdown and did something awful.'

Sophie wore a look of horror. 'Yet you say he was just flustered when he eventually arrived?'

Lyn looked at the oil-stained floor. 'That's the creepy thing about his illness. He can be in a rage, then the next minute, behaving as if nothing happened.'

'He's that good a fibber?' replied Sophie, not knowing how to respond.

'It's not that simple. I don't think he remembers what he's said or done.'

'You mean, he thought, like you, that the vicar was behind that door when he knocked on it?'

'I don't know what to believe anymore,' replied Lyn as tears trickled down her cheeks. 'Except that I'm trapped.'

Sophie reached over to touch Lyn's arm. 'Hang on. That's an odd thing to say after almost accusing Ant of harming the vicar, notwithstanding his possible mental distress. Why should you feel trapped? You had nothing to do with anything Ant may or may not have done. Come on, Lyn, out with it. I'll ask you again. What's going on in that head of yours?'

By now her companion was in floods of tears and inconsolable. No matter what Sophie tried. Sophie didn't push Lyn to feel better and left her alone. She took both mugs and washed them in the sink.

Eventually, Lyn's outward distress eased, until, at last, she lapsed into muted contemplation. At that point, Sophie reclaimed her chair, pulling it closer to her friend. She eased one of Lyn's hands from her lap and placed it between her own cupped hands.

'Come on, Lyn. I know you too well to think you believe for one second Ant has done anything so crazy. You've allowed Peter Riley's concerns to get mixed up with something else. For your own wellbeing, as well as any future you have with Ant. You need to separate the two things. What do you say?'

It took a while, but eventually, Lyn allowed her slim frame to relax. She lifted her gaze from the floor to Sophie.

'It's Ant's parents. They want us to take over running the Stanton Estate as soon as we're married.'

Sophie sighed with relief. 'Ah, I get it now. You're worried about your career?'

'It's not just that, although they haven't said so, but I know they'll want grandchildren. I love them both so much, but I know how these old families work. They expect a line of succession to be in place within twelve months of the wedding and I'm just not ready for that.'

Sophie squeezed Lyn's hand as a token of understanding.

'You know how hard it is for us to land the top jobs. I love Ant, but...' Lyn's voice tailed off.

'Then tell him. You know what blokes can be like. They're in a world of their own half the time. Tell him straight that you're happy to move into Stanton Hall after the wedding but won't sacrifice your professional career. If he loves you, he'll understand and support your decision.'

'But what about his parents? It will devastate them?'

'That's for Ant to deal with. And by the way, from everything you've told me about them, their response might surprise you.'

As Lyn allowed Sophie's words to sink in, she managed a weak smile and rubbed the tears from her reddened cheeks.

'Here, take this,' said Sophie as she handed Lyn a paper tissue. 'It's a clean one; well, almost,'

Just then, the booming sound of Fitch's recovery lorry crossing the garage forecourt could be heard. Both women turned to look out of the office's grimy window.

'There's Ant. He'll know I'm here once he sees the MINI. What am I going to do?' Lyn's panic was palpable as Sophie tried to calm Lyn down.

'Just talk to him. I'll drag Fitch away, so you're left in peace so you two can thrash this thing out.'

Lyn's agitation grew. 'You don't understand. I told Peter Riley I wouldn't say anything to Ant.'

Sophie glanced at the stationary recovery lorry to see both men about to jump from the ageing truck. 'Not to panic, shoot out the back way and they'll never know you were here.'

Lyn looked over her shoulder, 'What back way? And you're forgetting my car.'

Sophie smiled, 'I'll tell them you dropped it off while you nipped into the village. The door? It's our little secret. Move that curtain aside next to the sink.'

Sure enough, as Lyn followed her instructions, an old timber door revealed itself. 'It doesn't look as though it's seen the light of day in years,'

'To my knowledge, it hasn't, but I'm sure it'll still open.'

Lyn craned her neck to catch sight of Ant and Fitch strolling across the yard, looking as if they hadn't a care in the world. 'Now you tell me.'

She turned her attention back to the old door, turned a rusted key and gave the bottom a sharp kick as she pushed, hoping to see daylight. Lyn's effort succeeded too well as she stumbled forward onto the pavement beyond.

'In a bit of a rush, are we?' offered an elderly villager who just stepped back in time.

Lyn corrected her faltering arrival to the outside world in two strides and gave the well turned-out man an embarrassed smile. 'Sorry about that. I didn't think the door would open with such little effort.'

The villager smiled as he lifted his trilby in a sign of impeccable manners. 'Don't worry. You've not changed much in your habit of making a spectacular entrance since you were a little one. Now, I must be off. My dear wife will not be pleased if I do not return with her copy of Women's Weekly and two pounds of self-raising flour. Mind how you go, Lynda.'

Lyn watched the elderly man raise his hat once again before ambling towards the village centre. No one has called me by my full name for years. I can't think for the life of me who he is.

Things back in the office became frenetic as Sophie ran to close the door behind Lyn and pull the ragged curtain back into position. At that moment, Fitch and Ant entered the office.

'Where's Lyn?' asked Ant in a matter-of-fact tone.

'Lyn? Oh, her car's on the forecourt, isn't it? She's nipped into the village for some shopping and make a few house calls. I expect she'll be back in a couple of hours.'

Ant glanced at Fitch, then Sophie. 'Walked? Lyn doesn't walk anywhere if she can help it.'

Sophie attempted to divert the conversation by offering the two men coffee.

'Go on, then. You've twisted my arm,' said Fitch. His companion nodded and grabbed the more comfortable of the two chairs available.

'I'll never understand you lot,' said Ant.

'Don't even try. You'll lose your shirt every time,' replied Sophie as she finished making the drinks. 'Anyway, I assume you'll be wanting to take the Morgan?'

'Not until he's paid his bill, he's not,' laughed Fitch.

The two men exchanged a wry smile as they each took their coffee from a smiling Sophie.

'You know I'll see you right at the end of the month. You don't intend to keep a man from the love of his life, do you?' said Ant.

'Be careful. You mean the second love of your life,' said Sophie.

Ant flushed as he realised what he'd said. 'You know what I mean, I—'

'Stop digging and give me the spade,' said Fitch. 'Anyway, why should I wait until the end of the month for my money? It's not as though you're waiting for wages to go into the bank. We both know you live a different life than the rest of us. No wonder rich people stay rich.'

Ant didn't react, save to blow his hot drink and half-close his eyes as the steaming coffee made its presence known.

'See what I mean, Sophie? He's not a care in the world.'

Sophie perched on Fitch's lap, almost causing him to spill his coffee. 'Never mind, my little oily rag. Let the nasty lord have his coffee while I give you a cuddle. Anyway, he's no idea what I've put in his coffee.'

Ant smiled, then took a discreet sniff of his drink as a precaution.

Fitch was far too busy snuggling into Sophie to follow the conversation, or the amused glance she and Ant were exchanging.

The next few minutes passed in the sort of genial banter only secure friendships allow.

At that moment, Sophie realised she needed to decide on something she'd struggled with since their arrival, but she was uncertain about what to say. Should she say something to Ant about Lyn's unhappiness? She knew she couldn't talk about detective inspector Riley's covert meeting. Perhaps she might drop a hint about her friend's career worries?

'You know, Ant,' she began. 'It's all well and good us

larking about here, but I know someone who hasn't been happy for some time.'

Fitch untangled himself from his girlfriend as Ant held his mug of coffee mid-way between his lap and mouth.

'That can only mean you're talking about Lyn? What has she said to you?'

'Oh, nothing serious.'

Ant gingerly placed his coffee on the stone floor and fixed Sophie with a serious stare. 'Come on. You can't say something out of the blue like that without a reason. I know you two trust each other, so I guess there's not much she hasn't told you about what's going on.'

Sophie tensed, sensing her intervention was about to backfire. 'All I'm saying is—'

'It's what you're not saying that concerns me.' Ant's stern tone didn't waver.

'Hang on, Ant. You need to lighten up a little. She's only trying to—'

'Do what, exactly? Interfere?'

Sophie stood, her arms folded across her midriff, waiting for Ant to apologise.

Fitch's sharp intervention appeared to do the trick. Ant's glare softened. 'All I'm saying is—'

'Look, if I upset you, then I'm sorry,' said Sophie, with a slight edge. 'But life doesn't revolve around you and that car of yours. Remember what's important to you above all else, or do I have to remind you?'

'I don't need anyone to remind me of anything.'

Fitch got to his feet and stood over his best friend. 'Time to go before something's said we'll all regret.' He walked the few paces to a grimy chipboard panel that held the keys to all the vehicles in for repair. 'Here. Why don't you take these and cool off somewhere? You need time on your own.

You'll get no lectures from me. We've known each other too long, but I am telling you to sort yourself out.'

Sophie became horrified how events had unfolded, and how tenuous even the strongest of friendships can be. She tried to defuse the situation. 'Why don't you take a turn on Fieldsurfer? Lyn's always telling me how sailing on the Broads relaxes you.'

The mention of his fiance's name did little to calm matters.

'She's trying to help you, mate. Take it for what it is.'

Ant reached out to take the key to his car from Fitch, then turned to make his way to the door without responding to his friend's words of advice. As he crossed the threshold, he faltered.

'Do what Fitch suggests, Ant. Then talk to the person who loves you more than anyone else in the world,' said Sophie.

He half-turned to look at Fitch's girlfriend. This time, his gaze was softer. His manner, more reflective.

'She wants to be your wife. That doesn't mean she has to give everything else up for you, or your parents.'

'Parents?'

'You know what I mean. Yes, she told me.'

Ant leaned on the rickety door frame, his shoulders slumped.

'Everything will be OK, as long as both of you explain how you are feeling. I know it's hard for you, but think about Lyn for a second. How do you think she feels about…' Sophie realised what she was about to say and stopped herself.

Both men now looked at Sophie.

'Feels about what? Is there something you, or rather Lyn, aren't telling me?'

Sophie wanted to floor to swallow her up. How could she have made such a stupid mistake? And how would she get herself out of a sticky situation? She didn't know what to do as she watched the men exchanged confused looks.

'Tell me, Sophie. What's going on? Lyn hasn't gone shopping, has she?'

Sophie tried to buy time by gathering up the coffee mugs and taking them to the sink.

Fitch walked the few paces to join her and spoke in a whisper. 'Whatever it is you stopped yourself from saying, you need to tell him before he goes charging around for answers like a bull in a china shop. You know as well as I do what he can be like when things aren't going well for him.'

The atmosphere within the small, dank space grew more intense as each second passed.

Finally, Sophie stopped moving the coffee mugs around on the sink. She turned towards Ant, whose position remained frozen in the office doorway. 'Someone asked to meet her this morning. You'll have to ask Lyn who that was because it's not for me to say.'

Ant looked puzzled for a few seconds, then his demeanour changed. 'So that's why I couldn't get hold of her,' he muttered. Without saying another word, he closed the office door behind him and stepped across the yard, his shoulders hunched.

Sophie, followed by Fitch, crossed to the window to watch the dejected man. Before Ant reached his beloved Morgan sports car, he hesitated and looked over to Lyn's MINI and walked over to the small vehicle. When he reached the car, he placed a palm on the bonnet.

'Oh, no,' said Sophie.

'What's up?' replied Fitch.

'The bonnet will still be warm. He'll work out Lyn hasn't long since left and put two and two together.'

Fitch gently turned Sophie so that they were facing each other. 'You're not making any sense. He'll know what?'

Sophie wiped a tear from her eyes. 'That his world has just come tumbling down.'

Chapter Seventeen

WHAT'S THAT?

STANTON PARVA'S church remained the sanctuary it had been for almost a thousand years. Today, it extended its loving mantle around a solitary figure, hunched in a pew a few rows back from the front-most seating. This was a man who had cause to feel sad whenever he crossed the sacred building's threshold, yet here he sat, not knowing where else to turn.

It's not fair that my parents expect us to take over the running of the Estate as soon as we are married, thought Ant. He mulled over the events of the day and tried to work out who his fiance had met that morning. He came to a startling conclusion. If she told Sophie about the pressure she's under. Maybe she's at Stanton Hall now, telling mum and dad how things will be, not how they want them to be. What if she's fed up with it and instead told them the wedding's off?

Ant's subconscious momentarily ceased its cruel trajectory. His attention fell on water droplets splashing into a plastic bucket in the adjacent aisle. The rhythmic splodge provided a welcome distraction from his mental pain.

Instead, the interruption offered the calming balm of a metronome-like rhythm to which he could match his breathing.

I must get back to the hall. I've been unfair on Lyn and it's my job to put it right by telling them how we both feel. I don't know, perhaps I should give it all up. That way, we can both have the careers we want. There are plenty of relatives who'd sell their soul to control the Estate, and the titles that go with it. I don't want it. I never wanted it.

His thoughts meandered around how things were, to how his world could have been. Ant conjured up images of his elder brother and the accident that had deprived him of life well before his time. Anger swelled within him, as it always did when he thought about his elder brother's death.

Why should I feel guilty? I wasn't driving. I didn't go.

Ant knew the answer to his own question. Greg had offered to take Ant for a run in his new sports car. He'd said he was too busy and ever since, he'd tortured himself about his best friend losing his life without a living soul near him.

Once again, the rhythmic sound of slashing water came to his rescue. Perhaps Greg is telling me to get on with my life. But what to do? I know for certain I don't want to go back into the army. I just want to be happy and settled with Lyn. Am I asking too much? Then again, is Greg telling me to stop feeling sorry for myself and sort it? That's what he used to tell me.

His emotions fluctuated, going from confronting his parents to worrying about the village and its inhabitants. Deep in thought, Ant hadn't noticed the man now sitting directly behind him.

'How are you doing, my old mucker?' said Fitch in a quiet, reassuring tone. Gone was the anger displayed earlier in the afternoon. Now, he wished only to support his longest-standing friend.

Ant didn't react. Instead, he continued to hunch into a shape so that he occupied as little space as possible.

Fitch leaned forward; his hand placed on Ant's right shoulder. His friend failed to acknowledge the man's presence. 'You wallowing in your own thoughts isn't healthy with your condition. You know that.'

Desperate to find a way through, he retracted his hand, stood and made his way around his pew to sit next to Ant. 'You have to open up. If not to me, then certainly to Lyn. Hasn't it occurred to that self-absorbed brain of yours that she might think the same thing? Don't let hurt pride stop you from doing something you'll regret for the rest of your life. If it were Lyn sat here, I'd say the same thing to her. Both of you always were stubborn, except we're not kids anymore. What do you say?'

Both men stared straight ahead, making no effort to look at the other.

'I'll tell you for sure. If you're honest with her, you won't lose Lyn. Are you brave enough to do that, or stupid enough to miss your one chance?'

The stark ultimatum hit its target. Ant shuffled in his seat. 'It's too late. She thinks I lied to her, and I did.'

Fitch thumped the pew with his fist so hard that the sound reverberated around the ageless stone walls of the church. 'Listen, I've had enough of this "woe is me" stuff. You always were one for feeling sorry for yourself. And you with all that privilege. Grow up. You can think what you like. Invent any crack-pot theory that suits your mood. Until the both of you talk like you've never done before, you'll each get the opposite of what I, and everyone else in this village, want. For you to get married.'

Fitch's outburst caused Ant to jerk his head so that his blazing eyes bore into his friend. 'I told you; she knows I lied to her. How can I get her to trust me ever again?'

'Tell her, just tell her whatever the truth is. Is that so hard? I don't know. Have you lied to her before? Perhaps she's had enough for good reason. Your lot always want their own way, don't they?'

Ant sprang to his feet and glared down at Fitch. 'Stop it now. You're my closest friend, but you're crossing a line.'

Fitch stood square on to his friend. 'I won't stop until you understand you can't keep beating yourself up about a corrupt general.'

'Six of my men died out there,' screamed Ant. his eyes blazing with pent-up anger.

'And you saved another twenty from the same fate. Have you forgotten that?' So what if your commanding officer lied about what happened so you'd take the blame for their deaths? Everyone else who survived knew you, and you alone saved their lives. I know Lyn has spoken to several of those men, all of whom suffer as you do. She knows the truth, so do you think she'd willingly walk away from you now?'

The two men continued to exchange fearsome glares, their body language speaking to fight, not flight. Eventually Fitch gave Ant a way out of the situation by breaking eye contact and pacing the few yards to the altar rail. 'Now tell me what this "lie" is all about before I throw you over this lovely rail. Remember, I always beat you when we scrapped as kids.'

Ant relaxed. The immediate danger was, in his mind, over. 'As you said, we're not kids anymore, even if you always cheat.'

'In your mind, you mean. I always won fair-and-square.

Anyhow, you knew Lyn would always show up and thump me. That's two on one, and you say I cheated?'

The exchange caused both men to relax, with the beginning of a mutual grin emerging.

'Now come on. Tell me what you've been up to, so we can sort this mess out,' said Fitch. He sat on the altar rail, only to scramble to his feet as he felt the oak construction move.

'Do you think He's trying to tell you something?'

'Who?'

Ant lifted his eyes to the heavens.

'Don't be a daft lump. I don't believe in that stuff.' Fitch hesitated for a second as his gaze followed his friend's finger. 'You don't think that. I mean—'

'Hedging your bets, eh?'

'Hmm, hilarious. Anyway, at least you've got your daft sense of humour back,' said Fitch with a wry smile. 'So, what's been going on?'

Ant's grin disappeared, to be replaced by a concerned look. He glanced towards the altar, then busied himself following the outline of some ancient graffiti etched onto the top of the altar rail long ago. 'The truth is. I met the vicar a couple of hours before meeting up with Lyn at the church on Wednesday morning.'

All traces of levity vanished from Fitch's demeanour. 'That means... well, you know... you knew the Reverend Morton wouldn't be in the vestry when you knocked on the door?' with Lyn.

'No. How could I know? All I said was that I met him earlier; at his request.'

Fitch matched his friend's frown and shook his head in confusion. 'You don't have to be Einstein to know how this looks. Peter—'

'Peter? Ah, now I see. Lyn met Peter Riley earlier today. That's what her strange behaviour is all about, is it?'

'Hang on, Ant. Don't go blaming Lyn, and as for Peter, he's doing his job?'

'What's that supposed to mean?' Ant's temper got the better of him. 'So you believe him and not me? Some mate you are.' He broke off eye contact and reverted to tracing the old graffiti with an index finger.

'Will you leave that stupid thing alone and look at me? All I know is what Sophie told me, and all she knows is what Lyn told her. Get a grip, will you, before the upshot of your little escapade gets out of hand with the police? I've no idea what they know about your movements. My guess is that they've found out you weren't where you told Lyn you were. You worked in intelligence. You must have known they'd check up on us all.'

Ant's face flushed as the truth of Fitch's words sank in. 'One mistake. That's all this is about. One daft fib. Because I agreed to the vicar's pleading, I wouldn't tell anyone what I'd agreed to do for him. Look where it's got me.'

The men looked at each other in silence. Ant was the first to break eye contact.

'Don't start fiddling with those scratchings. Time to come clean, mate, before they arrest you for something you didn't do. What on earth did the vicar ask you to do that was worth jeopardising your relationship with—'

'But that's the point. I didn't know things would turn out the way they have. How was I to know the reverend would disappear into thin air, still less, that a man connected to him would be murdered?'

'And how do you expect Peter Riley to react?' shouted Fitch, his voice reverberating around the old church like a celestial chorus shouting, guilty. 'You'd better tell me what the vicar asked you to do, if for no other reason than that Riley can't be far behind me. I saw him pulling up at the garage as I rounded the corner to come and find you. Sophie's great at keeping things to herself when she needs to, but he'll wear her down. You know what a good copper he is. So—'

'Fitch, give it a rest, will you? I know I'm up to my neck in it?' Ant paced along the altar rail like a caged lion, looking for a chance to escape and devour its tormentors.

'No, I will not. And for the sake of my sanity and vertigo, will you please stand still?'

Ant obliged the request and instead plunged his hands into his trouser pockets. He fixed his gaze on the effigy of a large brass eagle with wings spread wide. 'He told me about the letters, and that someone had threatened his life if he didn't do as they asked.'

'You mean Cynthia Hake?'

'That's the trouble. He didn't say. Just as he was about to give me a name, the telephone rang. He looked terrified. After he put the telephone down, I asked him what the matter was. He clammed up and wouldn't say. I kept trying to tease a name out of him. In the end, he pleaded with me not to tell anyone about our meeting.'

'And you just agreed. Especially after everything that's happened since?'

Ant stiffened his posture. 'He made me swear on my family's name.'

'What?' replied Fitch, his face etched with alarm.

'He's known the family for a long time and knows how people like us tick. He knew that if I gave my word as a gentleman, I couldn't break it.'

Fitch shook his head and made for a pew, flopping onto the hard wooden seat like a rag doll. 'Gentleman? People like us? You do know it's 2023, don't you? Are you telling me you posh lot still live by some medieval code of ethics? Next, you'll be telling me you're spending the weekend slaying dragons in full armour on your trusty steed.'

'Don't be stupid.'

'Me? I'm not the one facing arrest by the police for kidnap and murder. Are you actually telling me you'll lose everything you have, simply because you gave your word to someone? If you are, then you don't deserve Lyn, and you're making fools of what few friends you have. Anyway, you still haven't explained why you were late in meeting up with Lyn. You say you met the vicar much earlier in the morning. Where did you go? And don't tell me your honour is at stake, so you can't say anything. If you do, I'll hand you in to Peter Riley. Do you understand?'

Ant looked exasperated. 'All I did was check a couple of things out. It took much longer than I expected.'

'What? About who might have it in for the reverend?'

Before Ant could defend himself, a voice boomed from the back of the church. 'Stay where you are.'

Ant didn't need to look up, he knew who the voice belonged to. 'What makes you think I'm going anywhere, Peter?'

The detective strolled down the aisle as if he hadn't a care in the world. Ant knew there was more to Riley's appearance than passing time before heading home for the day.

'Are you going to tell him, or will I?'

'You'll say nothing if you value our friendship,' replied Ant, giving his friend an intense stare.

'Tell me what?'

'It doesn't matter.'

'It does if you want to stay out of prison,' replied Riley

in a concerned tone. 'I assume you know I'm not enjoying this? I have a job to do and no matter how well we get on, I will do my duty.'

'Save me from people who take oaths. What's the matter with you two? You're acting as if you've never met before, or caught criminals together. Will you please both just grow up?'

Fitch's intervention appeared not to touch the sides of either man, who continued to lock eyes.

'You can talk. Ant has clearly told you something directly connected to the case. A bit like "pot calling kettle", don't you think?'

Fitch stood. For a second, it looked as though he was about to leave. He hesitated and turned back to the two men, who now stood facing each other less than six feet apart. 'I'm not the one facing jail time.'

'You are if I discover you've withheld information having the effect of frustrating a police investigation,' snapped Riley.

Fitch exploded with rage. 'Right, I've had enough of this rubbish. Ant, either you tell him, or I will.' His friend remained resolute in remaining silent, while continuing to glare at the detective.

'OK, you've had your chance. Peter, I assume you've discovered my thick friend wasn't where he told you, was that—'

'Help. Please someone, help me.'

The faint voice stunned Fitch into silence. The attention of all three men turned to discovering where the strangled cry emanated.

'Did you hear that?' asked the detective.

'It came from the altar,' replied Fitch.

Ant's eyes darted from one spot to the next as he tried to

home in on the wretched sound. 'No, it's nearer to us than that.' His voice was strong, assertive. It was as if something deep within him had re-emerged. He moved towards a pair of narrow doors built into the altar rail at the same height to conceal their presence. With a push from his knee, the doors swept back, allowing access to the most sacred part of the church.

A scratching sound permeated the near distance.

'The pulpit?' suggested Fitch.

The three men stood in a huddle, trying to discover the sound's origin.

'You're right,' said Riley, bending over the set of four stair treads that allowed the vicar to reach the speaking platform of the pulpit.

A hush descended as the trio waited impatiently for a further sign someone was attempting to draw attention to themselves.

'There it is again. Do you hear it?'

Fitch shook his head. Ant knelt at the foot of the bottom step and leaned inward, like a cat stalking its prey. He pulled at each, one after the other, then at the inside face of the pulpit.

'What are you doing?' urged Riley.

He didn't answer, instead his urgent investigations continued. At last, he felt the stairs move. He realised he needed to pull the bottom step up and towards him, rather than push down. Suddenly, the entire staircase lifted. Ant sprang backwards to give the construction room to complete its silent manoeuvre.

Riley sprang forward to peer into the darkness of the abyss-like void. His eyes widened. His face etched with horror. The detective covered his mouth with a hand, as if not wanting to speak the words. 'We're too late,' he gasped.

———

IN A CROWDED COTTAGE HOSPITAL, the men waited while a receptionist tried to help anxious people inquiring about their loved ones.

'You two should wait here while I get up to his room. And Fitch, it's down to you to make sure Anthony doesn't do a runner. Just so as you know, two bobbies are on their way to take up position outside the entrance, and another around the back. '

Fitch looked crest fallen. 'Don't be like that, Peter. You know we wouldn't let you down.'

'I don't know any such thing. I've already broken the rules by not taking him straight to the station. Think yourself lucky that this is an emergency. Time will tell if he put the reverend in here. Either way, he's got some explaining to do.'

With that, Fitch and Ant scanned space for seating. 'Looks like we're standing,' said Fitch.

'That's the least of my worries,' said Ant.

'There you go again, feeling sorry for yourself. Why don't you put yourself in Peter's shoes for a minute or two? He's right, you know. From his perspective, you should be in a cell waiting for him to interview you. If I were you, I'd keep my head down and shut up.'

Ant's situation went from bad to worse as a petite woman ran through the open entrance to the hospital and sped to the still-busy reception desk.

'And I mean, shut up,' said Fitch as he pointed to the tail-end of a queue. 'Despite what I said before, this isn't the time and place to have it out with your fiance.'

Ant didn't respond as he watched his friend saunter over to the woman and gently touched her forearm. He watched as she shot him an angry stare. Within seconds, the two stood feet apart, with Fitch separating the two aggressors with his muscular body. The trio soon settled into a routine in which Ant and Lyn refused to look at one another, with questions from either, filtered through Fitch.

A young police constable stood outside the private room of Reverend Morton, watching for any sign of the person who had locked up the vicar.

'All quiet?' asked Riley in a formal tone.

'Yes, sir,' responded the young officer and resolutely not meeting his superior's line of sight.

As a clinician emerged from the stricken man's room, Riley pounced on the woman. 'Am I able to speak to the Reverend Morton? It's important that I interview him.'

The tall, immaculately turned out professional in her matron's uniform stopped in her tracks and fired the detective a stern look. 'And you are?'

Riley fumbled for his warrant card. 'Yes, of course,' he responded as he flicked open the small leather wallet with practiced aplomb. Detective Inspector Peter Riley is based in Stanton Parva and reporting to Norfolk headquarters in Wymondham.

'So I see,' said the matron as she interrogated Riley's identification with forensic attention to detail. 'I'm afraid your questions will have to wait. The patient is extremely unwell.' Her steely voice left little to the imagination.

'Matron, I must insist—'

'Insist? Inspector, I do not recognise such a term, other than in a medical emergency … and that is precisely what we have. The gentleman is unconscious, and we are uncertain he will ever wake up. Do you understand?'

Riley's professional demeanour confirmed he'd understood the message. 'I'm sorry if I exceeded my authority. It's a tendency most police officers have. I—'

'I understand only too well, Inspector. My husband works for the police... not Norfolk, so you won't know him. Look, I know why you need to speak to my patient. The issue is, for you to do that, we'd have to wake him up. At the moment, that is too dangerous for us to attempt.' The matron's approach softened as she spoke. 'Look, the best I can do is to tell you is that the reverend will undergo several scans over the next couple of hours. If the results are favourable, we'll be able to wake him. If you let me have your business card, I promise to ring you.'

Riley's mood lifted so that in his eagerness to find and pass a card over, he dropped the oblong shaped object. His effort to retrieve the property met with sharp rebuke.

'I think not, Detective Inspector. A clean one, if you don't mind.'

'Of course, err... Ah, yes, here we are,' replied Riley, his cheeks flushing with embarrassment as he fumbled for a replacement.

'As for my other half,' began the matron. 'He's bad, but not as insistent as you.' With that, the practitioner turned on her heels and disappeared back into the reverend's room.

A minute later, he rounded the corner of a corridor which led back to reception. As he neared the others in the busy thoroughfare, he tried to contain the smile.

'Good news?' asked Fitch, while the other two looked on in expectation.

'Hello, Lyn. How did you know we were here?' said the detective, ignoring the question.

'The village is rife with rumours. They think a thief fell off the church roof trying to steal some lead again. The fact there's a police guard at the entrance has convinced them that The Gaffer is going to spring his man and whisk him away right under your nose. I didn't believe any of it, so I called into the station. You know what Burt is like for gossiping. Isn't it wonderful news?'

'What, that my desk sergeant likes to gossip, or that the vicar is here? I'll have to have a word in his shell-like. Anyway, to answer the question; yes… and no,' replied the detective.

'Whose question are you answering?' asked a confused Fitch.

Riley looked at the mechanic, then Lyn, while studiously avoiding Ant. 'Both. Yes, it's good news that the vicar's here, and he's alive. The bad news is that they've put him into a coma to give his brain time to recover from the trauma he's suffered.'

'But that's good news and better news, isn't it?' said Lyn.

'Not for a copper trying to interview a victim to see what they can tell me about his assailant.'

As the three friends discussed a man's fight for life, the work of the hospital went on as normal, with people coming and going from the reception area. Most seemed happy, or at least content with their visit. Only the occasional man or woman close to tears gave away the fact that the building was no ordinary place for people to gather and chat the day away.

'Then why were you smiling when you came back from trying to see the vicar?' enquired Fitch.

Riley thought for a second as he ruminated on the question. 'Oh, nothing. Just something someone said.'

Fitch blinked twice, as if trying to compute a suitable response. In the end, he gave up and shrugged his shoulders.

'Anyway,' continued Riley. 'There's nothing we can do

here until they think it's safe to bring him round. The matron promised to ring me when they do.'

Lyn grinned and wagged a finger at Riley. 'Ah, so it was her that said something to put a smile on your face. Are you in love?'

Riley fidgeted with his mobile without looking at his interrogator. 'I don't know what you're talking about. Anyway, she's married.'

'Is she now?' laughed Lyn. 'So, you know that much about her?'

'I've nothing more to say on the matter. Now, I suggest we call it a night. If anything changes, I'll be in touch.'

Even Ant joined in the group's laughter at their friend's embarrassment, which didn't go unnoticed.

'And you? Do you want to spend a night in the cells, or in your own bed? Remember, our friendship is the only thing keeping you at large.'

Ant's grin waned, as did his colleagues. As the foursome dodged a constant flow of people arriving for visiting hour, on their way to the exit, Riley's mobile rang. He looked at the display. It wasn't a number he recognised.

'Detective Inspector Riley.'

The others acted on instinct and stopped walking.

'I see. That's good news. I'll come straight away.'

Lyn was the first to break the ensuing silence. 'Is it something to do with the case?'

Riley allowed his police officer's practiced stern look to morph into a wide smile. 'He's woken up on his own. They're withdrawing his medication now so they can control things better.'

The other three let out a group cheer, causing the reception area to come to a momentary halt.

'Let's get up to his room before we cause more trouble,' said Lyn.

Riley shook his head. 'No. I want to speak to the vicar on my own. Tell me where you'll be, and I'll be in touch as soon as I have any news. If my hunch is correct, we shall be busy over the next twenty-four hours.'

The call Ant, Lyn, and Fitch were on tenterhooks for came two hours later. Lyn answered her mobile and confirmed they were at her house. She listened to the caller with intense concentration, giving out the occasional, 'Yes, I see', and 'Okay'. After the brief call ended, she turned to the other two. 'Peter is on his way. He didn't say much, other than tell me, 'The game is on,' and to make sure not to speak to anyone before he arrives. Apparently, a national newspaper reporter is on holiday in the area. He heard about the rumours and thinks he's onto a scoop about a London 'Mr Big' operating in Norfolk.'

'Hmm,' mused Fitch. 'Reporters have the same affliction the coppers have. They're like a dog with a bone and never off duty. It gets my goat.'

'What, even Peter?' replied Lyn.

'Yes, if you must know. I always get the feeling he thinks I'm up to something dodgy when he comes to the garage.'

'That's because you are, sometimes,' said Ant, in his first intervention since leaving the hospital.

'Look who's talking.'

'Now then, children. Stop it or I'll put you on litter duty in the playground for a week.'

No sooner had Lyn made fresh coffee and placed a generous number of her special shortbread biscuits on a large plate than the front doorbell rang. For once, not even the temptation of her biscuits could divert Ant and Fitch's attention. Both waited impatiently for Lyn to welcome Riley to their gathering.

'I've just made the coffee. Want one?' asked Lyn.

'Have you anything to go with it? I'm pegged out.'

Lyn gave the detective a wry smile. 'If you mean alcohol, yes, but you're not having any. You'll have to make do with a biscuit ... and don't turn your nose up like that. I made them.'

Riley appeared to think better of replying. Instead, he helped himself to a coffee from the burbling percolator and relieved the plate of two shortbread treats.

The others sipped their drinks and took the occasional nip from their biscuits, all the time looking at the detective and waiting for him to explain all.

He's making us wait on purpose, thought Lyn.

As the minutes passed and coffee mugs emptied, Riley, at last, made his move.

'Getting the vicar to talk was hard work. He's still poorly, and his voice weak. However, what he said is enough to make me believe we have a better than even chance of finding whoever abducted him... and the killer Ian Greenacre. The trouble is, there's one or two gaps in my knowledge that leave me feeling it could all go horribly wrong.'

His friends exchanged tense looks.

'It?' asked Lyn. 'What do you mean?'

Riley's concern deepened. 'That all depends on what we do here tonight. Each of us needs to set out their understanding of what has gone on this last week. I don't care how irrelevant or daft you think sounds. We have to get it all out to see if one of us spotted or heard something the others have missed.'

'It'll take hours,' said Fitch.

'We've plenty of time. The memorial service at the church doesn't start until six-o-clock tomorrow evening.'

'The service? What's that got to do with anything?' asked Lyn.

'I know,' offered Ant. 'That's when virtually the entire village will turn out. Not something the perpetrators can miss even if they want to. They'd stand out like a sore thumb by their absence.'

Lyn still couldn't bear to look at her fingers. Instead, she took a biscuit from the plate while asking her question. 'More than one? I mean, you used the plural to describe whoever did this?'

'He's right to think that way,' interrupted Riley. 'I hope that when we've finished our work here tonight, the answer to that question will become clear.'

As the evening wore on, and coffee mugs came, went and continued to be refilled, the gathering worked through the exhausting agenda set out by Peter Riley. By close to midnight, they completed their work. Before them lay a single sheet of lined paper. A dull pencil lay at right angles. Its tip pointed at a particular detail.

'Are we all agreed, then?'

Three heads nodded in perfect synchronicity.

'Then we put my plan into action. Here's what I want each of you to do.'

The inspector addressed each person, giving a clear set of instructions, which he required repeating back to him. When all three had their orders, Riley downed the last of his coffee, stood, and stretched as if he's just got out of bed.

'We meet at the garage at four-thirty tomorrow afternoon to complete our plan. If, in the meantime, any of you discover something that could compromise our plan, you must contact me immediately. Is that understood?'

Again, three heads nodded.

Chapter Eighteen

A GATHERING

AS A SULTRY SUNDAY afternoon gave way to the darkening sky of early evening, Ant ran across Fitch's garage forecourt to dodge the coming downpour.

'I'm glad I beat that lot.'

'Beat what?' replied Fitch, as he shoved an untidy pile of paperwork to one side of his cluttered desk.

'The tornado.'

'The what?'

'Will you please stop doing that? It drives me insane,' said Ant while rubbing his forehead to emphasise the point.

'Doing what?'

'There, you're doing it again. I know it's on purpose, so pack it in.'

Fitch gave his friend a wry smile and looked out the grubby office window. 'How do dark clouds and a bit of wind make a tornado? As for driving you insane, you've done that all by yourself.'

Just then, a tremendous gust of wind blew a black plastic waste bin over and scattered the contents across the forecourt and beyond. Seconds later, a heavy squall of hailstones danced on every surface they touched like a demented popcorn maker.

'What were you saying about dark clouds?' asked Ant as he glanced at the white torrent beyond.

Fitch sniffed the air as a sign of defiance. 'I don't think Lyn or Peter will thank you for your prediction.' He pointed with an oil-stained finger at two hunched figures running towards the office.

Soon, the office door crashed open as the soaked pair almost fell into it, scattering beads of ice before them.

'Fitch told me there was nothing to worry about. It was only a dark cloud.'

Neither newcomer replied. Instead, each gave the garage owner a contemptuous look as they shook themselves free of hailstone.

'Coffee?' asked Fitch in an innocent tone, making no comment about the pair's bedraggled appearance.

Peter looked at his wristwatch. 'No time to dry out, never mind a coffee. Are you all clear what to do once we get to the church?'

The detective's insistence on getting down to business made the others give up on the idea of a relaxed chat over a biscuit. Instead, the group nodded in unison. The mood in the cramped space morphed from light-hearted banter to a serious focus on what was about to unfold.

'Oh, Anthony, thank you for ringing earlier. The information you shared reinforces my view that we're on the right track. But tell me, do you ever sleep?' said the detective.

'Not that early, was it?'

As Lyn and Fitch gave Ant a curious look, he smiled for the first time in a long time. 'The land never sleeps, or to be more precise, animals can't tell the time. Anyway, not that early, was it?'

Peter yawned, setting the others off. 'I don't suppose six-o-clock is early for a sheep or cow, but it is for me on a Sunday.'

Lyn held up a hand as if she were taking the morning assembly at work. 'Excuse me, but if we're to work as a team this evening, don't you think Fitch and I deserve an explanation? Anyway, why should we believe anything he has to say?'

Ant gave Lyn a nervous glance as she stared at him.

The detective looked at the grimy floor and plunged both hands deep into his trouser pockets. After an age, he re-engaged the warring couple. 'This has to stop. I know you have your differences, and my actions haven't helped, but I want it left here. Tonight is far too important for me to risk it going wrong because you've fallen out. My job is on the line and for that reason, I'll leave you here while Fitch and I continue with the plan. So, what's it to be?'

Peter Riley's threat brought the bickering to a halt. The only sound interrupting an awkward silence related to the heavy rain, which displaced hailstones clattering against the office window.

'That's better. Now, let's get down to business, shall we?'

The detective kept a tight grip on the room as he ran through their plan for the evening, covering every point in minute detail. 'Right, unless I've missed anything?' Peter checked with each. 'Good, then let's make our way to the church. Remember, we each take a different route and make sure you enter the vestry on your own. I don't want any suspicions raised. I've had officers in plain clothes in that church since nine this morning, so no one has entered or left without me knowing.'

As they exited the garage via the office rear door, Ant, and Lyn exchanged a sad, lingering look.

———

BY FIVE-FORTY-FIVE, all four had arrived in the vestry, each having got there via a different route. Luck was on their side as the rain eased to a drizzle for their journey. By the time they met, only the glistening of a dew-like film covered their outer clothes.

'Avoiding the villagers wasn't easy, was it?' said Lyn.

'You're right there. Did you see how many villagers were on their way?' replied Fitch.

Ant remained aloof, while the detective looked distracted, as if running through the plan one last time.

'It's awfully quiet, isn't it? You know, considering there's so many people in the church,' Lyn pointed to the vestry's connecting door to the chancel.

No one answered her comment. Instead, Peter looked at his wristwatch again. 'Right, time to take up our positions.'

Ant quietly opened the inner door, through which he and the detective disappeared into the space beyond. Fitch walked the opposite way and left via the external vestry door to take up his position in the vicarage. Lyn was now alone in the small space. She meandered around the small space. Now and then, she'd choose a book from a standing bookcase, flip a few pages, then return the dusty book back to its neglected resting place.

She caught sight of a black and white framed photograph on the far wall. It showed the Reverend Morton on the day of his accession to the priesthood.

He looks so happy, thought Lyn.

Her attention moved to the outside door as she heard

the latch being lifted, followed by the appearance of the Alison King carrying a leather Gladstone bag.

'Oh, Alison. I hope you didn't get too wet?'

'Not one bit. God is on our side this evening.'

Lyn gave the photograph one last look before she covered the few paces it took to reach Alison and help take off her heavy raincoat. 'Well, I can't argue with that. It's been a horrible week for everyone, hasn't it?'

Alison hardly drew breath before she opened the leather bag to retrieve her cassock and stole. In seconds she'd slipped the ecclesiastical robe over her head and allowed it to fall free, so that the hemline rested just above her ankles. Next, she placed the richly decorated stole over her head, making sure it sat neatly in place.

'I know the cassock we wear for day-to-day services is black, but I thought I'd wear the white version as a symbol of the light God shines on his flock. What do you think?'

'What a lovely touch, Alison. Oh, and by the way, thank you for stepping in at the last minute. I thought we had it sorted, but it turned out our reserve had double booked himself.'

Alison smiled. 'Not at all. It's my privilege to give something back to the community, even if they don't know I'm here, so to speak.'

Lyn had to think about Alison's remark until she connected it with the refuge the vicar ran in almost total secrecy.

'Well, all the same, thank you, but have you had enough time to prepare? You'll have hundreds of eyes on you in a few minutes. Doesn't that intimidate you?'

Alison smoothed down her cassock and checked again to make sure her stole rested just so. 'You're a teacher, so you know people like us step up to the challenge. Anyway, my sermon almost wrote itself. You know, considering what's happened. Anyway, I thought I'd concentrate on two themes: forgiveness and hope.'

Lyn felt uncomfortable. 'What, you mean to forgive the person who killed Ian?'

'Don't misunderstand me. Whoever did that dreadful thing must account for the act according to law, but if they truly repent, God will surely embrace them. As for your dear vicar, hope must remain in each of our hearts that he's found safe and well.'

Lyn's eyes glistened.

'Please don't upset yourself. We all live encompassed by God's love. We must take heart from that. Come here, time for another hug before we go in.'

Lyn responded in kind to Alison's act of kindness. 'It's just me being silly. You're right, we must look for the best in people and trust all will be well.'

For the next few seconds, the two women embraced, until the soothing sound of the church organ announced the start of the service.

'Much as I'd love to spend more time with you, our audience awaits. Are you staying for the service?'

'I'll stay here for a minute or two, then I'll join the congregation,' replied Lyn as Alison opened the inner door and began her sedate progress to the transept.

Within a minute, Alison was in position and began her welcome to the packed church. Lyn took her pre-arranged position sitting on a hard-backed chair next to the altar, tucked just out of view from most of the congregation.

Soon, Alison concluded her opening words and turned towards the pulpit. Despite her long robes, she navigated the wooden steps, elevating herself above the seated crowd. She opened her arms wide and showed her open palms to the heaving gathering. 'Welcome to God's house. We come together this evening for two different reasons. Neither brings joy, yet I ask you to open your hearts to the Lord, for He hears and sees all.'

Many bowed their heads as if in prayer. Others nodded in agreement. After a pause to allow her words to sink in, Alison continued. 'This evening we mourn the tragic death of Ian Jefferson, and trust that they bring the perpetrator to justice.'

She turned her attention to the detective who sat in a front row pew. 'We are fortunate indeed to have Detective Inspector Riley and his officers to keep our community safe. I know from experience, and many of you can, I'm sure, testify that their commitment comes at considerable risk to their own safety.'

Several calls of "Hear-hear" came from the congregation.

'And so, we give thanks for Ian's life and his devoted service to the church. Let us pray,' continued the vicar.

Lyn, Ant, and Riley synchronised their actions. They checked their wristwatches and nodded at each other to show that everything was going according to plan.

As the prayers ended, Alison King again held her arms wide open as if gathering her flock. 'At this difficult time, I want to talk to you about forgiveness. By that, I mean finding that special place in our hearts that allows us to forgive those for wrongs inflicted. Doing so sets us free instead of being trapped in a vicious cycle of negative thoughts. We can then grow in God's love by seeing the better side of others.'

The congregation listened intently as Alison continued with her homily. As the minutes passed, Peter Riley prepared to make his move.

No going back now, thought Lyn.

She watched the detective get to his feet and make his way to the low communion rail that separated the nave from the chancel. As he did so, a quiet murmur spread around the church as the congregation fixed their attention on the tall, slim figure of Detective Inspector Peter Riley.

Alison stopped mid-sentence as she looked down on the unfolding events.

Riley grasped the initiative. 'Forgive me Reverend King. I know this situation looks odd, but with your permission, I'd like to address the congregation.'

The vicar's confused expression convinced the congregation that this was an unplanned intervention. She extended a hand to signal her agreement.

'In the minute it took the congregation to quieten, Riley gathered his thoughts. At last, a stillness fell over the church.

'On Wednesday of this week, our vicar vanished. Despite the efforts of many, that remains the case.'

He turned towards the vicar, still high in the pulpit. 'And thank you, Reverend King, for leading us in our prayers this evening.'

Alison King responded with a dignified nod.

'However, the statement that I have just made is, in fact, untrue.'

The villagers erupted into a babble of voices as one turned to another to elicit their thoughts on the matter.

Alison looked confused, but then gathered her thoughts to proclaim, 'Praise the Lord for delivering your dear vicar back into his fold.'

After acknowledging the priest's words, Riley continued, 'I should explain. We found Reverend Morton today and took him to the hospital, where he remains in a critical condition.'

'How poorly is he? Is he going to be alright?' shouted a man from among the throng of villagers, eager for more information.

Riley raised his arms to quieten the eager crowd. 'He's doing as well as expected after his ordeal. Whether he recovers, well, that's another matter. Physically, yes. Mentally, that's more difficult to say. He will try his hardest to practise what he preaches. To forgive whoever hurt him. If he can do that, all will be fine.'

Riley's response settled the congregation down, except for a woman who demanded to know what had happened to their vicar.

'That's a brief question about a complicated situation, but to explain how events unfolded, we have to go back several weeks. To do that, let me invite a woman who everyone knows and respects. Please, Miss Blackthorn, will you join me?'

As he turned towards the altar, Lyn was already half-way down the chancel and spoke before she reached the communion rail.

'Anthony Stanton and I realised something untoward when we visited the vicar for a meeting on Wednesday morning. We called the inspector right away. They discovered incriminating evidence against certain individuals who betrayed our vicar.'

As the congregation erupted, Lyn found it hard to make herself heard, 'What I mean to say is that his ordeal emanated from three people known to you all.'

Heads turned to right and left as the villagers tried to make sense of their trusted headteacher's sensational accusation.

Lyn waited for the tumult to subside. All eyes now rested on her.

'In the end, it all comes down to greed. What I mean is, the length some people will go to as they seek financial gain, no matter the effects or consequences on others.'

'Then you've identified the culprits?' enquired Alison.

'That's a matter for the police to comment on,' replied Lyn as she turned to face the vicar. 'However, one thing I can say is that sometimes the thing that seems furthest away is, in fact, right under your feet.'

'I don't understand?' said Alison.

Lyn pointed to the pulpit. 'I wonder if I might ask you to step down for a few minutes. I've something novel to show everyone.'

Once again, a murmur rippled through the congregation, and those who couldn't see what was going on strained for a better view.

Alison frowned but agreed to the request. Standing on one side of the wooden structure gave Lyn all the space she needed to begin her demonstration. The church fell into muted anticipation of what was to happen next. Moving closer to the pulpit, Lyn crouched to rest on one knee as she felt for a button under the second tread lip. A muted click sounded as the staircase lifted.

Alison let out a gasp as a small, dark space revealed itself as the stairway completed its journey. Only those parishioners sitting to the far right of the left of the church could see what was happening. Others made their feelings clear.

'What's happening?' demanded one. 'What's going on?' insisted another.

Lyn knew she had to get a grip on things before the situation got out of hand. 'This is where we found Reverend Morton.'

And that's how Ian Jefferson disappeared within seconds

of leaving the vestry the other day. He *went to check on the vicar*, thought Lyn.

A man who had a clear view of events stood. 'They've found the secret passage. See, the rumours were true. My old dad was always saying when this place was part of the monastery, a passage led from the church to the pub. Now we know it's true.'

A small section of the congregation laughed, which soon spread. 'Your old fella was always spinning tales when we were kids. He liked his beer, didn't he?' said a rotund man sitting behind the speaker.

'Do you mean to tell me those monks were supping beer instead of making it?' said another man.

'No wonder King Henry did away with the monasteries, if that's what they were up to,' shouted a woman from the back of the church.

'Stop it. Cease this nonsense now and remember where you are.' Alison's tone made it clear she expected compliance. Her remarks hit the spot with the congregation falling silent in an instant. 'I do not apologise for my words, but I am sorry I shouted.' She paused before continuing. 'Let us remember the seriousness of the situation. We don't know yet whether your vicar will fully recover. So please, allow Lyn to continue.'

That's told them, thought Lyn as she prepared for her next move.

'Whether the passage leads anywhere we do not know, and frankly, it's of no relevance.'

Alison nodded.

For a split second, Lyn panicked. What if we've got this wrong, and the passage leads to the Wherry Arms? Anyone could have put the vicar down there?

She knew she had to get a grip. Everyone, including

Peter Riley, was waiting, but she'd frozen. Lyn could hear her words, but nothing came out. The room spun. I can't faint ... I can't.

As Lyn felt her knees beginning to give way, a gentle but determined hand supported her. She attempted to turn her head, but that made matters worse, except she knew something stopped her from falling. A voice comforted her. Was she imagining it?

'You're OK. I've got you,' a whispered voice said. 'You'll be alright, they don't know anything's wrong. Just lean into me.'

As her head cleared, she recognised the voice.

'Don't talk,' he whispered, 'I'll take over. You'll be as right as rain in a few seconds.'

'I want each of you,' began Ant, 'to imagine being in that dark and damp space. Not just for a minute, or an hour, but for days, without knowing if you would ever escape. Imagine the terror of hearing people a few feet above you and being unable to make contact. As one day turns into two, then three, you think, that's it. But even worse, knowing a person you had implicit trust in put you in that horrible place. How would that make you feel?'

At first the congregation remained silent, then a man shouted, 'I'd try my best to get out, then make myself heard ... then set about whoever put me down there.'

A brief round of applause and man shouting, 'You tell 'em, Geoff' encouraged the man to continue, until the woman sat next to him pulled the man into his seat.

Ant pointed at the man to draw attention to his comment. 'And that's what the vicar tried to do. He made himself heard at least twice. The first time to be dismissed as the mental terror of a man struggling with the loss of his wife. On the second occasion, to be confused with the noise of water falling from the beams above us.'

Ant looked over his shoulder to see Fitch giving a thumb's up sign. 'And who is the man who we dismissed as unwell, when he was telling the truth all along? Let me introduce you to Mr Greenacre.'

The man entered the chancel, a lonely figure. His haunted demeanour made him appear much older than he was. The man made his way to a seat by the communion rail facing at right angles to the pulpit.

A woman sitting next to inspector Riley spoke up. 'How are you doing? Are they looking after you?'

Greenacre didn't respond. Instead, he kept his gaze straight ahead.

As the scene unfolded, Lyn, now recovered from her earlier wobble, made her way back to the vestry door to check all was in place. 'And here's someone else well known to you all.' Lyn held out a hand of encouragement, and from the vestry stepped Cynthia Hake.

The woman, looking nervous, hurried to a chair next to Greenacre. Neither exchanged glances.

Lyn rejoined Ant before addressing the congregation again. 'Cynthia is a woman who the police almost arrested for the abduction of our vicar, and murder of Ian Jefferson.'

Before Lyn could continue, the congregation erupted, with people shouting and pointing at Cynthia. The temperature reached such a level that a worried-looking Riley got to his feet to consult with Ant and Lyn. After a brief conversation, they continued, rather than abandon the plan.

Alison King, who had returned to the pulpit, stepped in to calm the crowd. 'Please, please everyone. This is not the way to behave in a place of worship. I ask you to sit and listen to what is being said. I also want you all to consider how much of an ordeal this must be for Cynthia.'

Her words did the trick, allowing Peter Riley to take up the story from a police perspective. 'Cynthia emerges as a woman manipulated by others, and here I must speak ill of the dead. The person who cruelly used Cynthia was Ian Jefferson—and before you all shout again, I'll hand over to Ms Blackthorn to explain.'

'We know Cynthia has been the source of gossip for some time. This is a small village, and rumours, which some of you excel at spreading, can cause a lot of distress. In this case, that Cynthia became infatuated with the Reverend Morton. Even worse, she'd been seen arguing with the vicar the day before he vanished.'

'Then she tried to kill him?' shouted an indignant parishioner.

'He told me he loved me,' shouted Cynthia, as she stood to face a hostile congregation.

'There, I told you. A crime of passion. That's what it was,' said the man who'd spoken earlier.

'No, no. You don't understand. He tricked me,' pleaded Cynthia as she collapsed back into her chair in a flood of tears.

A young woman took over the role of an unofficial spokesperson for the crowd. 'That's not the vicar we know. You must be telling lies?'

Lyn stepped forward to shout over the unsettled crowd, 'She not talking about the vicar. She means Ian Jefferson.'

The noise abated within seconds.

'We now know Ian used his influence over Cynthia to persuade her to write several affectionate letters to our vicar. And to be seen shouting at him in public. She didn't help herself by telling me she was at home watching her favourite soap. In fact, a quick check with the TV listings confirmed the programme aired on Monday, not Tuesday evening. Add to that the perfumed letters … the same perfume Cynthia uses, almost led to her arrest, especially after she said her father had bought it for her. We soon discovered that not to be the case through a discarded receipt.'

'Then she's banged-to-rights for Ian's death, yes?' asked a man with a muted voice near the front row of pews.

'I've taken some convincing that is not the case,' responded Peter Riley. 'My duty as a police officer is to follow the evidence, without fear or favour. Here, Cynthia Hake appeared to have reason to hate the vicar, yet this was an act. In fact, the focus of her attention was Ian Jefferson. But why kill him? And that still doesn't explain the vicar's disappearance.'

'Then how did you break the case?' asked Alison King, still high in the pulpit.

'An abandoned church; a bottle-top, and a man whose job it is to record the donation envelopes parishioners give at church services.'

'I don't understand?' said Alison.

'No, neither did we at first,' replied Riley. We know Cynthia and Ian both attended the service at St Peter's on the Water recently. The donation envelopes confirm it. As you know, each one has a number printed on it, and that number corresponds to its owner. It was easy enough to match the number to the person.'

'I get it,' shouted a parishioner. 'Cynthia showed Ian the scent she'd bought to put on the letters?'

'The other way around, sir,' replied Riley. 'Ian attempted to hand over the bottle he'd bought for Cynthia to use. In the confusion of falling debris from the abandoned church roof, he dropped it as those attending gathered around the altar. He couldn't retrieve it, and so there it remained, trampled underfoot and broken.'

'That meant Ian had to buy another bottle,' interjected Lyn. 'And that is the bottle found by the police when they searched Cynthia's house. Ian knew she wouldn't throw an expensive bottle of perfume away once she'd used it on the letters. He knew it meant the trail for the vicar vanishing would lead straight to Cynthia's door. And it nearly worked, because that's how I came to smell the aroma on her when I visited Cynthia earlier this week and matched it to the envelopes.'

In an unexpected development, she turned to Cynthia. 'Did you kill Ian?'

The woman turned pale as the entire congregation looked at her with angry eyes. Riley didn't help her predicament, giving the signal for a constable to secure the exit. He then walked at a brisk pace along the chancel, ignoring Cynthia, then vanished into the vestry. After a few seconds, he re-emerged to give a single nod to Lyn and Ant.

Cynthia sprang to her feet. 'So you've been using me all along like everyone else,' she screamed at Lyn. 'I know I told lies. He made me. You believe me, don't you?'

Chapter Nineteen

THE RECKONING

THE CHURCH DOOR opened on its ancient wrought iron hinges. Heads turned to see who dared interrupt the intense drama unfolding in front of them.

After a brief pause, the constable stationed nearby to stop anyone from leaving stepped outside to check who was there. Seconds later, he returned to shrug his shoulders at his superior. He pulled the heavy door closed and made sure the latch sat in place before resuming his station.

Before Lyn could continue interrogating Cynthia, the door opened once again. This time, a rumour spread like wildfire that a criminal gang was intent on helping whoever abducted the vicar and killed Ian to escape.

'What's going on, Constable?' shouted Riley. The abruptness of his tone ensured the young police officer dashed outside in double-quick time.

When he returned, he wasn't alone. Standing on either side of the tall bobby were two boys.

Lyn recognised them straight away. 'Robert Ploughman; Timothy Laidlaw. What are you two up to?'

The boys looked at their old headteacher with sheepish eyes. 'Nothing, miss, said Timothy.'

'Don't give me that. You're old enough now to know right from wrong, so out with it, why are you playing knock and run with the church door?'

The young constable encouraged the two to speak by clearing his throat. The action was enough to encourage the boys to speak.

'Someone told us they saw you crying in your car outside the church. After you found us at that old place, and paid our bus fare home, we wanted to pay you back. We heard there was a big meeting here tonight, so we thought we'd come and check on you.'

Lyn wasn't sure how to answer Robert without adding to her embarrassment. She knew everyone was looking at her.

Wouldn't they all like to know? she thought.

'I see,' began Lyn. 'That's very sweet of you, but the thing is, boys, it isn't the sort of meeting children should attend, and we've so much to get through. Do you think you might get yourselves home before your parents miss you?'

Both boys beamed. 'Can we ride in a police car? We've always wanted to do that, haven't we, Timmy?'

The other boy nodded and wore an eager grin.

Lyn shifted her attention to Riley, who she could tell was trying hard not to smile.

'Well boys, you should be careful what you wish for, but alright. Just this once.' The detective glanced at his constable. He ushered the boys outside to arrange a car, before re-entering and closing the creaking door behind him.

If nothing else, the brief interruption broke the tension that had been building for the last hour. It also gave Cynthia Hake time to compose herself after her fraught outburst.

Lyn knew she hadn't replied to Cynthia's plea before the interruption and held her counsel for the time being.

Riley, however, was keen to get back to business. 'The police are used to being lied to. In fact, we expect it. We take nothing at face value, whether it be a witness statement or physical evidence. Our motto is to check and check again. It's the hard grind of cross-checking statements. Also, the movements and background relating to persons of interest, and finding long-lost records. You get the idea, I'm sure.'

'Then are the two crimes linked to the same person?' asked someone from the back of the church.

'They are. In fact, each linked to Cynthia Hake and Ian Jefferson. Were they in it together? No, they are guilty in one respect, and that is the persecution of your vicar. And yet this is a case of everyone involved being used, except the mastermind behind it all.'

The congregation fidgeted, unsure what to make of the detective's analysis.

'Talk sense, will you, Inspector?' shouted a man.

'I'm sorry. Let me try that again. Think of it as a pyramid of misplaced affection. Cynthia thought Ian Jefferson loved her, and she was prepared to do anything to prove her love for him. He exploited Cynthia's loyalty to deceive the vicar into aiding fraud. Of course, Cynthia did not know this. In turn, Ian acted to prove his love and devotion to—'

'So, is she guilty or not?' interrupted Alison.

'That will be for a court to decide, but given the circumstances, I doubt any jury would convict.'

Ant stepped forward. 'And that leaves us with Ian Jefferson However, he's not here to defend himself. It would be easy enough for the police to claim they've solved the crime to help their "clean up" statistics. But you see, Peter Riley is not one of those detectives who takes the easy win. He knew something didn't add up.'

'You're right there, he's dead,' shouted a parishioner.

'But was it intentional?' said Ant.

The congregation was stunned by the thought the well-liked villager might have taken his own life.

'Perhaps I should direct that question at Alison?' asked Ant.

The familiar sound of collective murmuring filled the air as Alison gave a reassuring glance to the congregation.

'That's an interesting question and thank you for asking my opinion. I hardly knew Mr Jefferson, so I can only make a generalised comment. I'm not sure if he had any under-lying issues, but it's true that intense stress can make people feel hopeless. This can make them look for a way out that, under normal circumstances, wouldn't cross their mind.'

The congregation looked thoughtful as they considered Alison's words.

'And would you say at such times, a person might look for help from the one they think is most close to them?'

Alison nodded; her expression wide open. 'Yes, Anthony. Are there not moments when we all require help?'

Lyn listened to the exchange. She knows about his PTSD.

'Then wouldn't it be natural for Ian to have contacted you?'

Alison remained unruffled by the line of questioning. 'It's not in my nature to tell fibs, Anthony, so yes, as a pastor, I gave him all the help I could in the absence of his own vicar.'

'But you didn't see fit to tell the police about your contact?'

'Anthony, you know only too well that what passes between a priest and a member of their flock is bound to secrecy and known only to God. I dare say that your own vicar has counselled many of his flock. Who knows, perhaps even you. Are you suggesting he should share such conversations with organs of the state?'

Ant smiled. 'That's an interesting way of describing the police.'

'It is the case,' responded Alison.

'Then you are unlikely to admit that you injected Ian Jefferson with an overdose of drugs?'

The church fell into anarchy as the ramifications of Ant's question sank in. Fear crossed Alison King's face as she watched the anger of a baying crowd fall on her.

It took an instruction from Riley for a constable to blow his whistle to bring order where chaos ruled. After several shrill blasts, the congregation settled.

Inspector Riley moved a step nearer to the pulpit. 'Let me explain the background to what Anthony is getting at. After you came to my office to support Cynthia, you aroused my curiosity. Your attending seemed plausible, yet you were so new to the village that I wasn't aware of your arrival—especially given the apparent nature of your work.'

'I've been open with Lyn. She knows what my calling is and why I devote my life to it.'

Riley shrugged his shoulders. 'That's fine, if true. But it isn't, is it, Reverend King… or should I call you by your real name? Karen Stokes? I know the church unfrocked you seven years ago for committing fraud. Isn't that so?'

'That's not the case.'

'The archbishop says it is, and I know who I believe. Anyway, let's stick to Alison King for now, because you've been up to much nastier things than changing your name.'

In an extraordinary move, Alison clasped her hands together and turned to the congregation. 'Let us pray for the Inspector. That he sees the injustice of his words, and so we may ask God to bless him.'

Several parishioners moved to a kneeling position. The vast majority sat ramrod straight in their seats while looking at Peter Riley.

'Novel, I'll give you that, err, Alison. However, it won't wash. I know too much about you. Like the fact that you'd worked in a London drug rehabilitation unit to administer controlled drugs to the patients. Except you didn't have the correct qualifications. When you thought they were onto you, you scarpered. Isn't that correct?'

'Have you ever seen someone in the throes of withdrawal?'

'Many times, Ms. King. You forget what I do for a living. Was it seeing your brother die from an overdose that drove you on to help others?'

'Is that such a terrible thing?'

'Not at all, Ms King. Unless you turn the caring aspect on its head and use your skills to kill.'

Alison shook her head and looked towards the congregation. 'This is all stuff and nonsense. You're blaming me for a terrible act in the absence of actual evidence. And you have no right to bring my brother's death into this, especially in this Holy Place.'

A portion of the congregation appeared sympathetic to her plea. Others looked down to avoid making eye contact with the pastor.

'Oh, but Ian's death is only a consequence of your actual intentions. I've uncovered the way you work, Ms King. You move into a new area in the guise of a pastor, having already checked out the opportunities for land fraud.

Next, you find yourself a willing male accomplice, who, having fallen under your spell, will do anything you ask. In Ian's case, it involved tracing a land transfer deed for the place you purloined by spinning a yarn about it being a shelter for mothers and small children. Ingenious, if I say so myself. Who would challenge such a situation... except for the true owners of the property?'

Lyn couldn't contain herself. 'When I visited, you said the house was empty because you were only just setting up. I heard a noise from upstairs, which you dismissed.' Alison turned to Cynthia. 'Who was that, I wonder?'

The woman stood, restrained anger distorting every muscle of her facial features. 'It was me. She told me to hide upstairs when she saw you walking up the drive.'

'That's not true,' said Alison in a calm, controlled tone.

'As you keep reminding us, remember where you are,' replied Lyn in an equally controlled tone. 'Go on, Cynthia.'

'It's true, I went to see her because of a half-burnt note I found in Ian's fire-grate.'

'And what did it say?' asked Lyn.

'There wasn't much left, but enough for me to think they were having an affair. How could that be if he loved me? I went to confront her, but she's so clever and convinced me I was imagining things.'

Alison stepped down from the pulpit and confronted Cynthia. 'So you admit you were jealous? Is that why you murdered Ian? Tell the truth. You killed him, didn't you?'

Lyn gave Riley an anxious look. The evening wasn't supposed to go like this.

Cynthia was in bits as Alison's relentless accusations continued.

'Enough,' shouted Riley. 'It's over. You should know we executed a search warrant on Radley House this morning.

Within minutes of you leaving, my officers began a forensic search of the property.'

'Don't be ridiculous,' replied Alison, her tone still flat and without emotion.

Riley shook his head. 'Stop this charade now. What you don't know is that we found the remains of a needle under the sofa on which Ian died. Oh, you made a good job of clearing everything away. But this time, you missed one tiny piece of evidence. We knew Ian couldn't have administered the substance himself. The position of the puncture mark made that impossible. For a time we thought the Reverend Morton might have injected him out of kindness, because he knew Ian had a serious drug habit. We didn't think he'd have killed on purpose, but calculated the dose incorrectly, then panicked. Of course, the timing of events made that impossible.'

'So why blame me?' retorted Alison.

'Because we found this.' Riley retrieved a clear plastic evidence bag from his inside pocket. 'This needle has a unique design and hasn't been used for several decades.'

Alison remained unruffled. 'Not alone, Inspector. Cynthia has admitted visiting me and hiding upstairs when Lyn visited. She omitted to say it was her idea to sprint upstairs out of concern that Lyn might see her.'

Cynthia made a move to stand again before Lyn gestured for her to remain seated.

'Now you've lost me,' said Riley.

'Simple, Inspector. I did not know those needles existed. Cynthia obviously discovered a syringe and used it to inject Ian for betraying her.'

'Admit it, Alison,' countered Riley. Getting someone else to inject Ian would have allowed you to escape a murder charge.'

The pastor shook her head. 'You have no proof. It's a fantasy of your own making.'

Riley felt in his jacket pocket and brought out a second evidence bag. Inside was a small rectangular object with a chrome tip at one end.

Alison reacted by unconsciously patting her right hip.

'It's not there, Alison. I suppose you think you assumed no one would look for a memory stick, because you didn't use computers. At least that's what you told Lyn when she visited you, wasn't it?'

For the first time, Alison struggled to come up with a credible response.

Riley turned to the congregation, holding the evidence bag. 'This memory stick contains all the information she gathered about Radley House. By that I mean its history of ownership. We owe a debt of gratitude to Anthony and his father for working through the night to find the documents we knew existed. The same documents Alison King thought were in the church document chest and made Ian force the vicar to open it, except they weren't there. Unbeknown to anyone at that point, they rested in the substantial family archive of the Stanton family. Anthony's only issue was that the family failed to make a proper record of the archive. This meant he and Lord Stanton had to check hundreds of old documents by hand.'

'And why would I want a pile of old documents?' asked Alison.

'Because you sought to register a change of ownership. You knew the original owners had gifted the property and land to a charity. What you didn't realise was the Stanton family made the gift. Which was fortunate for them, given the lengths you've gone to locate those deeds.'

'This is a fantasy. Nothing more,' replied Alison, her voice now not so self-assured.

'Is it?' said Riley in a terse tone. 'I bet you couldn't believe your luck when you discovered Ian had a terrible substance addiction. You gained his trust by facilitating his habit. Because of that, he convinced himself you loved him.'

Cynthia could contain herself no more. Rushing over to Alison, only to be restrained by the detective, she spat out her feeling towards Alison. 'How could you do that to Ian? How could you do that to anything living? You're mad, that's what you are.'

Alison's confidence returned. 'I have used no one. I'm not responsible for what's inside your head. You should be the one apologising for your sins. Don't forget, you were the one who mistreated the vicar for personal gain, not me. In fact, I've never met your vicar.'

Riley was quick to jump in. 'I'm afraid I told a second untruth this evening when I said the vicar remained in hospital.'

'As I say, I've never met the vicar, or Ian Jefferson. Let's see, shall we?'

Riley turned towards the vestry. 'Fitch, it's appropriate you join us.'

Right on cue, Fitch exited the vestry, pushing a wheelchair in which sat the Reverend Morton. As the vicar came into view, the congregation erupted into a chorus of applause. Everyone got to their feet, as if welcoming home a long-lost hero.

As Fitch reached the communion rail, the frail-looking pastor began to speak. The congregation hushed so they could hear what he had to say.

Fitch turned the wheelchair so that the vicar looked

Alison in the eye. 'I have listened to every word spoken in this Holy Place this evening. I ask in all humility, how could a woman who serves the church have fallen so low?'

Alison fidgeted with her cassock and avoided eye contact with the seated vicar.

'You know full well you first contacted Ian and me three months ago to introduce yourself, and to outline the work you were doing with mothers and their children. On reflection, I thought it strange that the bishop had said nothing before you contacting me. I assumed, wrongly, that it was because of the delicate work you undertook.'

Alison's face contorted into a rage. 'I did no harm to you.'

The vicar, struggling to gather strength to continue, hit back. 'But you corrupted Ian. A man you knew full well to be vulnerable. Your sinful plan meant he believed you loved him, and to reciprocate, he went along with your evilness by pretending he had feelings for Cynthia. He even attempted force to make me unlock the church's document chest. That poor man caused me an injury out of character with the gentle soul he possessed. Can you imagine the torment he must have gone through forcing me into that dark place? Do you not understand the harm you've done?'

The fragile vicar turned to Cynthia and tried to hold out a bandaged hand, but failed. In return, Cynthia gave him a smile of thanks and reassurance.

Fitch turned the wheelchair back to face Alison. 'However, I forgive you, provided you repent.' He waited for a sign of remorse from the woman.

Before she could respond, Riley stepped in. 'Alas, the law does not take such a benevolent view of heinous crimes.'

Alison gave a broad smile before it morphed into twisted

rage. 'That woman is stupid. I just put the idea into the man's head and off he trotted like an obedient lapdog. How could she have fallen for such a stupid idea, and then wear the scent? She did what he told her to. And no, I didn't kill that man.'

Ant stepped forward. 'Ah, yes. The scent. That would be the bottle you bought from "Maribelle's of Norwich" for Ian to give to Cynthia?'

'What are you talking about? I did no such thing.'

'No? Do you remember writing your mobile number down for Lyn when she visited you?'

Deep furrows appeared on Alison's forehead as she digested Ant's question. 'Yes, of course. Why do you ask?'

Ant smiled. 'Well, for all your meticulous planning, you made a mistake. You see, the scrap of paper Lyn tells me you took from your handbag was, in fact, a sales receipt for a bottle of Amore Amore. As you might expect, the receipt has the exact date, day, and time of issue, so it'll be easy to check the store's CCTV.'

'Preposterous,' spat Alison.

'Perhaps. Anyway, let's move on. It's interesting you've stopped calling Ian by his name. Is that because he meant nothing to you? You detest substance abusers, don't you?'

Alison exploded. 'No one helped my brother. Not the doctors, and especially not the church.' she gave a throaty laugh as she scanned the ancient building and its astonished visitors. 'Especially the church. They abandoned him when he needed them the most. I swore to get my revenge.'

'Ah,' replied Ant. 'That would be in London, you know, the place you told us you'd never visited. Believe me when I say I'm sorry for what happened to your brother, but that's no excuse for killing an innocent and vulnerable man. That can't bring your sibling back.'

Alison fell quiet, as if the true gravity of what she'd done had, at last, dawned on her.

'You saw the opportunity to transfer the ownership of Radley House to yourself - and we have proof that you searched the land records. You specialise in what might be called "hands-off" fraud by manipulating others to do the dirty work, ensuring that nothing leads back to you. This time you found Ian Jefferson, who, on your instructions, recruited Cynthia Hake. Your sophisticated plan went as expected until Cynthia thought he was cheating on her with you. That's when you decided they both had to go. Ian was easy. He had a problem you could feed, literally. As for Cynthia? Well, you did everything in your power to convince her she had killed the man she thought loved her. Well, it's over.'

Alison smirked as she turned to the Reverend Morton. 'I told him to finish you. I warned him if they found you, he'd cop for everything, but the stupid man didn't have the guts to do it.'

She turned to Cynthia. 'And you. If you had kept your mouth shut, both of us would have been OK by blaming it all on a dead man. You deserved one another.'

This time, Cynthia remained in control of her emotions. 'I'm not scared of you anymore. I know what I did and I'll have to live with that. Can you live with what you've done?'

Riley looked over at the constable guarding the entrance door. 'Read this woman her rights, and remember to use her real name, Karen Stokes. Now take her away.'

Epilogue

A WEEK HAD PASSED since the arrest of Alison King. To mark the successful conclusion to the case. Ant and Lyn hosted their three close friends to a restorative cruise on Stanton Broad.

'Fixing up Field Surfer was your dad's best decision,' Lyn said as she sat arm-in-arm with Ant mid-ship, keeping an eye out for any shift in the single large sail.

'He might have something to say about that, but yes, if he hadn't bought it, she'd have rotted away by now.' Ant's tone with his fiance was relaxed. They'd spent the week talking about their future and discussing the Stanton Estate with his parents, which had helped heal recent wounds.

'Oh, and by the way,' began Lyn. 'Who's been a busy boy this week? A little bird tells me you're setting Bootsy up with a clay pigeon business. Who's an old softy, then?'

He blushed. 'Alright, no need to tell the world about it. All I've done is offer the man an outbuilding we no longer use and put a bit of finance behind him.'

'Not to mention leasing him the right to a parcel of land to shoot birds.'

Ant gave Lyn a sideways look. 'Stop it. You know perfectly well it's got nothing to do with harming wildlife. The clue is in the word, "clay". Anyway, I'd rather he used his shooting skills to obliterate round bits of clay than pointing a shotgun at you or me again.'

'You know what?' said Lyn. 'I know why you didn't fight back at school when Bootsy bullied you. You felt sorry for him, and you still do, even though he lied to us about seeing the vicar arguing on Tuesday evening. I reckon he picked the gossip up and used it to cover his tracks about stealing lead from the old saddlery.'

'Don't talk daft, and as for him telling fibs, who knows? Anyway, you're one to blabber on. I saw you with dad and our land agent the other day. That little bird you mentioned also called on me. You know what? It said you'd had a right go at the agent for threatening to evict Clive Greenacre. Let me guess, Clive now has a life tenancy on his cottage?'

'That was your dad's idea, not mine.'

'If you say so,' replied Ant, as the two lovers exchanged a lingering look.

Elsewhere, Fitch and Sophie occupied the bow of the proud vessel, their feet dangling over the deck edge as they larked about like a couple of teenagers.

Peter Riley stood alone, tending the rudder to guide the silent progress of Field Surfer around a series of gentle bends in the broad. As the old boat entered a long, straight stretch of water, he tied the tiller off and called for everyone's attention.

'I wanted to say a few words about the case.'

His words brought back painful memories as warm

smiles faded and the boat took on an altogether more serious purpose.

'The police … that is, I couldn't have cracked the investigation without the help of you four. The woman is safely under lock and key. We must now let justice take its course.'

'See what he did there? Take its course, you know—'

'Yes, we get it, Ant. No need to over-egg it,' said Lyn, to lift the general mood.

'If you ask me, I've had enough of this amateur sleuth malarkey,' said Fitch. 'Give me a blocked carburettor or iffy timing belt anytime. That's what I say.'

Sophie moved so that she could wrap her arms around the mechanic. 'I do love you, my little oily rag.'

The detective smiled. 'Well, there goes my speech, but for one thing.' He turned to Ant. 'You almost gave me a heart attack when your alibi didn't check out. Lucky for you, the vicar backed up what you said about meeting him, and how abruptly he'd finished the discussion with you. My advice, although you shouldn't need reminding, is to always tell the truth. That way, you can't be compromised. Yes?'

'I suppose I deserved that,' replied Ant in a reflective tone.

'Enough, Peter,' chipped in Lyn. 'Here, have a beer and enjoy the scenery. You'll soon be back chasing villains … which, thinking about it, is what I suspect you'd rather be doing right now.'

'I couldn't possibly comment. Cheers,' replied Peter as he lifted his Fen Bodger Pale Ale.

Amidst a serene landscape of yellow oilseed flowers and a setting sun, a cheerful response resonated as Field Surfer glided elegantly along Stanton Broad.

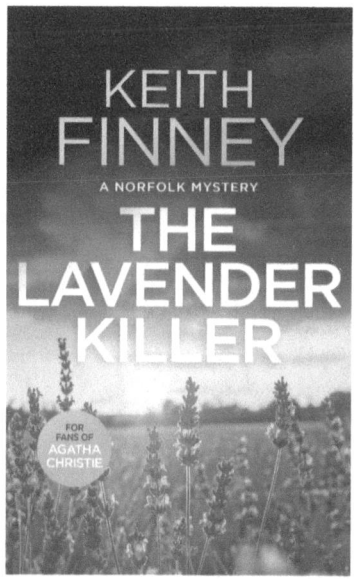

vinci-books.com/lavenderkiller

Beneath the beauty of the lavender fields lies a chilling murder waiting to be solved.

A body among the lavender fields reveals dark secrets in a tranquil Norfolk village. As Ant and Lyn investigate, they uncover betrayal and hidden motives in this suspenseful cozy mystery packed with twists and turns.

Turn the page for a free preview…

The Lavender Killer: Chapter One

A DISCOVERY

Ant Stanton and Lyn Blackthorn strolled through the sun-dappled lanes of Stanton Parva, arm in arm, as they made their way to the Wherry Inn. The village was a picture-perfect scene of English country life. Georgian red-brick houses stood proudly alongside thatched cottages and Victorian mews houses. The picturesque surroundings added to the excitement of celebrating Lyn's birthday at their favourite pub.

'Can you believe it? Another year older,' Lyn sighed, her eyes twinkling as she squeezed Ant's arm affectionately.

'Age is a number, don't you think?' Ant replied with a warm, playful smile, 'and besides, you're like a fine wine—only getting better with age.'

Lyn laughed; her cheeks flushed with a rosy hue. 'You can stop with the cliches.'

As they approached the Wherry Inn, the sounds of laughter and chatter spilled out onto the streets. A welcoming atmosphere enveloped the couple as they stepped inside and met by familiar faces who wished Lyn well on her special day.

'Happy birthday, Lyn,' called out the cheery Janice, polishing a pint glass behind the counter as others raised their drinks in unison.

'Thank you, everyone,' Lyn responded, beaming at the show of camaraderie. 'It's great to see you all.'

Ant led Lyn to a corner table, where he had secretly arranged for a bouquet of her favourite flowers to await her arrival. She gasped with delight, taking in the fragrant scent of roses and lilies. 'Oh, Ant! These are beautiful!'

'Only the best for you, love,' Ant replied, his dark eyes shining with adoration.

As they settled into their seats, the village came alive around them. Neighbours gossiped, friends shared stories, and laughter filled the air. An unmistakable sense of community wrapped itself around Ant and Lyn like a warm embrace. This was the Stanton Parva the couple loved.

'Here's to another wonderful year,' Ant said, raising his glass in toast. 'Happy birthday, Lyn.'

'Thank you, Ant,' she replied softly, her eyes glistening with emotion. 'I couldn't ask for a better way to celebrate.'

Ant glanced up from his drink, catching sight of the Wherry Inn's owner as he emerged from the kitchen. Jed, a stocky man with a salt-and-pepper beard, ran a tight ship while keeping his pub a welcoming place, making it the heart of the village.

'Evening, Ant, Lyn,' Jed greeted them gruffly, but not without a hint of a smile. 'Happy birthday, young lady. How is the school treating you?'

'Thank you, Jed,' Lyn replied warmly, sipping her lemonade. 'The school's been wonderful. The children are really responding to the new curriculum.'

'Ah, that's grand.' Jed nodded approvingly. 'Education is important. Don't you forget that.' He gave her a wink before turning his attention to Ant. 'And what about you, lad? Is that Morgan of yours holding up?'

'Still leaking water, as always,' Ant confessed with a chuckle. 'But it wouldn't be the same without its quirks, would it?'

'True enough,' Jed agreed, clapping Ant on the shoulder before excusing himself to serve other customers.

As they resumed their conversation, a diminutive, black-clad figure approached their table. Her hat perched precariously atop her silver hair. It was Phyllis, the village gossip, who could never resist the opportunity to spread her own unique brand of news.

'Ant! Lyn!' she exclaimed, her voice a blend of delight and conspiratorial intrigue. 'I simply must tell you the latest. You won't believe what happened to poor Mrs. Green at the post office!'

'Hello, Phyllis,' Lyn greeted politely, exchanging a knowing glance with Ant. 'What news do you have for us?'

She looked around as if scanning for spies, then leaned into Lyn, grunting as she did so and holding a hand to her left. 'I'm a martyr to my hip. I am. Isn't that right, Betty?'

Her best friend, who towered over her vocal companion, began to formulate a response. She knew Phyllis had no intention of listening, so gave up.

'Well,' began Phyllis, lowering her voice to a dramatic whisper. 'Mrs. Green went to collect her pension, as she does every week. But this time, there was a mix-up. They accused her of trying to claim someone else's money.' She paused for effect, eyes wide with theatrical horror.

'Goodness!' Lyn feigned surprise, playing along. 'What happened next?'

'Apparently,' Phyllis continued, relishing the attention, 'It turns out Mrs. Green had picked up Mr. Thompson's glasses by mistake. They look so similar, you see. So, she couldn't read the forms properly! The whole thing got resolved in moments, but not before Mr. Thompson had threatened to call the police!'

'Ah, well, misunderstandings happen,' Ant chimed in, hoping to defuse the situation. 'I'm sure everyone involved got a laugh out of it afterward.'

'Perhaps,' Phyllis conceded, although her expression suggested she would've preferred a more scandalous outcome. 'Well, I must be off. More stories to uncover. You know how it is.' She gave them a conspiratorial wink and bustled away, leaving Ant and Lyn to share an amused eyeroll.

'Never a dull moment with her around,' Ant mused, taking another sip of his drink.

'Indeed,' Lyn agreed, smiling. 'But it wouldn't be Stanton Parva without a bit of excitement, would it?'

'Speaking of excitement,' said Betty, sidling up to Ant and Lyn with a warm smile. 'I understand you two have been busy solving another one of Stanton Parva's little mysteries.'

'Ah, Betty, ever the voice of reason in this village,' Ant chuckled. 'We do what we can, but let's not give Phyllis any more fuel for the fire.'

'True enough,' Betty agreed, her eyes twinkling mischievously. 'Though it would be nice to learn of some genuine news instead of her... tall tales.'

'Genuine news?' Lyn asked with a light laugh. 'Well, I suppose our upcoming wedding may count as that.'

'Indeed!' Betty grinned. 'I'm sure Phyllis will spin it into a thrilling tale of intrigue and romance. But seriously, I'm so happy for you both.'

'Thank you, Betty,' Lyn replied warmly.

At that moment, Fitch, Ant, and Lyn's best friend, burst through the door of the Wherry Inn, grease-stained overalls and all. 'Sorry I'm late!' he exclaimed. 'Had to finish fixing Old Man Jenkins' tractor. The man never learns that duct tape isn't a permanent solution.'

'Ah, Fitch, our resident mechanical genius. How goes the world of engines and oil?' Ant enquired, shaking his hand.

'Busy as ever,' Fitch said, grinning. 'You wouldn't believe the number of people who come in with their cars held together by hope and prayers. Speaking of which, Ant, when are you bringing your Morgan in for a tune-up? She's been sounding a bit off lately.'

'Has she?' Ant frowned, concern for his beloved vintage sports car evident in his expression. 'I hadn't noticed. I'll bring her in tomorrow.'

'See that you do,' Fitch advised, wagging a finger. 'You don't want her breaking down on you during your honeymoon, do you?'

'Definitely not,' Lyn agreed, shuddering at the thought.

'Alright, Fitch, that's enough car talk for one evening,' Sophie interjected, looping an arm around his waist, and planting a kiss on his cheek. 'Let's not bore everyone with our 'Little Oily Rag's' endless knowledge of engines.'

'Fair enough,' Fitch conceded, allowing himself to be led away by his girlfriend. 'But remember Ant, tomorrow!'

'Tomorrow, I promise,' Ant replied, raising his pint in a mock toast.

Lyn smiled as she watched their friends move off,

leaving her and Ant to enjoy the cozy atmosphere of the Wherry Inn.

Detective Inspector Peter Riley entered the Wherry Inn, causing everyone to stop talking. The locals fell quiet when they saw his short grey hair and serious expression, but Lyn didn't want to assume his visit was anything other than social. She noticed her heart skip a beat.

'Evening, everyone,' Peter said, waving to the room at large, before fixing his gaze on Lyn with a mischievous glint in his eye. 'Don't worry, folks. I'm not here on official business. Just came to arrest Lyn for the heinous crime of getting older.'

The tension in the room dissipated as quickly as it had formed, and laughter bubbled up around them. Ant chuckled, wrapping an arm around Lyn's waist. 'Well, she'd best behave then, hadn't she?'

'Indeed,' agreed Lyn, smiling up at Peter as he approached the pair. 'Though it's rather generous of you to let me off the hook just this once.'

'Ah, well, I suppose I can make an exception for today,' Peter conceded, taking a seat at their table. 'But only because it's your birthday.'

Lyn was fascinated by the way the candlelight played on the tables and stained-glass windows. It cast a warm, golden glow that enveloped the inhabitants of the Wherry Inn like a comforting embrace.

As she gazed around the pub, she looked at the faces of her neighbours, each one a testament to the powerful sense of community that pervaded their village. Old Mr. Higgins propped up the bar with his customary tankard of ale. Young Rosie, who'd just turned eighteen, perched herself on a stool beside her young man, sipping a glass of white wine.

'Alright,' Peter said, clapping his hands together. 'Now

that we've established that I'm not here to rain on your parade, what say we raise a toast? To Lyn. May your day be filled with laughter and good company.'

'Thank you, Peter,' Lyn replied, touched by his senti-ment. Raised glasses, and the sound of clinking glass filled the air as the gathered friends and neighbours celebrated the birthday girl.

'Cheers,' Ant whispered in her ear, squeezing her hand beneath the table. She returned the gesture, even though there was an undercurrent of tension in the air whenever Peter walked into a room. He was a police officer. Tonight was about friendship.

And as the evening wore on, laughter filled the pub. Music spilled out onto the cobblestone streets beyond. Lyn realised she wouldn't trade this moment for anything in the world.

Jed came out from behind the bar with a huge birthday buffet after the toasts to Lyn's birthday ended. The aroma of warm sausage rolls, cheese, and onion quiches, and a variety of sandwiches filled the air, mingling with the earthy scent of mudded field-boots.

'Jed, this looks fantastic!' Lyn exclaimed; her eyes were wide at the array of food that now adorned the long wooden table.

'Only the best for our birthday girl,' Jed replied gruffly, though his eyes twinkled with pride at her reaction.

Ant guided Lyn towards the buffet, where they both loaded their plates with the delicious offerings. He sneaked a few extra cocktail sausages onto Lyn's plate, knowing they were her favourite. While enjoying the sumptuous feast, Ant took a hearty swig of his beloved Fen-Bodger Ale, savouring the rich, malty flavour and smooth texture. Lyn, however, opted for lemonade, as she had a visit from the education department of the local authority scheduled for the following morning. She needed to be alert and at her best for their inspection of the village primary school.

'Have you tried these bread rolls yet?' Ant asked, picking one up and giving it a curious sniff. 'They've got something inside them, but I can't tell what it is.'

'Ooh, mystery rolls,' Lyn teased, playfully flicking a stray crumb at him. 'You'll have to try one and report back.'

Before Ant took a bite, Phyllis swooped in like a bird of prey, interrupting their light-hearted banter. 'My great-niece makes the most marvellous stuffed bread rolls,' she began, not waiting for an invitation to join their conversation. 'She once won a prize at the Norfolk Show Ground for her cheese and bacon filled ones. They were a tremendous hit!'

'Really, Phyllis?' Ant responded with feigned enthusiasm, secretly sharing an amused look with Lyn.

'Of course, I taught her everything she knows about baking,' Phyllis continued, puffing out her chest with pride. 'I've always had a knack for it, you see. I dare say these rolls here are nothing compared to hers.'

Lyn bit back a smile as she watched Phyllis attempt to monopolise the conversation, steering it firmly towards her own interests. She knew to count on the village gossip to provide some entertainment at any gathering. It seemed that Phyllis's love of attention would never wane, especially when she believed herself to be particularly close to Ant.

'Phyllis, your great-niece's rolls sound absolutely delightful,' Lyn interjected, trying to steer the conversation back to a more inclusive topic. 'But I must admit, Jed's bread rolls here are delicious as well. Don't you think?'

'Indeed,' Ant agreed, finally taking a bite of the mysterious roll. 'It appears we have sun-dried tomato and onions in this one. An interesting flavour combination.'

'Ah, sun-dried tomato and...did you say onions?' Betty exclaimed. 'I remember when Jed first introduced those rolls at the village fete last summer. Everyone was, er, curious about-.'

'Speaking of the village fete,' Phyllis interjected, cutting across Betty. 'Did I ever tell you about my award-winning marmalade? It's all about the oranges, you see. You simply must use the finest—'

'Phyllis,' Ant interrupted gently, 'We've all listened to the story of your marmalade more times than we can count. We should give someone else a chance to share an anecdote?'

Lyn smiled gratefully at Ant and agreed as they spent the next hour mingling with friends and sharing stories from their youth.

'It's almost nine-thirty and it'll be dark soon. We promised each other a quick stroll before turning in. Do you think they'd mind?' Lyn scanned the room anxiously.

'We'll soon find out.'

Before Lyn had caught her breath, Ant called for everyone's attention by tapping a fork on the side of his empty pint glass.

'Ladies, gentlemen...and Fitch. Your attention, please.'

What's he going to say? thought Lyn.

'Lyn has suggested she and I take a turn about the village to stretch her legs. Now, at her age, it's of the utmost importance to keep those muscles moving to stop 'em seizing up. So, without further ado, we shall take our leave of you, so that Lyn's new healthy life routine may commence.'

A friendly roar went up at Lyn's expense, who stared knowingly at her fiance.

'Thanks for nothing,' Lyn giggled as Ant held the pub

door open for her, stepping into the warm night air from the Wherry Inn. The setting sun seemed to rise and fall behind the higgledy-piggledy roofscape of the village. Each appearance led the pair on to the ultimate destination as they walked together down the High Street. Once past the buttercross and last of the cottages, they reached a flat landscape leading down to Stanton Broad.

'Let's walk past the lavender fields,' Lyn suggested. 'There's something magical about them of an evening.'

'Good idea,' Ant replied, squeezing her hand affectionately. They strolled on, leaving behind the soft laughter and chatter from the pub.

As they approached the Manningham's lavender field, the unmistakable scent of the purple blooms filled the air. The fragrant flowers swayed gently in the lightest of breezes, creating an almost hypnotic effect against a reddening sky.

'Isn't it beautiful?' Lyn whispered, pausing at the edge of the field to take in the sight. Ant nodded, equally captivated by the scene before them.

'Certainly,' he murmured. 'Do you remember us doing this as kids?'

'I remember us nicking the odd bunch like all the other kids, if that's what you mean.'

'Passion killer,' chuckled Ant.

Lyn smiled, but as her gaze swept across the field, something caught her eye in the near distance. A chill ran down her spine as she squinted to get a clearer view.

'Ant,' she whispered, her voice suddenly tense. 'Do you see that?'

'See what?' Ant asked, concern furrowing his brow as he followed her gaze.

'Over there,' she pointed. 'There's something...not right.'

'Over there. Do you see it?'

Ant squinted, trying to make out what Lyn had spotted. The failing light made it difficult to distinguish anything beyond a vague shape.

'Maybe it's just an animal,' he suggested, attempting to dismiss Lyn's unease with a light-hearted tone. 'A deer or a badger, perhaps?'

Lyn shook her head, her eyes never leaving the spot. 'No, it's not that... I can't explain it, but —'

'Let's look?' Ant suggested, his curiosity piqued by Lyn's concern.

'Alright,' Lyn agreed hesitantly. 'Be careful.'

They cautiously approached the spot where Lyn had noticed the disturbance in the lavender.

'Something's definitely been here,' Ant commented, crouching down to examine the crushed flowers. 'Or someone.'

'Look, over there,' Lyn whispered, her voice barely audible. She pointed towards a shadowy figure, partially obscured by the tall lavender stems. The figure was bent forward on its knees, as if about to pick a bunch of the fragrant crop.

'Who could that be?' Ant wondered aloud, his voice betraying a hint of concern.

'Shh,' Lyn hissed, grabbing onto Ant's arm. 'They've heard us.'

'I'm not leaving until I find out who it is and what they're doing here. He's no kid pinching flowers for his mum. You wait here while I see what he's up to.'

Lyn watched as Ant made swift progress towards the stranger.

'Be careful,' she whispered.

'Hey, what are you doing? Who are you?'

Ant's attempt to startle the man and gain an advantage failed. Instead, the stranger remained still.

'Watch out. He may have a knife,' shouted Lyn, all pretence at stealth now abandoned.

She watched as Ant continued his speedy progress, lavender parting in a rhythmic wave as he forced his way through the lush crop.

'I said, who are you? What are—'

The Lavender Killer: Chapter Two

UNSEEN EYES

Ant and Lyn stood over the body; their faces etched with disbelief. The man lay hunched over in the middle of the lavender field, his limbs arranged in an unnatural pose beneath him.

'Perhaps he had a heart attack and...Boom?' Ant suggested, scratching his head as he tried to make sense of the scene. 'Or a stroke?'

Lyn frowned, her keen blue eyes scanning the man's face for any signs of injury. ' There's a neat wound between his shoulders. It looks like a bullet entry point. But how and why did he end up here? We both know everyone in the village, and we've never seen him before.'

'True,' Ant conceded, rubbing his chin thoughtfully.'

Lyn stepped closer to the body and pointed at the small round tear in the man's jacket. 'Blood. We need to call Peter.'

Detective Inspector Peter Riley was not only their close friend but also an experienced detective. He'd be able to help them figure out what had happened to the stranger.

'I'll give Peter a ring. It won't be the first time he's come across this sort of thing.'

Lyn nodded. 'Of course,' she replied, her eyes never leaving the man's lifeless form. 'We owe it to him, whoever he is, to find out how this happened.'

As Ant pulled out his mobile and dialled Peter's number, Lyn continued to study the body, her mind racing with questions.

Who was this man, and how had he met such a tragic end? What secrets lay hidden beneath the fragrant lavender blooms? And what would they discover as they delved deeper into the mystery of the stranger's death?

'Peter,' Ant said, his voice serious as he relayed the situation to their friend. 'We need your help. There's a body in the lavender field—Yes, the one at the end of Cowgate Drove. We don't know who he is or how he got here. He's been shot by the looks of things.'

Minutes after Ant's call, the distant sound of police sirens grew louder. A brief time later, Detective Inspector Peter Riley's familiar car pulled up at the edge of the lavender field. The driver's door opened, and Riley stepped out. His tall frame and short-cropped grey hair were immediately recognisable even in the failing light.

'Thank you for coming so quickly,' Lyn said, relief clear in her voice.

'And so here we are again. And on your birthday, too!' Riley replied, scanning the scene with a keen eye. 'Now, what have we got here?'

'He's just as we found him about twenty minutes ago,' Ant explained, gesturing to the lifeless body. 'We were just discussing how he may have met his end.'

Lyn added, 'And neither of us thinks he's a local.'

'Interesting,' Riley mused, approaching the body with

caution. 'No doubt about it. That's a bullet wound. Not much blood. All the damage will be inside the body. Poor bloke.'

Ant nodded, watching as Riley crouched down beside the body, examining the man carefully. His professional demeanour put them both at ease.

I'm glad I don't have the responsibility of sorting this mess out, thought Lyn.

'Look at the way he's positioned,' Lyn whispered, as if in church, her eyes filled with concern. 'It's so unnatural.'

'Remember what Peter said—no jumping to conclusions,' replied Ant. 'Let him do his job and see what he discovers.'

As they watched Riley work, Ant admired his friend's methodical approach to the investigation. It reminded him of his time working for military intelligence. He was confident that, if anyone might uncover the truth behind this mysterious death, it was Detective Inspector Peter Riley.

'Alright,' said Riley, standing up and looking at his friends. 'It's murder alright.'

Lyn gasped, her hand covering her mouth in shock. 'Oh, no.'

'Poor man,' added Ant.

Peter agreed, his eyes narrowing. 'But that's not all. I've found something interesting.'

He held up a small slip of folded paper, which he had discovered in the deceased man's jacket pocket. Unfolding it, Peter read aloud:

'Meet me in the centre of the lavender field at 4.00 pm exactly. Don't be late this time.'

'I tell you what, though. Whoever wrote this has a flair for posh writing,' Peter added.

'Heavens,' Lyn murmured, her concern for the victim

intensifying. 'That sounds like an order, not a request. What say you?'

'It certainly does,' added Ant. 'It was a meeting of equals. What time do you reckon he met his end, Peter?'

The detective glanced down at the body. 'Most likely within minutes of his arrival,' answered Peter, tucking the note into an evidence bag. 'This poor soul expected trouble, but not to die. What made him show up, I wonder?'

'We need to find out who this man was and why someone wanted him dead.'

'Absolutely,' Lyn agreed, her voice filled with shock.'

'Well, we'll need to wait for the post-mortem to confirm the cause of death, no matter what my view is just now. In the meantime, I'll have my scene-of-crime team examine the vicinity and body, and get this place cordoned off. The station will also check the missing person reports for anyone matching this chap's description.'

'Is there anything we can do?' Lyn asked, eager to assist in the investigation.

'Actually, yes,' Riley said, eyeing Ant and Lyn thoughtfully. 'First, I'd like you to speak with the landowner. I bet he's a friend of your family?'

Ant reflected for a moment. 'I hadn't considered that, but yes, that would be old Thomas Whitaker. He leased the land to one of the local farmers for years to grow lavender. We'll pay him a visit and see if he knows anything about our unfortunate victim here.'

'Excellent,' Peter nodded. 'And while you're at it, try to find out more about the people connected to this lavender crop. There might be someone who's seen or heard something.'

'Understood,' Lyn said, her eyes scanning the crime scene meticulously. She carefully stepped around the body, making sure not to disturb any potential evidence. Her keen gaze took in every detail, from the crushed lavender stalks beneath the man's lifeless form to the disturbed earth near the toes of his scuffed shoes.

'Be cautious when speaking with the locals, though,' Peter warned. 'We don't want to cause panic or give Phyllis reason to spread any gossip before we have all the facts.'

'Of course, Peter,' Ant assured him. 'We'll be discreet.'

Ant felt a pang of sadness as they left, seeing the trampled lavender flowers at the crime scene. He stooped and gently picked up a single intact blossom, inhaling its soothing scent. It was a poignant reminder of the beauty that persisted amid the darkness that had befallen their quiet village.

'Come on, Ant,' Lyn said softly, touching his arm. 'Let's go talk to Thomas and see what we can find out.'

'Right,' Ant agreed, pocketing the lavender blossom as a symbol of hope. Together, they walked back towards the village to pick up Ant's vintage sports car.

As they walked together, the sun dipped below the horizon, casting long shadows across the lavender, seeming to merge earth and sky into a purple haze. The crime scene, illuminated softly, stood as a testament to the mystery in Stanton Parva. A mystery that Ant, Lyn, and Detective Inspector Peter Riley were determined to solve, despite the challenges ahead.

Peter continued his meticulous examination of the crime scene. He knew that every detail could be crucial to solving the puzzle they now faced—and he wasn't about to let anything slip through the cracks. He took a deep breath, steadying himself for the task ahead.

'Right', he muttered, 'let's see what we can find.'

Riley meticulously inspected the tragic scene, navigating

through the rows of crushed lavender plants. His instincts, honed over years of police work, guided him as he searched for even the smallest detail that might prove significant.

Ant and Lyn turned to watch their friend from a distance.

'Peter will be out there a while yet,' Lyn observed, her gaze never leaving the detective. 'Do you think he'll find anything?'

'Hard to say,' Ant replied, his own eyes scrutinising Riley's movements. 'But knowing him, if there's something to be found, he'll discover it.'

As they watched the detective surveying the scene, Lyn noticed the sound of a distant rumble. She looked up at the darkening sky and felt drops of rain splatter against her cheeks. 'We'd better hurry before we get soaked.'

'Good Idea,' Ant agreed, pulling his coat collar up around his neck.

'I've got a class of six-year-olds waiting for me in the morning. They're a handful on the best of days, let alone when I'm sleep-deprived and soggy.'

'Ah, the joys of teaching,' Ant teased, winking at her as they quickened their pace.

Detective Inspector Riley caught up with them, having raced to beat the oncoming squall, breathing heavy from running.

'I suggest we all meet back at the station in a couple of hours to discuss our findings.'

'In a couple of hours? That'll be midnight. I've got to work tomorrow, unless you're volunteering to run my school for me?' Lyn said.

Peter thought for a moment. 'On second thoughts, perhaps we'll catch up over your lunch break?'

'A wise choice,' replied Lyn, wearing a wide smile.

At the edge of the field nearest the village, the trio passed a scene-of-crime team. Four soaking individuals gave an official acknowledgement to their superior.

'Good luck. We need all the evidence you can find,' said Peter in an authoritative tone. 'I know you won't let me down.'

The team continued to trudge forward carrying an array of heavy equipment to complete their investigation.

'Pulling rank Peter?'

The detective allowed a half-grin to form. 'I've done my fair share of getting soaked when I was a young Bobby. It's their turn now.'

As the trio approached the detective's police car, he offered his fellow investigators a lift.

'Thanks Peter,' said Lyn, 'But we'll call off on Whitaker and get back home to dry out. By the time we get in your car and soak your seats, we could be at my place. Listen, we'll see you tomorrow, yes?'

Peter smiled as he pulled his collar up against the driving rain before disappearing into the car.

'Why did you say that?' asked Ant, as he blew droplets of water from the tip of his nose.

'Don't be such a baby,' replied Lyn as she stepped up her pace, leaving Ant for dust.

Ant and Lyn, now drenched from the rain, approached the Old Schoolhouse to seek refuge and gather their thoughts. As they neared the Wherry Inn, Ant's resolve for a pint of Fen Bodger pale ale got the better of his desire to dry out. 'Shall we? Ant said as he opened the door to allow Lyn through.

'It doesn't look as though I've got a choice, does it? You are a daft lump. OK, but just a quick one, or it'll be you taking morning assembly tomorrow, not me.'

The door creaked open, revealing a cosy, dimly lit room filled with the familiar faces of villagers seeking solace from the storm.

'Ah, the birthday girl's back. I won't ask what you two have been up to. A pint of Fen-Bodger is it, Ant. And what about you, Lyn? You're not still on the lemonade?' Jed's enquiry met with a raucous reception from the locals, who had been busy demolishing Lyn's birthday buffet.

'Too right about my pint, Jed,' said Ant, acknowledging their friendly reception.

'I am, because the inspectors are still coming tomorrow,' lamented Lyn as she shrugged her shoulders at their host.

As they settled into a corner table, the weight of the day's events seemed to bear down on them. Their laughter subsided, replaced by contemplative silence.

'Ant,' Lyn began hesitantly, her gaze fixed on the dancing flames of the freshly lit wood fire in its huge dog-grate. 'Do you think one of the villagers could have killed that chap?'

'Let's not jump to conclusions,' Ant replied, rubbing his temples. 'What is Peter always saying? Follow the evidence? No matter where it takes us.'

'Right,' Lyn sighed, taking a sip of the lemonade the young bartender had slipped onto the small round table. 'It's just hard to take in that the village is about to discover its peace is about to be shattered by such a terrible crime.'

'We don't even know if that's the case yet,' said Ant as a reminder to his fiance.

An uninvited guest interrupted their conversation as he slid into the seat next to Lyn. 'Evening, folks,' he said with an inscrutable grin. 'I hear there's been a commotion this evening.'

'Has there? And you would be?' Ant replied cautiously, eyeing the newcomer with suspicion.

The short, stocky man grinned again. 'My name. Forgive me. What must you be thinking? It's Simon Broadbent. As for what I'm doing here. Well, it's to help you.'

Lyn eyed the man from tip to toe. 'Why us? The pub is full of people?'

'Indeed it is,' said the man with an enigmatic smile. 'But only one person around here is Lord Stanton, who is engaged to the local headteacher. Am I correct?'

Ant's temper got the better of him. 'That'll do, fella. Time you were on your way.'

The man didn't move a muscle. 'No need to be like that, Lord Stanton. Oh, I forgot, your PTSD gets the better of you sometimes, does it not?'

Lyn sensed the stranger knew how to trigger Ant's condition. Instinctively, she placed her hand on his thigh to reassure him, and not rise to the bait. Lyn's tactic worked as she noticed her fiance relax back into his chair.

'Time to leave, Mr Broadbent,' said Ant in a calm tone. 'I don't care what you think has happened, or that we may know about it. It's best you pop into the police station. They'll be happy to take a statement from you. At least that's what I'm told.'

'Of course,' said the stranger, raising his hands in mock surrender. 'I'm just a curious bystander, like everyone else. Well, I'll leave you to your evening. Oh, I almost forgot. Happy birthday, Miss Blackthorn.'

Broadbent's parting gift was a sickly smile to Lyn as he vanished into the crowd of the packed pub.

'What a horrible man,' began Lyn. 'And he knows a lot about us two. Creepy or what?'

'That stuff is simple to find out. All he had to do was

sweet-talk a couple of villagers or check us out on social media. You can't keep your life out of the public eye, even if you wanted to.'

Lyn finished her glass of lemonade and spent several seconds twirling its accompanying slice of lemon around the bottom of the glass.

'The question is, was that bloke trying to see what we knew, or just playing with us?'

'What do you reckon?'

Ant acknowledged Fitch, their closest friend, who had just entered the pub on the far side of the building. Lost in the loud hubbub, he couldn't hear what Fitch was trying to say.

'Are you listening to me?' said Lyn, unaware of the mechanic's arrival.

'Of course I am. All we can do is tell Peter Riley when we meet him tomorrow, because as sure as eggs are eggs, that bloke isn't going anywhere near a police station.'

As the night wore on, Ant and Lyn couldn't help but scrutinise the other patrons in the pub. A woman of around 28 years of age caught their attention. She continuously whispered to a man older than her while occasionally glancing at the pair.

'Something's off about her,' Ant whispered. 'I can't put my finger on it, but we should keep an eye on that.'

'Are you sure it's not that she's caught your eye?'

'Hilarious,' replied Ant, making sure his fiance hadn't meant the remark too seriously. 'Anyway, let's call it a night before we suspect everyone in the pub. Don't you?'

'Hang on a minute. Now you've drawn my attention to her, I want to check she's OK.'

'Eh? I'm confused.'

'It's the way she's looking at the bloke she's with. Perhaps she wants to leave, but he's keeping her here. Oh, hang on, it looks like she's off to the ladies. I'll be back in a minute,' said Lyn, getting up and following the young woman before Ant had a chance to comment.

Several minutes passed until the two women re-emerged into the bar. Shortly after, Lyn returned to Ant as the young women re-took her bar stool and smiled at her companion.

'Can't be much wrong between those two. They're all over one another,' offered Ant.

'Well, yes…and no'

'Priceless, Lyn. Do I get an explanation? '

'The good news is that you're right. Those two are madly in love. The downside is that her relative is dead set against the chap. That's why she's been looking around the pub. Her other half has said he's not bothered and is intent on sticking around the village.'

'Not bothered about what?'

'I couldn't get that out of her, Ant. All she said was her family is, how did she put it…snobbish. It seems she tried to reason with the relative, but to no avail.'

'Do we know who this mysterious person is?

'She wouldn't say, but it's clear him or her holds a lot of influence over her. I did well to get her first name out of her. It's Wendy.'

Ant turned to look at the couple at the bar. The woman still looked nervous. 'Well, listen. We've got enough on our plate without you turning into an agony aunt. Come on, let's be off.

Exiting the Wherry Arms, they missed saying goodbye to Fitch amid the chaos. As they stepped onto the pavement, a man rushing past caused Lyn to lose her balance. Only Ant's quick thinking avoided his fiance from slamming against the white lime-washed wall of the pub.

'Hey,' shouted Ant, to catch the hurried man's attention. Within seconds, the fellow rounded a sharp turn into an alleyway and was out of sight.

'What's wrong with the village tonight?' said Lyn as she smoothed down her still damp clothes from their earlier adventure. 'We find a dead man. Then we're harassed by a bloke who knows us inside out. Now we get poleaxed by a man who apologises, but who couldn't look me in the eye?'

'It means it's time for some rest,' replied Ant, trying to cheer Lyn up with an affectionate smile. 'We can start fresh tomorrow. We have a long day ahead of us.'

As the pair sauntered up the High Street and past the village church, a figure watched from the shadows as the duo disappeared into the darkness.

Grab your copy...

vinci-books.com/lavenderkiller

About the Author

Keith lives in, and writes about, the evocative county of Norfolk, England.

"I've had an interesting working life, from selling ice cream to teaching management studies on cruise ships," says Keith.

Having started in the construction and furniture-making industries, Keith spent the final twenty years of his career lecturing in further and higher education, eventually becoming Assistant Principal in a large Norfolk college. Now happily retired, Keith spends his time writing mystery stories and making a nuisance of himself at home and with his grandchildren.

Acknowledgments

A special thank you to Peter R, Jo W, and Mike D, without who *Double Cross* would not have made it to publication.